Praise for

Relentless

"In typical Lauren Dane fashion, *Relentless* will sweep you away to a place where passion and romance rule the day . . . Pick up *Relentless* and discover why Dane made my auto-buy list long ago."

—Anya Bast, national bestselling author of *Witch Heart*

"Dane's *Relentless* is exceptional for its realism, because she quite capably articulates a class-based society in an intriguing alternative world. Dane gives us a down-to-earth pairing of decent, appealing individuals who struggle to find peaceable solutions for their people, while hoping for the chance of an enduring love with one another."

—Joey W. Hill, author of *A Vampire's Claim*

"Hot romance, detailed world-building and a plot focusing on righting injustice make *Relentless* a page-turner. With passion and politics, Dane delivers again!" —Megan Hart, author of *Tempted*

Praise for

Lauren Dane and *Undercover*

"Lauren Dane deftly weaves action, intrigue and emotion with spicy, delicious eroticism. *Undercover* is a toe-curling erotic romance sure to keep you reading late into the night." —Anya Bast

continued . . .

Relentless

lauren dane

heat I new york

THE BERKLEY PUBLISHING GROUP
Published by the Penguin Group
Penguin Group (USA) Inc.
375 Hudson Street, New York, New York 10014, USA
Penguin Group (Canada), 90 Eglinton Avenue East, Suite 700, Toronto, Ontario M4P 2Y3, Canada
(a division of Pearson Penguin Canada Inc.)
Penguin Books Ltd., 80 Strand, London WC2R 0RL, England
Penguin Group Ireland, 25 St. Stephen's Green, Dublin 2, Ireland (a division of Penguin Books Ltd.)
Penguin Group (Australia), 250 Camberwell Road, Camberwell, Victoria 3124, Australia
(a division of Pearson Australia Group Pty. Ltd.)
Penguin Books India Pvt. Ltd., 11 Community Centre, Panchsheel Park, New Delhi—110 017, India
Penguin Group (NZ), 67 Apollo Drive, Rosedale, North Shore 0632, New Zealand
(a division of Pearson New Zealand Ltd.)
Penguin Books (South Africa) (Pty.) Ltd., 24 Sturdee Avenue, Rosebank, Johannesburg 2196,
South Africa

Penguin Books Ltd., Registered Offices: 80 Strand, London WC2R 0RL, England

This is an original publication of The Berkley Publishing Group.

PRINTING HISTORY
Heat trade paperback edition / May 2009

Library of Congress Cataloging-in-Publication Data

Dane, Lauren.
    Relentless / Lauren Dane. — 1st ed.
        p. cm.
    ISBN 978-0-425-22760-2
    I. Title.
    PS3604.A5R46 2009
    813'.6—dc22   2008047108

PRINTED IN THE UNITED STATES OF AMERICA

10 9 8 7 6 5 4 3 2 1

This one is for the boy with long hair and a muscle car who now wears suits and plays field trip dad.
Always.

Acknowledgments

While you'll often hear writers talk about how solitary and isolating it can be to write books, I'd never be able to do this if it weren't for oodles of people in my universe:

Laura Bradford—my agent and my friend. She is made of shiny awesome sunshine and rainbows. She also loves Ann Stuart as much as I do and never gets bored when I blather on and on about Linda Howard.

Leis Pederson—wonderful editor and a most fabulous person!

Megan Hart—Pong Cocktail. That is all.

Anya Bast and Ann Aguirre—for the friendship and writerly advice, and for being there to snark with and bounce ideas off of.

Renee Meyer—because no acknowledgment would be complete without thanking you for being the best darned beta reader in the world (as well as a wonderful friend). And Mary—for being so unfailing in her enthusiasm at my message board where she moderates, and also for her wonderful beta reads! Fatin—you give me lots of book love; I appreciate every mention! My Vixenreaders and those ladies at my Yahoo! group as well—thank you for your unfailing support.

My readers and the romance community in general—there's no divide, just lots of wonderful and supportive people who love romance and reading. Thank you for making romancelandia a better place to be.

Lastly, thank you to Daniel Craig, who played Roman Lyons in my head. I promise neither Abbie or I sullied you too much.

Relentless

Chapter 1

The tensions sweeping through the Known Universes belonging to the Federation had brought sharp focus to the issue of the lack of parity between the Ranked Family members who made all the leadership decisions and the unranked—the majority of citizenry—who had no voice at all.

Many times over the years, she'd tried to get some decent vid coverage to address the issue of the lack of representative democracy and had failed or had been relegated to times when everyone was sleeping. Finally, so many people had had enough that she'd been able to catch some attention and garner enough interest to become the subject of several vid interviews much like the one she was just about to do.

Abbie Haws had worked for justice her entire life, and she was smart enough to know the time for real change had never been better. Things didn't just *happen* to you; you *made* them happen.

Everything she'd ever achieved in her life came from hard work and grabbing an opportunity and making it her own.

Hoping someone in the gargantuan Governance Council chambers was watching, she smoothed a hand over her hair, making sure it was securely in the knot at the nape of her neck, adjusted the front of her suit jacket, stood tall and put on her serious barrister face right before the cameras honed in.

"We're here with Abigail Haws, spokesperson for the Movement for Representative Democracy." The host sent her a flirty smile. "Ms. Haws, please tell us why you're here today outside the municipal complex."

"In light of the recent shameful activity on the part of certain Families, it seems to us, to many of the unranked, that the time for this hoarding of power must end."

"What do you propose, then?"

"We, that is, the Movement for Representative Democracy, say it's time for the Ranked to share with the rest of us, with the majority of citizens in the Federation Universes, what is rightfully ours. We want the right to have a voice in our own governance."

"Ms. Haws, the Families have led the 'Verses, they say quite well, for millennia, why call for change now?"

She loved it when they asked her questions like this. Abbie looked up at him, a smile curving her lips. "If not now, when? We are not pets, we are humans with brains and wills and we are not content to let things happen to us any longer. We cannot simply trust that the Families, that the Governance Council, are acting in our best interests. This is lazy and it garners us a situation like the one that's sent us reeling these last months. Sedition! Treason by Family members resulting in the deaths of hundreds of citizens. For what? We were harmed in a play for power far above our heads.

"You ask, why now? Ask Gretel Mortan why now. Ask House Kerrigan why they'd persecute a woman who has served them, has raised their children and grandchildren with love and care, only to be accused of theft on the eve of her retirement. In our legal system, she has less power than her accuser simply because her accuser is Ranked."

Abigail Haws paused and looked from the host and straight into the camera.

"The time is now because we are not content to be ignored and unheard any longer. What threat does it pose to actually seek the input of the people you govern? Why does the idea of letting us have a say in our lives scare them so? Ask them why *not* now."

"Thank you, Ms. Haws and good luck. I'm Penn Even. Good evening."

The host turned to Abbie and smiled. "Thanks for doing this on short notice."

As if she'd be angry that she just got some prime coverage on the vids during the important end of workday hours? "Not a problem. Thank *you* for comming me and setting this up. We really appreciate it."

"I think you're doing a very good thing. Good luck with it and I'll be in contact soon."

Abbie smiled at his retreating back. All in all, despite the horrifically long and pretty much totally frustrating workday, things were looking up. Hells, someone over at the Council offices might actually take her comm after this. A girl could hope anyway.

The Council chambers quieted when Roman Lyons rapped the tabletop with his gavel. He slid a hand through his hair at the temple,

the only outward sign of his agitation with the assembled group
and the lovely but annoying Abigail Haws. Anything else would be
weakness and a loss of control.

The room was large, dominated by a very long table where
Familial representatives sat in the flesh or monitors bearing their
images were placed. Lion's heads, the sigil of House Lyons and also
of the Familial Council, were mosaicked into the table and also pat-
terned in the marble on the floors. The space was soaring, majestic.
Roman found comfort there, comfort in the grooved spaces in the
table where hands had held it to push a chair back over and over for
generations. The shapes the patterns in the stained glass threw on
the walls and furniture as the day passed marked the time in a way
so familiar that it was part of his life as much as the chair he sat in.

He'd occupied the space at the head of the table for twenty-three
years, since the age of seventeen when he'd taken over from his father.
The position was an indication of his rank and the Rank of House
Lyons. *The* House, the one that came first and had held the most
powerful seat in the Council since it was formed millennia before,
when the first settlers had come through from Earth.

Ravena was the Center of their world physically, powerwise and
symbolically as well. Many Familial representatives came in person
to the meetings of the Governing Council if they could, but none
missed a meeting, even if they had to come via vid screen.

Right now, in the wake of the scandal regarding Ranked Family
members working with the Imperialists, the pressure to govern ef-
fectively and fairly was paramount. On the verge of the first treason
trial, things were even more dire. Most of his brethren understood
that fact. Others, well—they were drunk with power and their behavior only made his job harder.

"All right then, let's move to the point of contention and get this over with. I have a full day and enough of my time has been wasted with this tantrum."

Ash Walker hid a smile behind his steepled fingers. Roman figured he'd had enough, too.

"Roman, as the head of the Ranked Council, it's your responsibility to deal with this rabble-rouser. She has been on the vids nonstop over the last days and her group on and off for months." Leong Khym was usually a voice of reason but Roman saw the strain even over the vid link.

"Just have the bitch arrested! Why are we tolerating this nonsense? This is treason." Saul Kerrigan stood up, red-faced.

"Sit down, Saul. You're being ridiculous. This group isn't calling for you to be killed, they're calling for reforms. That's not treason and we can't just have people arrested when they say things we don't like." A steady pounding tattooed behind Roman's eyes. Saul Kerrigan was the reason for this damned problem, and yet it would fall to Roman to fix. "This has been going on for hours. Just make a motion. Do something, because I have had it with all this whining."

"You're not a full member of this body, Kerrigan. Associate Houses are not recognized to speak without leave," Ash said. "And frankly, you're the root of the problem here. Your behavior with the old woman was the impetus for this."

Saul fumed but kept quiet. Roman liked Ash Walker even more at that moment.

"I move House Lyons meets with Abigail Haws or some representative of the—" Leong looked down momentarily. "Movement for Representative Democracy to hear their grievances and attempt to appease them."

The rest of the group agreed and Roman sighed. "Fine, then. I'll have my assistant make arrangements. Now let's move on."

The sky above her pinked toward night as Abbie made her way back to her office from a useless day spent in the Administration of Justice building. Not a single one of her motions made it to the lead administrator's desk. An utter waste of her time. And yet, sadly, not an unusual occurrence in her life.

Still, the walk in the fresh air at the end of her day made up for it in a small way. Ravena edged toward the cold season so the air had a bite, but not enough to warrant a cloak just yet.

Her mind raced. Abbie had a list of things to do as long as her arm and an ex who thought he was entitled to sleep with her when he got bored or lonely, and sometimes she was lonely enough to consider it. Her father needed to be reined in every few weeks. He tended to like agitating for causes more than patience, preferred to demonstrate rather than negotiate. Now was not time for rushing. Now was time for a fine hand and a patient heart, time for someone with a temperament like hers. Abbie had done the rabble-rousing and now it was time to step slowly and carefully so she could negotiate.

But right then with the sky looking like the inside of a purri fruit, she could be satisfied.

She'd been on the vids that day and the day before, addressing the way domestic workers had been treated by some Families. The latest case was that of Gretel Mortan, a woman who'd served House Kerrigan for forty-five years and who, just shy of her retirement, the Family had accused of theft. Domestics serving a Family for thirty-five standard years or longer were entitled to a pension but theft would render the agreement null. The amount of credits would be nothing to a Family like the Kerrigans but would mean everything to Gretel Mortan. But instead of paying what they owed morally and legally, they'd accused her of stealing from them.

Ridiculous. And anyone looking at it would know so as well. Gretel was nearly eighty years old. She'd pretty much raised the Kerrigans' children and grandchildren and there had never been a single problem with her until she filed to retire.

When Abbie had received word of the charges from someone in her office and then had spoken with the other members of the Movement for Representative Democracy, it had been decided to take an aggressive approach. The MRD had been working quietly, diligently and civilly for four years and had been rebuffed. Then they'd moved their tactics up a bit, become more vocal. Still nothing. And then came the horrible scandal of the Family betrayal and treason. The unranked finally began to really speak with each other and demand change. The time had never been better to force the hand of the Family Governance Council.

Luckily, one of the people within MRD had a contact with the media and Abbie had been the face of the movement. All she could hope for was that someone would just meet with her, give her the chance to talk to the Families about what was happening.

The Society for the Defense of the Accused offices loomed ahead, a tight, cramped warren of desks and file cabinets. A place she'd called close enough to home for the last six standard years. She'd started as an intern when she was completing her training and they'd brought her on as a barrister once she'd been awarded her license. Her agitation smoothed again as she ascended the steps to the SDA's large front doors.

The guard in the lobby looked up and when he saw it was her, relaxed and smiled. "Evening to you, Abbie. It's awfully late for you to be at work. Then again, all that time you've been spending on the vids making people mad must keep you busy." He winked.

She laughed. Long days were pretty common to barristers in general, even more so for ones who represented the accused. "Someone's got to fight the good fight."

"Well, don't stay too late. A young woman like you should be home with her family."

She waved at him as she stepped into the lift.

The building was old, the floor coverings frayed and tattered, but the ceilings still shone with hand-done mosaics, and donated art decorated the walls. The scent of papers and old books greeted her as she unlocked the front doors to the main area and made her way back through the narrow hall to her workspace.

Logan waited for her in her small office. "Abbie, Gretel Mortan has been taken to lockup."

She stopped, pulled up short by the sight of Logan, still so pretty to look at even after she knew the less-than-pretty parts of him, and at the news her elderly client had been incarcerated.

"What for? Surely not the theft charge? That charge had nothing to back it up at all."

"Come on, Abbie, you can't be surprised by this. It's not the first time the Kerrigan Family has done something like this. And the MRD has made them angry I expect. I just thought you should know."

Heart heavy, she nearly fell into her chair. "Angry? Oh, I'll show them angry. They have no idea what angry is. *They're* the ones who betrayed the rest of us and they have the audacity to be like this?" She blew out a breath and began to twist her hair up and out of her way. "I'll get started on the paperwork right away," she said by way of dismissal.

"You look tired. Why don't we leave? You can work on this later after I've relaxed you a bit."

She flicked her glance up, knowing that tone. "I appreciate you coming by to tell me, Logan, but I'm not fucking you."

White teeth flashed a perfect smile. The smile of a man who always got what he wanted, which only served to make her more frustrated, more angry. Couldn't anyone have some sense of what was decent and right? When a man like Logan, a man who could make far more credits working for a large corporation, worked instead for the SDA, you'd think he'd be a good catch. But the man didn't know how to say no. Not to other women while he was engaged to her, not to too much drink. He simply didn't have any concept of moderation in anything. Which made him a great barrister but a failure as marriage material.

"Why not? You're not seeing anyone." He sent her the sexy head cock, the one he used over and over, she was quite sure, to stellar success.

"Which should make me unattractive in your eyes. Now go before I get mean."

He laughed and sauntered out. She knew he'd be back another day. They had an attraction still. One she was sometimes weak enough to indulge. But not just then. Just then she was angry, and the fires of that stoked her passion far better than he would have. And at least she wouldn't hate herself in the morning.

By the time she stumbled into her apartment long after the moons had set, she'd left the motion that needed to be filed on her assistant's desk, and had placed several vid calls to the people who needed to hear the news.

Something needed to happen. The Families were abusing their rule, and had been for some time. Arresting an old woman because of sheer greed was just a prime example of their behavior. It had to be exposed and she would continue to call attention to it until Gretel was freed and someone from the Governance Council agreed to meet.

Chapter 2

A bbie adjusted the button on her suit jacket as she waited for her audience with Roman Lyons. She'd been waiting half an hour already and each second that passed angered her even more.

The opulence of the outer office was designed to soothe as well as impress. The couch she sat on was plush, the fabric covering it soft and luxurious. The colors were rich and sumptuous. Tasteful art hung on the walls.

There had been a reception area in the entry, an attendant on the lift, as if she were unable to push a button on her own, another reception area when she'd made it to the lofty floor where Roman Lyons's personal office was located, and yet another desk in there with an assistant.

A handsome one though. At least she could look at him as well as the art while she waited. And then waited some more.

"I do apologize, Ms. Haws. Mr. Lyons is dealing with an unexpected problem. Are you sure I can't get you something to drink?"

Abbie had to give it to the assistant: the man had been very professional and courteous. If she hadn't dealt with this sort of situation repeatedly in her time as a barrister, hells, in her lifetime as an unranked person trying to succeed, she'd have believed Roman Lyons was truly dealing with something unexpected instead of sitting in his office having a snack and laughing to himself about how he was making her wait.

"No, thank you." She glanced at the chrono on the wall near the impressively huge desk the assistant occupied. "I cannot wait much longer. I have my own appointments to attend to." Which wasn't a lie. She'd had to get coverage for all her afternoon cases so she could come to this meeting.

The man nodded and went back to the door and slipped inside. Just a few moments later he came back out. "Mr. Lyons is finishing up and he asks for you to stay just a bit longer."

And so she waited nearly another half an hour and finally got up. Keeping her features bleak and severe, she addressed the assistant, "Tell Mr. Lyons when he's decided to take meeting me seriously, he can contact my assistant. I do not appreciate having my time wasted."

The assistant stood up quickly. He'd been sneaking peeks in the door and had been on the comm panel to what Abbie figured was Lyons's desk on and off since she'd arrived well over an hour and a half before.

"I cannot apologize enough, Ms. Haws. Honestly, Mr. Lyons is not playing games. He's very sorry, I am sure."

She raised a brow but it wasn't this guy's fault. "He can make it up to me. *He'd better make it up to me.* But for now, I'm leaving. Thank you for your hospitality."

She stormed out, anger coursing through her system, but she didn't have the luxury of a good mad. She had to get back to work and that included a call back to the interviewer who had been handling the stories about Gretel's case.

*R*oman finally disconnected the video conference and made sure to smooth down the front of his shirt before rushing out to the front office. The Haws woman had been waiting nearly two hours and Marcus had continually poked his head in and sent notes via comm that she was nearly out the door.

"She left twenty minutes ago, Roman. I told you she wasn't going to wait around all day." Marcus shook his head.

"Do you think I wanted to deal with this nonsense with House Turgev? Idiots." House Turgev, the House controlling Perea, several slips through the portals away, had been using chemicals to treat their salt water to convert it to potable drinking water. A good thing for such an arid 'Verse. But as the scientists had warned, the chemicals were unstable and a warehouse housing them had exploded, killing several workers and spilling so much of the fluid it had rendered the water undrinkable. He'd had to arrange with neighboring 'Verses to get water to Perea. It wasn't as if he was having a manicure and watching a vid.

"She said you should contact her when you're ready to meet her. She was very angry and very frustrated."

"I can't stand any more tantrums, Marcus. I get enough from the Council. I don't need it from her, too. Does she think I have free time running from my fingertips? She had an appointment with me. I made the time. I can't simply drop everything to suit her schedule."

Marcus pursed his lips. "My, aren't we very important. Have you been associating with your brother again? You don't think Ms. Haws has a busy schedule? She's a senior barrister so she's got caseloads backed up for years. She waited nearly two hours past your appointment time and she showed up fifteen minutes early. She did come on time. She waited long after you would have if your positions were reversed. Accept it, Roman. You're the one who needs to make amends. I can call her assistant now and reschedule if you like."

"My brother? Marcus, that was low." Roman hated it when his assistant was right. Still, it was a sharp blow to bring Alexander into the discussion to make his point.

"Yes, you're acting like a spoiled prince. You are neither. You were born who you are. Do you want me to make the . . . Uh oh." Marcus's words trailed off once his attention snagged on the vid screen in the office.

Roman's stomach sank as he looked over Marcus's shoulder to see the screen. "Ms. Haws is a busy girl I see."

Marcus shushed him and nodded.

Well, he'd have to give it to Abigail Haws—she wasn't hard to look at, even if she was a bit severe with her hair pulled back so tight. He certainly didn't like what she was saying about House Kerrigan though.

The unranked were terribly unhappy and part of him understood that. In the wake of the scandal where it had been discovered that members of House Walker and House Pela had been working with the Imperialists, along with several Associate Houses, overall trust in the ability of Family Rule had been on the decline.

But it hardly seemed fair to give up when it had just been the actions of a select few. Family Rule had been the way of things for millennia. All the trouble this Haws woman and her little group stirred with this sort of agitation only complicated matters and made Roman's job harder.

It was easy to criticize. But she had a house and a job and he spent every waking moment leading people. He wished people understood what sacrifices the Ranked made instead of assuming they were all lazy, irresponsible fools.

Still, the stark idiocy of what Saul Kerrigan had done brought a flush of anger to his face.

"What in the seven hells? They had the Mortan woman arrested? I told Saul to back off. Get him in here immediately. He has less than half an hour and if he does not appear within that time frame have *him* arrested. Can you get Ms. Haws on the screen? I'd like to speak with her about this case."

"I told you two days ago about the arrest, Roman. And the file Ms. Haws sent over is on your desk marked *Information for Haws meeting*. I'll tell you right now, she's not going to be available."

Snapping his teeth together, Roman tried to take a calming breath but failed as he stomped from the reception area. *Like he didn't have enough to do already?*

This is where Abigail Haws lives? Roman took in the building. Not bad at all. He'd expected shabby once he'd left the Family living blocks near the municipal complex. While still within the first circle, he rarely got out this far. Roman realized he'd lived a sheltered life. He did get out from time to time, but it was usually on some sort of mission to view how the unranked lived, a visit to a school, something of that sort.

Listening closely, he knocked once he heard movement on the other side of the door. It was very late but he hadn't wanted to let the day end without trying to see the woman. Once he'd read the file and spoken to Saul Kerrigan he'd been livid. He wanted to hear Abigail Haws's side of the story.

"Who is it?" A pause as he heard the viewport on the door slide open. "Oh, you. What in the seven hells are you doing here?" she snarled as her door flew open. A tiny sprite of a woman stood before him, long, dark hair hanging loose to her waist, big brown eyes flashing behind a pair of spectacles. He hadn't seen spectacles very often. Most of the time surgical treatment repaired vision problems.

"I'm—"

She had the audacity to grab his arm and yank him into the apartment, slamming the door behind them both. "I know who you are. Why are you in my house?"

He looked around, again, surprised. The place was lovely. Plants exploded from pots hanging, draping, perched and placed on the windowsills. The furniture was nice, not expensive like his, but it fit the space.

He sniffed, trying to keep it to himself, but a redolent, heady scent hung in the air. It came from her kitchen where a pot sat on a cooktop. She cooked, too? Pictures sat in frames on shelves and on tables. Abigail Haws led a full life, and suddenly, he got a whole different perspective on her.

"Hello?" She snapped her fingers in front of his face, jolting him from his inner thoughts. She may have had a lovely apartment, but her manners left something to be desired.

"Please don't do that." He stepped back. "I'm here because you left before I could meet with you today. Marcus, my assistant, assured me you'd be home and that your assistant had told you to expect me. Apparently that did not happen."

"I was before an administrator all afternoon. After you missed our appointment. I met with several of my clients at the lockup, did research at the library and came home. I haven't even eaten yet."

"You left out speaking with a vid crew."

She had the audacity to laugh and he had the audacity to be charmed in a startled sort of way.

"Oh, that's right. Yes. And I spoke with a vid crew about yet another instance of a Family using the system to harm the unranked. I nearly forgot that part. Thank you for reminding me."

She turned, pushing that dark river of gleaming hair over her shoulder and headed to the kitchen. The scent of her soap wafting in her wake met his nose. Light, feminine, not much like her personality at all.

"Why are you using spectacles?"

"Why aren't you using manners?" she countered, ladling the fabulously aromatic concoction into two bowls. "Would you like some stew? It's nothing fancy but it's good."

He wanted to say no but he had to speak with her and he hadn't eaten in hours. "Thank you."

"*Hmpf.*" She placed the bowls on the table in the corner of her kitchen and turned again, returning with a pitcher of juice and some bread. "Sit."

He did, surprised by how quickly he'd simply obeyed her order.

*G*ood gods, Roman Lyons was ten kinds of delicious even as waves of privilege rolled from him as he sat at her table.

Still, she was going to have to beat Tasha for not forwarding notice of this little meeting to her home comm system. Here she was, keyed up and in need of quiet and some dinner and all of the sudden she had this at her table, eating her food and looking like a man who would most likely look even better without clothes. Inwardly, she sighed. She should have taken Logan up on his offer. If she went too long without sex, she got antsy. And sex with Roman Lyons fell under two categories: unrealistic and ridiculous. Unrealistic because he was not only Ranked but was *the* most powerful Ranked individual in the Known Universes. While she wasn't. And ridiculous because, well, refer back to the first point.

"So now that you're eating my food and drinking my juice, why don't you fill me in on just exactly what motivated you to come out here at this late hour."

"I wouldn't be here at this late hour eating your food if you hadn't run out on our appointment."

She sighed. "Let me guess. You sit in your office and look out over the city and you wonder why-oh-why the unranked are so ungrateful for all the work you do for them. You did me a favor by letting me travel in the midst of my workday to your office high in the clouds and it was then my fault that I didn't wait for you long past our appointed time. Because, you're very busy and really, I should be grateful anyone from House Lyons would meet with me to begin with."

"As it happens, I am very busy. I wasn't having a beauty appointment while you were waiting. I was dealing with a life-or-death crisis. I apologize if that offends your sensibility."

She smiled and tore a piece of bread from the loaf, using it to sop up the stew her sister had sent over. "Mr. Lyons, I expect you to do your job. But I also expect that if you should be two hours late for a meeting you'll let me know so that I may get on with my own busy schedule and come back another time. Instead you left me out there as if I only existed in moments when your attention was on me. So your annoyance that I left after *two hours* offends me far more than you blowing me off for that time."

"I did not *blow* you off. I explained that I was dealing with a life-or-death issue."

It figured he'd look handsome even when a vein in his forehead started to visibly throb. He looked, well, sort of feral. Interesting. He seemed so very controlled. It made her curious as to what lay beneath that exterior of his. That's it, she had to call Logan when Roman left.

"And *I* didn't miss our appointment. I have people depending on me as well. Gretel Mortan being one of them, and she had a hearing I needed to attend."

"This is very good. Thank you." Long, pale-gold lashes fluttered down over pale green eyes a moment as he delivered the compliment.

"Oh. Well, thank you. It's just a simple stew. My sister owns a café. She sent it over."

"Ah, well, it's still good. Tell me about Gretel Mortan."

"Do you want to hear about that, or about what the MRD is after?" She sipped her juice and watched him carefully. He'd put aside his general agitation and had slid into a bureaucratic face. It was disconcerting how quickly he could assume a different role.

"Let's start with Ms. Mortan since that's the news of the day."

So she laid it all out. She left the emotionalism of a life of service and the betrayal of a man Gretel had practically raised out of the discussion. It wasn't the time and Roman Lyons wasn't a soft touch anyway. He'd slipped on an impassive mask so she'd put on her own professional skin. Whatever it took to get Gretel Mortan out of lockup.

During her explanation, she'd dug into her case, pulled out the files and handed the pertinent paperwork to him. He read it all, listening to her carefully and giving her his complete attention.

He sighed when she finished. "You said she had a hearing today? If she's so innocent, why is she still in lockup?"

He'd been so polite up until then. Thank the gods for all her training. Still, she understood how difficult his job had to be, especially right then, so she would explain what she thought he should know already. "Mr. Lyons, how old are you? Do you mean to tell me you believe the justice system is perfect here in Ravena? The administrator who heard my motion this afternoon? His name is Paul Kerrigan. In addition to being a person Ms. Mortan raised from infancy, he's also Saul Kerrigan's third son." Even as jaded as she was, it had been shocking to her to see the love in Gretel's eyes for the boy she'd loved like her own even as he'd turned down Abbie's request for an emergency hearing.

"Are you saying he didn't administer the case fairly?"

"I'm saying that, looking at the facts, we've got a very elderly woman who has a spotless criminal record. She's worked for the Kerrigan Family her entire life, first as general help and then as their governess. She has a family of her own. Her children are all solid members of society. In a normal situation, based on the amount of evidence against her, she would not be in lockup. She would be free as she awaited her trial. Anyone her age with her record would not be held in lockup and a request for an emergency hearing to determine lockup status awaiting trial should have been heard. But none of that happened and I can't tell you why. I can only tell you what normally happens and my suspicions."

"What is it you'd like me to do?"

"I wasn't meeting you today about Gretel Mortan."

"I know that."

"I'm still going to want to speak to you about the MRD."

Was that a smile hinting at the corners of his mouth? A very sexy mouth, at that.

"I'm certain you do. Marcus will find a place for you in my schedule. Just call him. He likes you for some reason." He shrugged like he found it inexplicable.

"I'd like you to step in and sign the order to have Gretel Mortan issued an emergency hearing. And I would like to have any House Kerrigan members removed from the case in any capacity."

He cocked his head and examined her face. "I thought you'd ask me to free her."

"I'm not trying to get special favors. Or okay, so yes, it would be a special favor for you to step in at all. But all I'm asking is for her to have an emergency hearing so she can be freed while she awaits trial. You don't strike me as the kind of man who'd use his power to step in and free someone in a case like this. But if you'd look over the material I sent to your office and speak with Saul Kerrigan and urge him to drop the charges of theft, I would appreciate it very much."

He stood. "All right. I already spoke to the lead administrator of the courts and he happened to agree that Ms. Mortan should have received an emergency hearing. According to Cushing, she'll be on the schedule tomorrow morning."

Internally, she was impressed. Cushing. Alastair Cushing was the most powerful name in all of jurisprudence in Ravena and he was on Lyons's comm list. Obviously. "You knew this when you came here? And you still wanted my song and dance? Why?" Was she like a performing animal for him?

"I wanted to hear it from you. I wanted to get a feel for who you are. That you kept your request fair means something about your character. Now, it is late, as you mentioned, and I have early appointments tomorrow. Thank you for the stew, and for speaking with me so candidly."

He headed to the door and she tried not to gape at him.

What an interesting man he was.

Chapter 3

*I*n the hallway outside the hearing room, Gretel looked fragile, confused and very sad. It nearly broke Abbie's heart. But at least she could go home with her family instead of spending another night in lockup. The administrator who'd received the case was one Abbie knew to be fair and had been appointed for many years, and his rulings were unquestioned. It was one less thing to worry about in the short term.

"I will do everything I can to keep her free. You have my word," Abbie told Gretel's family, who'd assembled there for the hearing. They thanked her and she watched them walk away, relieved and united.

On Abbie's way to her next hearing, Saul Kerrigan stood in her path to block her. She sighed inwardly and braced herself. There was a bit of history between Abbie and the Kerrigans, so she knew to expect an outburst.

"Is there something I can do for you, Mr. Kerrigan?"

"You think you can just get your pet, Lyons, to fix things for you?" He yelled it so loud people stopped to stare.

"I have no idea what you are referring to. If you'll excuse me, I have another case to attend to." She attempted to walk past but he grabbed her arm to halt her progress and a cold chill ran up her spine.

"Look here, girl." His face was very close to hers and her arm began to hurt where he gripped it. She fought the panic, fought the memories and amazed herself by staying outwardly calm.

White noise filled her ears. It seemed as if she watched the entire scene from afar. She noted the way her hands shook slightly. The sheen of sweat down her spine, cold and flat, kept her anchored to the spot. Now was not the time to lose it. So she didn't.

"You need to unhand me this instant." Hmm, how very calm she sounded.

"Sir, is there a problem?" A security officer approached and attempted to get in between them. The guard knew her and Abbie realized he addressed Kerrigan first because he was Ranked, but he'd stepped in to protect her.

Kerrigan let go of her arm and she had to concentrate on not rubbing the spot where he'd gripped it so tightly. For an old man, he had a lot of strength. And a lot of audacity if he thought she'd just roll over and let him harm her. Her panic subsided, replaced by a growing rage that he'd just hurt her for no other reason than that he could.

"This woman is a traitor! She and all her little friends trying to overthrow Familial Rule. How dare she darken these halls?"

The guard stepped back, urging Abbie away with his body.

"I'm on my way to another hearing. If Mr. Kerrigan is done assaulting me, I need to be going." She kept her voice bored, even as she worked to tamp down her fear. An accusation like Kerrigan's wasn't anything to play around with. In the wake of the recent scandals regarding the Imperialists, calling someone a traitor wasn't an idle thing.

"Saul, come on. Let's get moving, we have a meeting." A nearly emaciated, stooped male about Gretel's age pulled gently on Kerrigan's arm, and Kerrigan sneered at her one last time before bustling down the hall, away from them.

"Abbie, are you all right?" Logan shoved his way through the crowd.

No. No, she wasn't, but she had no time to fall apart just then either. "I'm fine, thank you, Logan."

He saw her face and nodded. "I need to talk to you about a case. You have to be in Administrator Ubai's motions hearing, right?" He put a hand at the small of her back and ushered her through the crowd toward the sky bridge between the buildings, all the while chattering to her about meaningless things.

Marcus sailed into Roman's office and tossed a stack of papers and files onto the desk.

"Did Ms. Haws's office call to set an appointment? And have you heard any results of the hearing for the old woman?" Roman asked.

Marcus stopped and turned to look at him carefully. "My, you're very interested. She's cute, isn't she? That tiny little spitfire thing works for her. You know, I hear she's single."

Great, the last thing Roman needed was for Marcus to think he had a thing for Abigail Haws. "Stop it right there, Marcus. I asked because I wanted to be sure Cushing followed up. Ms. Haws's romantic status is irrelevant to me. The woman has no manners at all."

"You need that, Roman. You need a wild woman who will show you a world you haven't seen. A woman who doesn't need something from you other than some satisfaction in bed."

"Marcus!"

Marcus, his assistant of nearly twenty years, simply laughed. "Let me check and I'll get back to you."

His younger brother, Alexander, would probably frown at him for giving Marcus such leeway to say things like that in his presence but Marcus made him smile. Marcus respected him without taking him too seriously. Very few people apart from his children and a small circle of friends treated him like a person instead of *the* Roman Lyons. It wasn't so much that Roman gave Marcus the leeway to speak to him so informally, but that Roman preferred it that way and saw it as respect. Marcus was an employee but also a friend. That was a rare thing anywhere, much less in his world.

Roman had been standing at the window, reading a report, when Marcus rushed back in sometime later. "Roman, the old woman, Mortan, she was freed until trial. But the big news is that Saul Kerrigan grabbed Ms. Haws and screamed in her face, threatening her even, in the hall after the hearing had ended."

Roman gripped the sheaf of papers until they crinkled. "Grabbed her how? Is she all right? Has she spoken with the media? Where in the seven hells is Saul?"

"I don't know. I don't know. Not from what I can tell. Shall I send for him?"

Roman exhaled sharply. "This sort of thing only feeds the anti-Family party line. Get him in here immediately. And get me the vid footage of that hallway. I can't trust Saul to tell me the truth."

"Abbie, you've got several high-priority comm messages," Tasha informed her as she got back to her office. "Are you all right?" Tasha followed her into her tiny office as she asked in a hushed voice.

"Gretel is out until trial, that's a huge relief for her family." Abbie scrolled through the messages, stopping when she saw two from Marcus, Roman Lyons's assistant.

"He's not hard to look at." Tasha grinned.

"He seems very nice," she said absently as she watched Marcus request her presence in Roman Lyons's office as soon as possible.

Another comm, this one from Roman himself.

"Now *that* is one handsome male. Looks like he'd smell very good."

"He does. But he has terrible manners. I should hit you with this"—Abbie held up a hole punch briefly—"for forgetting to tell me he'd be on my doorstep at a very late hour." She hadn't even been wearing a bra when he'd shown up. Not that he'd shown any interest in the state of her nipples at all, but still.

"I left you a note. You always come back here." Tasha raised one shoulder that told Abbie her assistant knew good and well Abbie wouldn't get that message. Tasha knew Abbie would have put a stop to the meeting if she'd known.

She sighed after listening to Roman Lyons ask her to come to his office immediately. It wasn't like she could say no. Not when she wanted him to listen to her pitch about the MRD and he *had* helped out with Gretel. But when it came right down to it, Roman Lyons had requested an audience and it wasn't one she could refuse.

"I need to go over to House Lyons. I'm clear schedulewise. Please inform Mr. Lyons's assistant I'm on my way and that I don't have two hours to waste."

"Um, he's had a conveyance sent. The driver is waiting for you."

"Tasha! You knew all this time and you didn't tell me?" She stood and tried to smooth down the front of her clothing. Quickly, she managed to tuck errant strands of her hair back into the knot at the back of her head and hid a blush as she dabbed on lipstain.

"Abbie, if I'd told you at the beginning you'd have insisted he was manipulating you. And look, Kerrigan is a monster to have handled you that way. Logan told us how he was. Roman Lyons seems to care about the situation, so why shouldn't you go over there? He needs to know what the Ranked get up to." Tasha handed Abbie her case with a smile that said she didn't feel a single bit of guilt.

"Logan shouldn't be telling tales. I have to go. I'll get even with you later." She waved over her shoulder as she rushed out and the House Lyons driver who'd been waiting stood and gave her a slight bow.

"Ms. Haws? Mr. Lyons says to bring you right over when you get the opportunity."

She smiled—what else could she do, she was raised to have manners, after all—and let him lead her to the conveyance waiting at the front of the building.

No one in the inner-circle part of the capital city had vehicles. Mass transit worked very well, and without vehicles other than trams and the subterranean trains, it was easy enough to walk through the municipal complex from one side to the other in less than half of one standard hour.

The Ranked, of course, did have vehicles, but even they didn't use them very often within the municipal ring. And yet here she sat, ensconced in the plush seats of the transport of the House Lyons, headed to Roman Lyons's office. It had been a total waste of resources and time, and a way to keep the upper hand but, at the same time, Abbie was glad she hadn't had to walk and be jostled by the crowd on her way.

She should have taken a relaxer but it'd been so long since she'd had an attack that she'd left them at home. And now, jittery and burning with adrenaline, she headed straight into the absolute worst place she could go.

Chapter 4

An angry violence coursed through Roman's veins after he'd seen the vid footage from the hallway outside the courtroom. He'd fixated on the look of panic flashing over Abigail's features and then nausea rose as he'd watched her panic fade into blankness.

Saul Kerrigan was a thug, and if, after the dressing down he'd received for nearly a standard hour, he did not change his behavior and stay the hells away from Ms. Haws, Roman would punish House Kerrigan severely, no matter what connection existed between them.

A man did not use his size and power to harm a woman. It simply wasn't done. Roman's wife had been such a sweet and fragile woman. He couldn't imagine having touched her in anger even if she'd been as tough as the petite Abigail Haws was.

He shoved that line of thought far away. Lindy had been gone twelve years, and it wouldn't do to think on that just before he was due to meet with Ms. Haws.

Once Marcus announced her arrival, Roman terminated his comm immediately and told his assistant to send her in.

He stood and met her at the door. "Ms. Haws, are you well?"

She sighed and the tension vibrated from her, concerning him deeply.

"Marcus, will you please bring us some refreshments? And hold all comm traffic please." He looked back to her. "Please, sit down." When he touched her arm she jumped. He slowly moved away, taking a seat after she did.

"I'm fine. I take it this is about the scene Saul Kerrigan made today in the hall?"

He nodded. Her voice was so flat, the spark in her dimmed. There was something *wrong* with her just then. She wasn't her usual combative self. "I saw the footage, Ms. Haws. Is your arm all right?"

She winced, holding it close to her body. He had to know.

"Did he mark you?"

"That's none of your business."

He narrowed his eyes. "Indeed it is. This is my damned 'Verse and I take care of my people. You'll show me your arm because I asked."

She jerked back, brown eyes flashing, face flushed, and satisfaction roared through him that she showed signs of her spark.

"I'm not one of your peasants as if you are a fief lord in the oldest sense. If you saw the vid, you saw an Associate House leader act inappropriately. Security came and he left. I went to the rest of my hearings and came back to the office. By the way, thank you for speaking to Administrator Cushing. Gretel Mortan is now home with her family. She'll still have to endure trial but at least the credits won't be an issue. Her case has been taken up by my office and paid for by an anonymous donor. Now, would you like to speak about the Movement for Representative Democracy?"

Marcus chose that moment to glide in and place a tray heavy with food and tea on the table between Roman's and Abigail's chairs.

While Abigail's attention was on Marcus leaving the room, Roman leaned forward and pushed her sleeve up. The creamy pale skin was marred by an ugly thumbprint bruise.

All he heard was a gasp before he found himself flat on the carpet. Abigail scrambled atop his chest, teeth bared.

Her hair had come unmoored from the nest at the back of her neck and her spectacles sat askew on her face. The uptight barrister had been replaced by a wild woman with a river of dark hair and big, flashing eyes. Her lips, why hadn't he noticed them before? Plump and juicy. He certainly didn't miss the heaving breasts. He'd pretended not to notice she hadn't been wearing a bra the evening before, but with them only inches away from his face, he couldn't pretend they weren't there. Large, fleshy and mouthwatering. The upper curve of her right breast was exposed at the neck of her blouse as she leaned over him.

The moment stretched between them. He knew Marcus must have heard but the door had not opened. Madness took hold in him chasing all rational thought away.

His control slipped, replaced by fascination at what she'd feel like. His hands found her thighs as she straddled his body, slid up until the edge of her stockings alerted him to bare flesh. Her breath hitched and then she froze.

"I . . ." She blinked as if awakened from a dream.

"You have very soft skin," he murmured, his thumbs sliding back and forth along the band separating bare, velvet thigh and the stocking.

She scrambled back, legs akimbo, giving him a perfect view of the slice of her body he'd started to yearn for. Red. Bright red panties and stockings underneath the sensible suit. Abigail Haws had a bit of insensible and a lot of sexy.

"I'm so sorry."

He moved, slowly on his hands and knees, until he reached her. "I shouldn't have startled you. I'm the one who's sorry." Clearly something had happened to her to make her respond that way. He wanted to know, wanted her to trust him to tell him but it wasn't the time.

"You make me feel . . . this shouldn't be happening," she whispered and the shadow of fear slid from her eyes, replaced by something else.

He caught the dark shadow of her nipples against the front of her blouse, even through her bra. A deep breath as he sought control brought her scent, her arousal, into his system. It had been a very long time since he'd felt this sort of raw need.

"It is." Reaching toward her very cautiously, he tucked some of her hair behind her shoulder. And fell. Fell into her, into her spell, into whatever delicious thing that had built between them. The soft, cool silk of the dark strands caressed his hand and arm until all he could do was lean in and kiss her.

Rather than gasp or pull away, she relaxed, sliding her arms up and around his neck, opening her mouth to him.

He tasted her, sampled the heat of her mouth, the softness of her tongue sliding against his. He hadn't kissed anyone this way for nearly fifteen years.

His cock brushed against her thigh and all he could think about was the top of the stocking. All he wanted to do was place a kiss there and it drove him crazy. Crazy enough his hands found that spot on each thigh, on the inside. Her breath gusted out as her hips canted forward.

The tips of his fingers brushed against her cunt, open and ridiculously hot and wet against the material of her panties. She panted and he returned her breath with his own strain to breathe. He needed to stop, this should not happen, but the soft, desperate sound she made into his mouth was his undoing.

He moved closer, on his knees between her wide-open thighs. He burrowed his fingers beneath her panties and nearly passed out when they slid between the slick folds of her pussy, and her clit, already hard and swollen, met his fingertips as he moved them up.

He opened his eyes, looking down into her face as he fingered her pussy. The sounds of his fingers sliding into her core and pulling out echoed against her whispered moans and the rustle of clothing.

Anyone could walk in at any time. This was fucking madness, but he could not stop until she came all over his hand. He had to have her orgasm. Her fingers dug in to his shoulders as she rocked against his fingers and he wondered how long it had been for her, but then realized he didn't want to know what other men she'd been with. Didn't want to know if anyone else had shared this exquisite tension with her.

She arched, breaking the kiss with a gasp as he felt her body find release in a hot rush. All through the moments he'd had his fingers buried in her, his gaze hadn't left her face, not wanting to miss that moment, and he wasn't sorry. The lines on her forehead smoothed as her face totally relaxed and her mouth opened on a sated sigh.

*　*　*

What the hells had just happened? Abbie slowly opened her eyes to find those sexy green ones looking back. Satisfaction etched his features, purely and utterly male, and she couldn't help but smile.

"Um . . ." What could she say? Thanks for the hand job? Do you regularly finger women to climax on your carpet with your staff right outside?

"Roman, I'm sorry to bother you, but Alexander is on the comm and he's insisting on speaking with you." Marcus's voice echoed through the office intercom, startling them both into action.

Wincing a bit—a glance at his crotch and Abbie saw why—Roman stood and held a hand down to her. Grateful he hadn't simply pulled her to standing, she took the hand and got up.

She was a total mess. Emotionally, well, she couldn't even think on what had happened that day. Physically, though, was her concern right then.

"You . . ." She nodded toward his cock, feeling bad she hadn't given him what he'd done for her.

"I'll be all right. A discussion with my brother will undo all your work, I'm afraid." He paused and slid a fingertip through the notch in her chin. "My bathroom is right through that door should you want to straighten your clothes up. I have to take this comm, but I would like to continue this discussion afterward."

Avoiding *that* for the time being, she simply nodded and headed into the bathroom, closing the door behind herself, leaning against it to catch her breath as she heard Roman bustle around and then his voice as he took the comm.

The woman looking back at her in the mirror started as she took herself in. "I look like a nineteen-year-old who just got fingered in her boyfriend's parents' house," she mumbled as she wet her hands to get her hair back in order. Which made her laugh because she *had* been a nineteen-year-old girl who got fingered in her boyfriend's parents' house, in the dark, in their family room after an hour of kissing.

Who kissed for an hour anymore? She'd like to kiss Roman for an hour, maybe two. Languid kisses, because they had the whole day to do nothing more than that.

Her knees were still rubber from the interlude. How completely unexpected it had all been. Him touching her like that, shoving her sleeve up to see the bruise Kerrigan had left. And when she saw his hand there, something slipped its moorings inside her and she rushed at him, shoving him to the carpet, wanting to harm before she could be harmed.

But he'd been still, looking up at her through eyes that saw right to her soul. Some part of him had seen her pain and he'd responded to that. And then when he'd caressed her thighs, good great gods! It'd been enough to ram the sense back into her to jump from him and get some distance. But then he'd uncoiled himself like a great male predator and moved to her with kind eyes.

She'd attacked not just a Ranked male, but *the* Ranked male, and he'd gently moved the hair from her face. Not as if she were so fragile she'd break, but as if she were precious. And then he kissed her and she couldn't resist, couldn't even recall the reasons she'd had for staying away from him to begin with.

She'd gone up there upset and afraid, but now something else had passed between them. He'd touched her physically, yes, but emotionally, as well, and the dark edge of craving began to sliver through her.

He'd kissed her like a man was meant to kiss. Intent in every movement, in every slide of lips and tongue. Want roared through her, and when he'd touched her thighs, the tips of his fingers brushing against her cunt, she'd nearly swallowed her tongue.

Yes, those moments on his floor had undoubtedly been some of the hottest in her life, and they absolutely could not happen again. Well, maybe once she—you know—evened things out between them.

He'd gone from hypercontrolled to hypersexual, and yet she got the feeling he still held back. She wondered what he'd be like in bed completely unfettered. She shivered; it wasn't for her to know. He was Roman Lyons. She was a woman from a professional family, yes, but an unranked one. It wasn't like that little interlude meant anything, and all she could really hope was that he wouldn't think less of her for it.

She waited a while but he still spoke in the other room, and the longer she waited, the more nervous she became. Eventually, she quietly exited the bathroom and inched her way toward the door to the outer office.

His eyes cut to her as he continued to speak in terse, tight sentences. He shook his head but she nodded and waved as she headed for freedom.

"Is he off the comm?" Marcus asked, acting as if she hadn't just had his boss two knuckles deep on the floor of his office. Gods, she hoped he had no real idea of what had gone on in there.

"Um, no. He's still on, but it's late. I need to go home."

A mysterious smile curved Marcus's lips before concern replaced it.

"Are you all right, Ms. Haws? I saw the footage and if I wouldn't be tossed into lockup, I'd be heading over to Saul Kerrigan's home right now."

She softened a bit. Marcus was quite charming. "Please, call me Abbie. And I'm fine. Really. And now I must go. Please tell Mr. Lyons I appreciate his concern."

"Okay, if you call me Marcus. He had Kerrigan in here. Yelled at him. Roman does not yell."

She blew out a breath, liking it more than she should that Roman Lyons defended her in some sense.

"Well, that sort of vid footage is bound to get out, and I'm sure he wondered if I'd go to the media about it."

"Why didn't you?" One eyebrow rose, taunting her.

She shrugged. "Who says I won't? Good evening, Marcus."

Chapter 5

"I can't believe it. Kerrigan needs a punch in the face." Her brother Daniel paced in her parents' living room. She'd gone straight there from Roman's office, knowing that scene with Kerrigan would most likely hit the vids. She didn't want them to be scared, worrying about her, so she thought she'd head it off. Not to mention, she wanted to be sure her father didn't hare off on some wild scheme.

Of course, it *had* been on the vids, and making matters worse, the others in the MRD had been looking for her as well. She had a lot to deal with and she had no idea how she'd explain that in two meetings with Roman Lyons she hadn't spoken about the MRD at all. Those messages she left to deal with the following day.

She'd hoped to get a little comfort from her visit home, but instead all her siblings were there and her mother had baked several cakes. The cake part wasn't so bad. Her mother would send at least one home with her and she could eat it instead of having sex with

Roman Lyons. Which would be wrong. Bad and wrong and stupid. And really hot, she'd bet.

"Typical. Typical privileged behavior. If you'd done that to him, you'd have been arrested." Clementine Haws, Abbie's mother, handed her a plate heaped with cake before sitting beside her. "Eat."

"Mmmm. Cake. Thanks, Mai." She dug in before she had to say another thing about it. She wanted to go home, drink something strong enough to stop the nightmares, and sleep.

"Are you all right? You looked so very pale in that footage from the hallway. I know it must bring up memories for you." Her oldest brother, Daniel, sat across from her, concern etched into his features.

"I'm fine. I told you all, I'm fine and I don't want to talk about that. I only came over because I knew it would be on the screens and you'd be worried."

"Well, not to seem heartless or anything, but you can certainly use this with Lyons now. He's certain to be more sympathetic toward you."

She'd been wondering when her father would bring it up. He was a creature of habit, after all.

"Gods! Dai, you're so out of line sometimes. It would be nice of you to think about your children as people instead of opportunities every once in a while." Nyna, her sister and best friend, threw an angry glance at their father.

"I'm just saying! I love my children, Nyna," Jonas, their father, looking slightly guilty, but Abbie didn't miss the light of a mission in his eyes. "She has an opportunity, why should she waste it? Abbie didn't get where she is today by letting things happen to her. She makes things happen for other people."

Her baby brother, Georges, snorted and Daniel sighed.

Abbie knew her father loved them in his own way. But she also knew *the cause* meant just as much, if not more, and so she wasn't surprised or even hurt by what he'd said. In fact, she'd been amazed by his restraint at waiting as long as he did before bringing it up.

"This was lovely. Thanks for the cake, Mai. I need to go home now." Abbie stood and her sister did as well.

"I'll go with you. I need to get home, too." Nyna glared at their father and Abbie pulled a strand of her sister's hair. "Ouch! What?"

"Leave him alone. It's who he is. He doesn't mean anything by it," Abbie murmured.

"I'll go with both of you. With Family members out in the halls of justice assaulting tiny women, what's next?" Daniel said.

"Jonas, you've chased her off. After the day our girl has had, you just had to bring that up?" Her mother spun on her father, hands on her hips.

"Mai, it's all right. I promise. I really do have to go home. I've been up for a very long time and I need to sleep. I have several cases being heard in the next few weeks, so I have to prepare." She let her father hug her tight and returned the kiss to his cheek.

"You know I love you." He looked so sad, for a moment she realized how very much he was like a sibling instead of a father. It wasn't his fault. He wasn't a bad person, he just wasn't totally developed as a father. His causes took higher priority than his family, and their mother had always been the one who provided the actual parenting. Sad but true, and certainly not going to change at that point.

"I do. I'm not mad. I really do need to go."

The lines on his forehead smoothed and he smiled. "Night then, Abbie."

With Daniel on one side and Nyna on the other, they took the tram back toward the city center where the three of them lived within a few city blocks. The night was clear and crisp, and the scents of her old neighborhood hung in the air. Bakeries, cafés, the trees lining the walk. Despite everything, it was a good 'Verse. Ravena was her home and she would fight for it.

Perhaps she was feeling sort of sleepy and content because of the orgasm she'd had earlier.

"You'd better give me some of that cake. Just because some old guy yelled at you and stuff doesn't mean you should get all the cake. And what are you smiling about?" Daniel winked at her.

"He needs to stop eating so much cake, that Saul Kerrigan. He looks like a giant, featherheaded meatball," Nyna said.

Abbie and Daniel burst out laughing. "He's an old fool who felt threatened. And it's over now." The three of them got off near Abbie's building and walked the last bit.

"Are you going to be safe? How serious is this? Be honest." Daniel stopped her, putting a hand to her cheek.

"I think I'll be fine. He was just upset because he felt thwarted. Roman Lyons apparently warned him off."

"But when you start agitating with the MRD again? What then? This is a dangerous path, Abbie." Daniel had a point.

"It is, yes. But what can I do? Stop working to make the 'Verses more democratic? Because some old man yelled at me and gave me a bruise? The time is now, Daniel. Things have never been so favorable for us before."

"He gave you a bruise?" Daniel's voice darkened, violence making it sharp at the edges. He'd served in the military like most of Ravena's youth, but he had done things he didn't speak of. Abbie was pretty sure he was still involved in military intelligence in some way. They didn't discuss it, but he often knew things and did things that only someone in the upper echelons of the corps would know. He would disappear for weeks at a time without a word. She knew it wasn't merely consulting, no matter what he said.

She stopped, grabbing his arm for emphasis. "Yes, but you're not responsible for it, nor do I want you to do anything about it. Understand? There is *nothing* you can do."

He was silent for long moments until he finally nodded and she and Nyna relaxed. The last thing she needed was to have to defend her brother on a murder charge for some piece of garbage like Saul Kerrigan.

"I'm going in now. I'll see you both at dinner in a few days. Thanks for the escort, and, no, you may not have any of my cake. Perhaps some yucky old man can assault you and Mai will make you some." She kissed both siblings and went into her building while they watched.

No more hot chemistry for her and Roman Lyons. He was completely and totally unacceptable. He was Ranked and certainly unable to marry her, even if he wanted to. And it wasn't like she expected marriage after a hand job either. But at some point, with a man, you wanted to think about the future. If there was no future *ever*, what would the point be? She was old enough to be past any silly nonsense of just having a fling. She was a serious person when it came to relationships. It was one thing to date, but another thing to date until a replacement woman suitable for marriage came along.

She couldn't imagine him taking a mistress, and she'd never actually be one. So it was a dead end. In this case it was best to just let it be a sweet, hot memory.

Her apartment was quiet when she let herself in. She noted the myriad messages on her comm but walked by toward the bathroom and her pills. The past had a way of creeping in and it had sunk its claws in deep that afternoon. A drink and a little white pill and she could only pray for a night without dreams.

Sweet gods, his balls ached. Roman shifted his weight in his chair yet again. Abigail Haws had worked him up and then escaped while he'd been in midargument with Alexander.

Alexander felt their allegiance belonged to House Kerrigan in this whole mess. Roman didn't blame Alexander too much; after all, right then, many Families had a siege mentality and it wasn't as if Alexander had much empathy or experience with the unranked. Still, Roman had enough problems and now his idiot brother had allied himself with Saul at precisely the wrong time.

On top of that, he needed to come and he hadn't even spoken with Abigail about what her group wanted from him.

Marcus had gone home for the day so Roman left him a note to contact Abigail again to set up a meeting to discuss the demands of her group. They should absolutely *not* have sex, even if it was everything he wanted at that moment.

Abigail Haws was unranked and unsuitable. She was beautiful and he certainly admired her intelligence and her integrity but Ranked first sons simply didn't marry unranked. When he made the choice to marry again, it would be the daughter of an important House because it was *how things were done*.

She could be a mistress, certainly. But he didn't believe in having a wife and a mistress. He felt it only demeaned all three people. Roman would take a wife and be faithful to her because she deserved that commitment from him. He had respected Lindy, had even loved her in his own way. She'd been the best wife and mother she could be, if distant at the end. Kind, gentle, compassionate. He couldn't have asked for more. Even passionate love, something he'd always imagined having someday, was more than he could have asked for with Lindy or anyone else. He'd had a satisfying marriage and a good family life. Now he had two wonderful sons who'd take his place someday.

Seeking solace between the thighs of a woman, even one as incredible as Abigail Haws, wasn't part of his plan, and he would have to have himself under better control the next time he saw her.

Chapter 6

"What?" Abbie stared at Georges as he told her the news. "You have to be kidding me." She'd stopped by the MRD offices on her way over to House Lyons's offices for her appointment.

"The vid said the Kerrigan Family had joined with Alexander Lyons in their opposition to the MRD and their goals. They said the group was spouting treason and should be banned. And they called for your license to practice to be revoked." Georges was her right hand at the MRD and quite often stood at her side when they planned and worked.

"Unbelievable! I have a meeting with House Lyons in a little while. We shall see what Roman Lyons's opinion on this matter is." And if he was behind it, she'd kick his ass. No matter how tasty it looked.

She'd only gotten the barest amount of sleep. Her pill and the drink hadn't helped much against the dreams. Stupid, so stupid. Each time she thought she'd gotten past it, something brought it up again and she wondered if she'd ever be able to throw the pills away.

So she wasn't in the brightest of moods as she took the lift to the soaring space where Roman Lyons ran his empire. Marcus did look handsome behind his desk, wearing a smile and sending her a flirty wink when she arrived, taking a bit of the edge off her mood.

"Why hello! Don't you look beautiful today?"

"Are you trying to soften me up? Do you think I haven't seen the vids today?"

"Ouch. I figured you'd seen the vids; you're an informed sort of person. And who doesn't like to tell a woman she looks good? But softening you up would be a nice by-product. Not all Lyons are the same. Just remember that." He said the last under his breath but she heard it just the same.

"Is he in now? And thank you. You look quite handsome yourself. But you know that of course."

He fluttered his lashes at her playfully, but still very sexily, and laughed. "I commed him that you'd arrived and he'll be out momentarily. And why do I know I look handsome?"

"Men like you know how good they look. It's why you're all so appealing." She shrugged.

"Is that so? Do you have a man in your life, Abbie?"

"Whyever do you ask?" How long had it been since she'd flirted? The pounding behind her eyes lessened.

"Well, as much as I adore lovely women, I don't poach on other men's territory. It wouldn't be fair."

"It's funny you assume I'd be with a man."

He laughed. "I'd be so very disappointed if that weren't the case."

"What would that be?"

They both turned to the voice in the doorway and Roman stood there, the light behind him casting a bright glow about the edges of his body. She remembered his hands on her, the way he kissed. Roman Lyons was divine, but not like that.

"Nothing at all, Mr. Lyons. Ms. Haws is here for your appointment." Marcus's lips twitched slightly.

"I see that, Marcus. Thank you. Ms. Haws, won't you come in?"

She waved discreetly at Marcus as she walked past and into Roman's office.

"You left yesterday without saying good-bye." He stood very close to her and shivers broke over her body.

She cleared her throat and reined in her hormones. "Okay, we're veering off topic here. Movement for Representative Democracy. My organization? Yes, they're going to ask me what we discussed and I can't very well say . . . well, I can't say *that*."

He sat down, indicating she do the same, and she winced, noting he wasn't behind his desk but rather in the more intimate, and closer together, chair and table set up near the windows.

"Here, have some kava. Then tell me what exactly you can't say." He smirked and she pursed her lips as she thought over what to say. Did he think she was some sort of shy flower? When it came to sex, she may not get it regularly, but she wasn't ashamed of what she liked and what she did.

"I can't very well tell them you fingered me to orgasm on the floor of your office. I mean, imagine what your brother and Saul Kerrigan would say about that."

He hesitated a moment but she didn't miss the way his pupils enlarged or the hitch in his breath.

"Let's leave them out of any discussion involving my office floor and my fingers in your cunt."

She might have lost her hearing for a moment, the words coming from him were so unexpected. His voice had changed from the smooth cadence he normally had. Instead, he said it low, rough, and her nipples hardened in response.

"All right. But, um, back to the topic of our meeting. Let's get this out of the way first. Do you support the ridiculous call from your brother and House Kerrigan to revoke my license to practice and to have the MRD declared a banned organization?"

"You tell me, Ms. Haws. *Are* you a treasonous organization?"

"Abbie. Ms. Haws is my mother. The MRD wants representative democracy. How is that treasonous?"

"How do you plan to make it happen?"

"Are you asking if I'm going to sell information to the Imperialists to fund my war against Family Rule?"

He took a deep breath. "What is it you want, Abbie?"

"I want real democracy, Mr. Lyons."

"Roman. And I'm fairly educated on forms of government over history both before the Diaspora and once we all settled throughout the Known 'Verses. From what I can tell, you enjoy democracy now."

"Do I? That's an interesting perspective. When I can't hold a job that you can, how is that democracy? I didn't vote for you, and yet Families make all the rules I live by. Why? Because you all had the credits and therefore the power when we first came through the portals. You weren't elected or chosen. You came through with the power and the credits and you've hoarded them ever since."

His brows lowered, annoyed. "I work hard to represent the needs of the people of Ravena and the rest of the Known 'Verses. Do you think it's fun? This job?"

She took a deep breath. "I'm sure you do work hard. That's not the point. This isn't a test of how hard you work, or what a nice guy you are. This is about the fact that the people of Ravena do not have a vote in who represents us. There's no one on the Governing Council who understands what it is like to be unranked. Your world and ours are vastly different. Why shouldn't we have someone who understands that voicing our needs?"

"You have a job. A good job that pays well. You live in a nice home. All citizens of Ravena receive an excellent education and vocational training. We have health care and many, many benefits that make life better for Ranked and unranked alike. There are no differences between Ranked and unranked. Not in the way you're insinuating!"

"Bullshit! Stop making this about how nice you are, you self-righteous ass. Of course there are differences. Huge ones, like yesterday, when Saul Kerrigan attacked me, the guard addressed him first. Spoke to him like I wasn't there. If *I* had attacked him the way he did me, I'd have been arrested immediately. No one even asked if I was interested in pursuing charges against him. Do you really, truly believe there are no differences between Ranked and unranked? Can you sit there and say such a thing without laughing?"

"Self-righteous? I'm listening to your grievances and I'm self-righteous?"

"The fact that it's considered special to have a leader actually listen to grievances is self-righteous, yes. The fact that your brother, a known womanizer to the extreme, and Saul Kerrigan, a corrupt, insane and violent man, can stand up and say to the public that I should have my right to practice taken from me because I dare to say there has to be a better, *fairer* way says yes, there are differences. You're telling me that your brother, with his string of mistresses broken and abandoned in his wake, is better at governing than I am? Or *my* brother or any other unranked citizen who actually works for a living? All because your name is Lyons and mine isn't?"

He pushed to stand and she did as well.

"You go too far. You don't know Alexander at all."

His green eyes blazed with anger and something else. What it was, she didn't know, and right then, she didn't care. He turned and went to the window. She followed and stood next to him, staring out at the city below.

"I know all I need to know about his type. Believe me. And that he associates with the likes of Saul Kerrigan, a man who'd put an old woman who worked for him and his family for generations into lockup rather than pay her what she's due says quite a lot."

"So you'll tear down the foundations of our society? Break it all apart because you don't like my brother?" He turned to her as he asked.

"You think I've spent the better part of my life working on creating a system of representative democracy because of your brother? Truly? Why are you making this about you? It's not."

He took her by the upper arms but it wasn't the same as it had been with Kerrigan. Not at all. Her knees turned to rubber even as she tried to be ashamed of how hot it made her when he looked at her the way he did just then.

"I'm in charge. How can it not be about me?"

"It's about something larger than you," she whispered.

He gave an anguished sort of growl. "Why do you do this to me?"

"I don't know. I thought you were doing it to me."

His mouth crushed down over hers, dominating, taking, tasting. Want slid over her, took her somewhere else and she let it.

"I want you, Abbie." He wrenched his mouth away, nearly panting as he waited to hear her reply.

"Please, gods, please. Touch me."

Like a switch going off, they set upon each other as if they simply couldn't get what they wanted quickly enough. Their lips never left each other as hands shoved and yanked to pull clothes off in frenzied action. Her suit jacket hit the ground and he shoved her blouse up under her arms, exposing her breasts. She wanted to cry out and demand more, but before she could, he gave it.

His mouth left hers as he pulled the cups of her bra down and teeth and tongue found her nipple.

Her fingers sifted through his hair, holding his head to her. The tension in his muscles radiated from him, up into her body. He was holding back.

She pushed and he moved his mouth from her. Never in her life had she seen anything so amazing and sexy. His eyes were lit with an inner fire and his shirt hung open, exposing the masculine beauty beneath. She shoved the shirt off, leaving him naked from the waist up, and looked her fill.

His upper body was beautiful. Substantial. Not bulked, but he had a broad chest with a smattering of hair the same color as the pale-blond hair on his head.

"You're holding back," she said. "Don't. I don't want it. I don't need it."

He shuddered.

She ran her palms over the muscles of his belly, down over his cock through his pants and he jerked forward into her grip. Squeezing just so, she kept eye contact. "What is it? Do you like it rough? I bruise easily, but it's consensual. I'm not going to break. I'm on fertility blockers. So do it. Fuck me, Roman. Take me. I'm all yours. You can't scare me with your desires. I can see you, beneath the skin. You're not bad. You're a good man."

"Damn it." He wiped his mouth on the back of his hand and stared at her long and hard. "Look at you there, your tits out, nipples dark and swollen from my mouth. I can smell you, Abbie. I know you want me."

She nodded and he bent over, his mouth on her nipples again, teeth abrading the tender flesh just hard enough to wrench a moan from her. She looked down, watching him, watching his mouth on her, and the thrill slithered through her. Somewhere in her brain she knew this was dumb but she couldn't seem to connect with that part. There was only one part of her thinking and in control now, and it wasn't her brain.

Each pull of his mouth on her nipple shot straight to her clit. She shifted to try and ease the ache there, and it drew his attention to her.

He shoved her back against the wall of windows and fell to his knees. Chest heaving, she watched as he shoved her skirt up and yanked her panties down. "A bare cunt. I should have known. I felt it yesterday, so smooth, but I didn't get to see it. Just those red panties. Are you a bad girl beneath the suit?"

"I'm a bad girl all over." Was that an insult? She guessed it wasn't, because moments later his mouth moved to her. The first long swipe and then swirl of his tongue against her sensitized clit brought a gasp from deep in her gut.

"You taste good. Wet and creamy. Gods," he murmured against her pussy. "I could eat this cunt for hours and hours. I might just do that. But not right now. Now I'm going make you come all over my face and then I'm going to fuck you against this window." He brought one of her thighs up to rest on his shoulder as he licked and nibbled on her pussy like she was a delicacy.

Two of his fingers stroked into her, fucking her mercilessly as he tongued her. She held on to his head and bit her lip to keep from speaking. That didn't stop the deep, guttural moans and the soft sounds of pleasure from drifting out of her body.

Pinned there between his clever, relentless mouth and the cool glass at her back, she held on and tried to keep her balance as pleasure began to burn in her muscles. Oh, seven hells, she was going to come and come hard. In his office. *Again*.

"Oh my . . . yesssss," she burst out as orgasm claimed her with a shock of electric sensation.

He stood quickly, mouth finding hers again and she heard his belt slither off and his pants slide down. She tossed a thigh over his hip as he thrust his cock deep and hard into her cunt. Her taste was sharp on her lips as he continued to kiss her.

"Damn it, you're so hot," he mumbled as he thrust, hard and fast. "Your cunt is tight and wet. I like that."

"I like it too, almost as much as that gorgeous cock," she said as he pinched and rolled a nipple.

"I can't believe I'm doing this."

"Thank gods you are."

He stopped a moment and then laughed, thrusting again. "My cock belongs deep inside you."

Oh dear gods, she loved dirty talk. Real dirty talk done by someone who felt it. Logan sounded ridiculous when he tried it, but deep inside, Roman Lyons was a very dirty man, and because he owned the words, they worked. Straight down to her toes.

"Does it? Mmmm. I'm not complaining, that's for sure." She leaned forward and grabbed his earlobe between her teeth and he groaned.

"Maybe if I keep you stuffed with cock you'll be too busy to make trouble for me."

"While your cock is talented, not to mention your mouth, my pussy is in charge right now. I'm still going to make you listen to our demands when we're done."

"I was afraid of that," he said and she laughed.

"Afraid enough to stop fucking me?"

"Hells no. I'm going to come inside you not very long from now." He turned to catch her mouth for a brief kiss. "I'm still a gentleman, so you will come, too." Reaching around her thigh, past his cock, the tips of his fingers found her clit and he flicked over it with a featherlight but fast rhythm that found her rolling her hips to grind into them and his cock.

So close to her last orgasm she didn't think she had another in her, but she was wrong. She gasped as her body seized up, clamping down on his cock.

"Yes, that's it. Give me another one."

She did, biting into the muscle of his shoulder to keep from crying out and bringing security in.

His eyes closed and he dropped his head to her shoulder as he pumped into her over and over so hard the vase on the table nearby began to rock back and forth. When he came, his head shot back as he thrust one last time, so deep the head of his cock bumped into her cervix.

A few moments later he opened his eyes and looked at her. "I can't believe that just happened."

Did he regret it?

Her fear passed when he smiled and kissed her softly, as he pulled out gently and dragged her into the adjoining bathroom.

He picked her up easily and placed her on the counter before pulling her bra back into place and smoothing her blouse down. Using a washcloth, he cleaned her up and then himself as she watched.

"I guess I'll have to call you Abbie now for sure. We're most definitely past the formal address stage."

*H*is attraction to Abbie befuddled him. Not that he didn't understand what made him look twice. She was beautiful, small but lush. Big eyes, juicy lips, tits that made his mouth water and an ass that made his cock twitch. Physically, Abbie Haws was a very nice package. Certainly she was intelligent and well-spoken, but in the past that was not what he'd been attracted to. He liked his women very soft, women who liked him to make the decisions. Abbie was not that woman at all.

And yet, she coursed through his veins just then. Her laugh made him smile just thinking on it. The way her eyes lit up when she argued, the strident tone of her voice, she was a tough woman and she'd be a worthy adversary should things get that far.

Get that far? Had he not just spewed all the dirty thoughts in his head as he fucked her, standing up, against the wall of windows in his office? He'd never done anything approaching that carelessness, but he'd do it again if he got the chance.

The question was whether he should avoid having a chance at all. This was dangerous ground. But knowing he couldn't have her in the long term didn't meter his desire to know her. However unlike him it was to actually throw caution out the window and follow a course he knew had a dead end, he didn't know if he could stop.

"You're very quiet."

He looked back at her. She'd hopped down from the counter and her hair was back in the complicated knot she wore at the base of her neck. Even all tucked in and buttoned up, she still looked like she'd been well fucked. Her eyes were bright and her cheeks flushed.

He rinsed his face and finger-combed his hair and pulled his shirt back on.

"I'm just thinking, wondering what the hells to do about this thing between us. We can't . . ." How could he say it?

She nodded, walking away. "Ah. Well, yes. I can see your conundrum. It's one I share. You're Ranked. I am not. I'm entirely unsuitable."

He took a deep breath and followed her out. "Don't say it that way. I don't regret what happened. I . . . I just . . ."

"It can't go anywhere." She shrugged and he nodded, miserably.

"I'll have Georges, my brother, deal with MRD stuff. We should stop meeting like this." She laughed, but the sound was brittle and tore at him. "You know what I mean. Being alone together can only end up naked and sweaty."

"I don't want to meet with anyone else."

"My brother is very handsome, but he doesn't like men. You'll be safe with him." She grabbed her suit jacket and put it on. "But I'm warning you, in all seriousness, do not back this attack on me. I won't have it. I have the right, even under Family Rule, to speak my views. I will do so without threats."

She went to the door and he clenched his fists to keep from reaching for her. Things had been so damned good just minutes before. And now, the blandness of his life threatened to swallow him again.

"Can you at least attend the meetings with your brother? I'll bring Deimos, my oldest son and the Lyons heir. Nothing will happen that way. I think you have a lot to say, Abbie, and I want you to say it."

She paused as she thought and then nodded shortly. "Yes, all right. That will work. When we meet next, I'll bring some proposals. A few ideas on how we'd like to see changes made and where."

"I can't guarantee anything. You know that."

"Of course I do. It's my job to persuade people, Roman. Have a good day. I'll see you soon. Um, thanks."

He watched her go, wanting to stop her, wanting to ask her to dinner, but knowing it was best he not. Never in his life had he hated his position but the helplessness he felt as her scent began to fade made him wonder how far away he was from that place.

Chapter 7

$\mathscr{A}$ bbie saw Logan just outside her door when she looked up. She called out to him and he came in, leaning against her doorway as she gathered her things.

"I never got the chance to thank you for helping me that day with Kerrigan. I appreciate it."

"I'm your friend, of course I helped. Why don't you come to dinner at my place tonight?"

She paused, searching for a way to say what needed saying. "I can't do dinner. We have to stop that. You need to find someone and I need to stop having sex with you when I get lonely."

"Why? For the gods' sake, why would you think that? I like having sex with you. We could be together as a couple again if you'd just trust me. But in the meantime, I don't see why we can't share some warmth from time to time. I know you enjoy it. I know I do."

"Because it's become a way for me to avoid moving on. We aren't meant to be. You don't love me like that and I don't want to be with someone who can't keep his cock where it belongs." She laughed. "Truly, Logan, I do love you. But we can't do this."

He pouted, genuinely confused by her refusal. "You say you love me but you won't be with me."

"I love you but I'd hate you if I was with you again. You hurt me. But we're friends now and I like that. You don't need me for sex. You can get it elsewhere. We're better as friends, less pain all around. Now shoo. I have a meeting to go to."

She put her hand on his cheek and he leaned into it. "You have become so dear to me, Logan. Truly. Thank you for being such a good friend."

"I don't understand you, but I'll always love you. Do be careful with all this agitation going around, all right?" He kissed her forehead and she walked past him, nearly ramming into none other than Roman Lyons, who made no secret of scowling at Logan.

"Mr. Lyons, I was just on my way to our meeting. My brother should be out front. Did I get the location incorrect?" Her heart sped at his nearness and she wanted to touch him, to smooth her hand across his forehead, to press her lips against the hollow of his throat.

But that would be very bad.

"I had to be in a hearing a few floors below, so I thought I'd bring my son over to get a tour. Do you have time?"

She looked around Roman to see a younger version standing there, wearing a big grin.

"Of course." She turned to where Logan now stood at her elbow. "Can you see if Georges is out front, and if so, let him know I'll be down in a bit? Oh, and let me introduce you. Logan Beltine, this is Roman Lyons. Logan is a senior barrister here."

They did that handshake thing where each man tried to squeeze hard but not seem as if that's what they were doing.

"Don't let us keep you, Logan," Roman said with a smile that didn't reach his eyes.

She wanted to roll her eyes but managed not to. Logan mumbled his pleasure at meeting Roman and then turned back to her. "I'll go and talk to Georges and I'll see you tomorrow, all right? Comm me later if you change your mind about what we spoke on earlier. Or if you just want to talk." Brazenly, he brushed a kiss over her lips and was gone down the long, narrow hallway before she could say anything in response.

"You must be Deimos, right?" she asked gamely, ignoring more scowls from the delicious Mr. Lyons.

"Don't mind him, he's forgotten his manners. Yes, I'm Deimos, the oldest, and most handsome, if I do say so myself. I find that information is often useful." He winked as he kissed her hand. If he'd been serious, he could have given Logan a run for his credits in the cocksure department, but instead he grinned as he joked and his father groaned.

"Dem, you're going to make Ms. Haws want to avoid all Lyons forever at this point." Roman looked back to Abbie. "Yes, this is my oldest. He got a lot of attention until Corrin came along. It's why, I'm told, he's got such a high opinion of himself."

"We're not all like my uncle Alexander," Deimos said under his breath.

"Thank the gods for all their favors then. Now, about that tour?"

She showed them through the tight warren of offices, the small adjunct hearing spaces, the law library still filled with people even at that late hour, and as they were wrapping it up, Georges met them in the main alcove near the lifts.

"There you are. I was beginning to worry. Did you still want to grab a bite before the meeting?" Her brother stopped as Roman and Deimos came closer. "Oh I apologize, I hadn't realized you were still giving the tour."

Abbie quickly introduced everyone and Roman shook Georges' hand.

"No, we apologize. I didn't know we were keeping Abbie, Ms. Haws, from her meal. Deimos and I haven't eaten either. Why don't we take our meeting with some food?"

Good gods, she loved the way he looked just at that moment. Smiling at Georges as he stood next to his son. All three so handsome and vital they took up every bit of space in the alcove. And the one who took her breath away smelled very good.

Which was, of course, very bad to even think about. *Bad, Abbie!*

"We all have to eat." Georges looked at Abbie briefly and shrugged his shoulders. "Our sister runs a small café nearby. I'm quite sure she can fit us all in in the back. It's private enough that we can discuss things without interference."

Roman's gaze snagged on her and caught for long moments. "Sounds better than a conference room in an office building. Shall we?" He indicated they precede him onto the lift.

Light from Nyna's small café spilled out onto the walk in front. Happy chatter filtered through the doors as they pushed inside.

Nyna saw them and grinned, moving quickly to envelop Abbie and Georges into a big hug. "I didn't expect to see you two. Oh, and hello there. Well, I can see we've got some special guests. It's a good thing I've just put on another big pot of salume. Bread is fresh; pie, too. Come and sit. I gather you'll want some quiet?" She looked to

Abbie, who nodded. "Well, come into the back. We just had a name-day party leave, so it's empty."

Nyna showed them into the small room at the back, separated from the main room by pretty latticed doors. Abbie quickly introduced Roman and Deimos to her sister, who flirted and ushered them to sit.

"I'll be back shortly with some drinks and treats to nibble on while I get the salume plated up."

Roman liked watching her interact with her family. The ease was something he envied, wished he had with his brother and parents. Thankfully, his sons shared it with him.

"I don't think I've ever had salume." This from his son. So sheltered. How had he raised a child in Ravena without ever having tried the spicy concoction of legumes, vegetables and fruits of the sea?

"It's the perfect time for it. When the east moon wanes and the weather cools it makes the shellfish very sweet. My sister is a very good cook. Her salume is legendary."

A local ale showed up in crockery pitchers along with juice and water. Large loaves of crusty bread and soft cheese appeared with pickled vegetables and spiced cakes accompanying them.

What Roman really wanted to talk about, as Abbie began to give them some basic history of their group, was who the hells Logan was to her. Or more accurately, *what* he was to her.

It had been stupid of him to go to her offices. He had been a few floors below with Deimos but they could have left. He *should* have left. They'd agreed to keep away from each other, and here he sat, just inches from her, watching the way she swiped her tongue over her bottom lip to catch a drop of the oil from the vegetables.

This café had been a surprise. He didn't get down to this part of the municipal complex very often, and when he did, it was usually a quick trip and he was back in his part of the inner ring.

She pulled him from his reverie. "So, we have several different proposals to speak to you about."

"How do you expect this to go, Abbie?" Deimos asked, moving closer to her. "Do you think the Families will just hand over all their power?"

"No, and I don't want that anyway. There are, right now, eighty-seven Federation 'Verses. All of them have varying forms of governance. Each 'Verse would have to take this issue up, or not, as they saw fit. We aren't interested in replacing one system that doesn't listen to the unranked with another that essentially does the same thing. But look, you're how old? Twenty standard?"

Deimos took a sip of the ale. "Twenty-one. My parents were very young when they married."

"Okay, so twenty-one. And you've never had the meal the overwhelming majority of the unranked eat on a regular basis for a quarter of the Ravena annum. Do you have any friends who are unranked? I mean, not people who work for you, but people you socialize with?"

"What's your point?" Roman leaned forward, feeling protective. Abbie leaned back, separating herself from both of them.

Just then, heaping bowls of rice and salume arrived, and the scent made his stomach growl. Once the room had emptied again, Abbie took a bite and then pointed her spoon at them.

"You know what I'm saying. How can you govern people you don't know? You only understand us as your employees. As your wards, in some sense. But you don't *know* us. You don't know how we live. We have no voice as people to the Families or the Council in general."

"But unranked don't care. In polls, apathy levels regarding governance issues are very high," Deimos pointed out. "This is delicious."

Georges smiled as he ate. Roman noticed he let Abbie do most of the speaking.

"Of course. It's that or burn things down. Right? I mean what choices are we presented with? We don't even have governance at the most basic of levels. Not at the city level or the province level like they do in some 'Verses. You turn off your feelings or they eat you alive."

"Why not just trust us to do the right thing? How many generations has House Lyons kept this 'Verse, hells the Known Universes in general, prospering?" Deimos asked.

"We aren't pets, Deimos," Georges said from his place at the table.

And how could Roman argue with that point? He didn't think of the unranked as pets, but he couldn't truthfully say there weren't other Ranked who did.

"So tell me one proposal. One you like most."

Abbie looked him square in the eyes and said, "Start simple with the addition of an advisory council. You have an adjunct council to the main Council. It would have elected members on it from across the Federation."

She took her time and began to tell him about what future she envisioned.

Abbie wanted to twirl and laugh under the clear night sky as they walked from Nyna's place. The night smelled delicious, a bit of spice, a bit of heady flowers from the nearby hedges and the masculine scent of Roman as he walked beside her.

He'd listened to her, truly listened. And she could tell she'd made some points with him. Just being with him made her happy, which was a mistake, because once he made a choice to back or not back the idea of an advisory council, she wouldn't be seeing him at all. At least not this often.

And she had to face that seeing him as often as she had was an anomaly and it would end. She was most likely alone in her excitement at being with him this way and it was dangerous to get attached. Especially when they had both stated neither could get involved.

And if something didn't move soon, she'd have a hard time holding back the more impatient wing of the MRD who wanted to see results after so many years of nothing. Her father and his minions had been agitating to step up their activities.

Things had been set in motion. It scared her even as it made her giddy. She wasn't prone to either emotion much. In the wake of swallowing so much fear and nearly dying, she'd found in the following years it was often as if her fear had been burned out of her except on very rare occasions when it came hard and fast, threatening to drown her.

The memories of that awful event threatened but there, under twin moons, with Roman at her side, the fear abated. Gods help her if she ever got used to the feeling. Roman wasn't hers, nor would he ever be.

Georges was pointing out the plaza nearby where the twice weekly markets were held when Roman leaned over to speak in her ear. "I wish I could touch you."

She nearly groaned. Instead she swallowed hard and nodded. "I do, too."

"I think perhaps it's best if I assign Deimos and someone else from my Family to these meetings. I can't . . . I have a difficult time remembering why we shouldn't be touching whenever I'm near you."

Her stomach plummeted. He was right, of course. This contact, even with others around, was torture.

"Yes, of course." Abbie thought about saying more but Georges and Deimos turned back to them, both speaking at once, and the moment was broken.

$\mathcal{R}$oman had been looking through Abbie's proposal for an advisory council as an adjunct to the Governing Council, his mind wandering, caught between his desire and his admiration, when a pounding sounded on his door.

He jumped up and moved to the entry, glad he knew the boys were upstairs and hadn't awoken yet. Pounding on a door so long before daylight never meant anything good.

A quick look at the entry camera and he saw it was Marcus. He opened the door and Marcus rushed inside.

"Roman, I'm sorry for intruding so early. It's Jaron, he's been taken into custody. He's in lockup and I didn't know where else to turn."

Jaron was Marcus's son. Marcus had raised him from infancy after the child's mother had abandoned him to take on life in a nunnery in Kwen-lun. Marcus had been barely older than a child at the time, a member of Roman's father's household staff and when Roman had married Lindy and ascended to run the Family, he brought Marcus with him as his personal assistant.

They'd been friends ever since. Abbie had asked, just days prior, if Deimos had any unranked friends, real friends. Jaron had been one just as Marcus had been a true friend to Roman. And his friend needed him right then.

Roman ushered Marcus into the living room and told the housekeeper, who'd come in during the door-pounding, to get some food and drink and then to awaken Deimos.

"Sit down. Tell me everything."

"They won't let me see him. I was there for hours but I don't know anything more than that they're charging him with murder. Murder, Roman. My son could not kill anyone. You know that. I don't know what to do." Marcus, so normally unflappable and capable, was breaking down.

"Dai? What's wrong? Hello, Marcus." Deimos came into the room holding the tray he'd commandeered from the housekeeper. The scent of kava and bread rolls with meat and cheese wafted from it.

"When did you see Jaron last?" Roman asked his son.

"Last week. Right after he was discharged and came home. What's happening? Is he missing?"

Roman pressed a mug of kava into Marcus's hands and explained all he knew to Deimos.

"That's ridiculous! Jaron wouldn't hurt anyone. Remember when we were children and he cried when the ball we'd been throwing knocked that nest down and one of the birds got killed?" Deimos stood, outraged, and Roman noted Marcus relaxing just a bit.

"Well, we need to get in to see him and find out the details. To do that we need a barrister." Roman knew what had to be done.

"Abbie? Does she defend murder adjudications?" Deimos asked.

"There's only one way to find out. She's bound to understand what we need to do next, even if she doesn't represent the case personally. I'll go to her flat. I know where she lives." He stood and went to the comm in the corner and ordered up a conveyance to take him to her place immediately.

"You do? How is that?" Deimos looked up at him, one eyebrow raised in a fine imitation of his father as Roman stepped into his shoes.

"I got the information from her assistant. They had a meeting some time back and your father was two hours late and she left. He went to make amends." Marcus's lips twitched a bit.

"She fed me, we argued, we made a plan to meet again in my office and I left."

"She's a beautiful woman." Marcus shrugged.

Yes. Magnificent. And not for him. "I'll return as soon as I can. Marcus, keep your comm with you at all times so I can contact you. Unless you'd like to come now? That way we can all go together to the lockup."

Marcus stood. "Good idea. Let's go."

The light, slowly brightening, spread over the rooftops and sides of buildings as Abbie watched from her window. The petition to have her license to practice revoked sat on the table. Her boss had been so angry when he received it, Abbie had worried he would pass out.

He'd then given her a promotion, making her one of the most senior barristers in the agency. A nice rise in her pay came with it, but more than anything else, it was a very open way of saying the agency supported her totally. In fact, her old mentor, a Ranked barrister held in very high esteem, had come out of retirement to defend her.

It was nice to know you had friends, and in high places even. It wasn't so much that she worried about the petition succeeding; she hadn't done anything wrong, and it really only made the Kerrigans and, in some part, the Lyonses look bad. But having people out to harm her bothered her. This was more than professional competition, she dealt with that every day. More than people not liking her. That was a fact of life doing what she did and also it came with being outspoken. But someone wanting to destroy her? All for defending a little old lady like Gretel Mortan? It got under her skin.

The knock at her door surprised her, pulled her from her thoughts, and she put her plate down to go see who it was.

Looking through the viewer, she got a very pleasant sort of tingle when she saw who it was. But it subsided just as quickly when she noted Marcus was with him and both men looked extremely upset.

She opened the door and stood aside. "This is unexpected. Come in, please."

"We need your help, Abbie." Marcus's voice was thready, unstable, and she recognized it, had heard it over and over when families came to her office or she met them at lockup.

"Sit down. Let me get something to take notes with. Roman, there's freshly boiled water for tea if you like, or kava. If you're hungry, bread and fruit are at my table."

She left the room to get her case and also to comm the office to let them know she'd be in late.

When she returned, they'd settled in at the table, the sun lighting Roman, softening him even as he remained a mysterious and unreachable thing. Gah! Enough with that.

"Okay." She settled at the table. "Tell me."

"My son, he's been arrested for murder. But they won't tell me anything. They won't let me see him. I didn't know what to do. Roman suggested coming to you. Will you help?"

She put her hand over Marcus's. "Of course, I will. When did they take him in?"

Marcus looked at the timepiece on his wrist. "Four standard hours now. Abbie, my son would not hurt anyone. He's a very gentle person. He just finished his military service. He fixed things, helped people. He wants to be a medic." His voice cracked and Roman reached over, squeezing his shoulder.

She nodded and hoped he was right. Lockup was filled with people who acted out of character, even just once. "Okay then. I'll go down to lockup right now, all right? They'll have the charging papers by this point. I can't imagine why they didn't let you see him before but we'll get it all straight. We'll get your answers, Marcus."

"Can I come too?" Marcus asked.

"Sure. If I can get you in to see him I'll need you to be calm and steady. And then, well, would you like me to take his case if that's the next step? There are people in my office who can do the job as well."

"What's your experience?"

"I defended high crimes for four standard years before I came to the lesser charges unit two years ago. My friend Logan is in the high crimes unit if you'd rather. He's very good."

"No. I know you. I trust you. Let's go. I promise to be strong for him if they let me in to see him." Marcus visibly pulled himself together.

She stood. "All right. Let's go. Roman, well, you might come in handy if you have the time."

"Handy?"

"You're the big name here. I'm not above getting doors opened faster with your help." She shrugged.

"Be useful then, Roman. I'm sure Jaron would like to see you." Marcus looked so vulnerable Abbie had to resist the urge not to hug him.

Roman chuckled in a humorless way. "All right, have your way with me." But then his eyes cut to her and they both felt the pull of his words.

𝓡oman stood back and watched, impressed, as Abigail Haws, barrister, went to work. Even as they hurried to the majestic and imposing lockup complex, she spoke on her personal comm, put her hair up on the lift out of her building, gave concise orders to those around her and commanded everything in her path.

He'd learned with a bit of surprise that she'd been promoted in the wake of his brother's attempt to have her license revoked, and she wielded her power with a clever hand.

"Just you. No others." The guard at the door sneered at Marcus and Roman.

"Is this a new policy?" Abbie asked, almost bored.

"It's what I think. I hear you're in some trouble, Haws. That's what happens to little girls who reach above themselves. They get smacked. But you'd know about that, wouldn't you?"

Abbie's eyes narrowed and she took a step closer, bringing her very close to the guard. Roman ground his teeth together, only holding back from speaking to save Marcus. Jaron needed him to be calm. But this guard would be finding out just who had overheard his comments very soon. And Roman wanted to know exactly what the slovenly fool meant about Abbie getting smacked.

"Haerv, the rules, Ravena Code 4.2.30 subsection b, state a senior, level A barrister may bring up to three interested parties into the lockup facility on related business during regular hours. And here it is, business hours. And here I am, a newly promoted, senior, level A barrister. You will stand out of the way and you will let me in and bring prisoner Jaron Mach to a holding room along with any related charging paperwork."

This Haerv looked as if he considered disobeying until Abbie reached out, grabbed the door and opened it. The guard grunted and took the handle, ushering them inside.

"You reach above yourself, Abbie."

"Most things are above your situation, Haerv. We'll be waiting in interview room three. Do be sure all cameras are off." She sailed past the guard and headed to the lift.

The halls smelled of strong cleaning compounds and fear. The place made him edgy. He rarely visited lockup. In fact, this was probably only the third time in his life he'd been here, and he was glad for that as the echoes of their footsteps pinged back at them as they headed into the lift.

Once the doors closed, the scent of machine oil, most likely from the internal workings of the lift, edged out the cleansers.

He wanted to comfort Abbie. Wanted to pull her into his arms and stroke his hand over her hair. Tension vibrated from her, taut, and he wondered how she'd release it. Wondered what made her that way. Wondered what exactly that brute at the doors below had meant.

But he couldn't reach out to her. Partly because he sensed she needed to forget about whatever it was and partly because it wasn't his place. No matter how much he wanted it to be.

"Abbie, that man downstairs . . ." Marcus took her hand. "Are you all right?"

Roman noted how pale she'd gotten but watched her pull it together as they rose higher.

"Thank you, Marcus. I'm fine. It's an old issue." She leaned in and let the scanner read her retina. The doors opened for them and two guards nodded at them far more friendlier than the one below.

"We'll be in room three. I need to see the paperwork on Jaron Mach, please. Along with Mr. Mach."

One of the guards nodded and then started once he caught sight of Roman. "Oh, Mr. Lyons. Yes, we'll get right on that."

Once they'd arrived in the appointed room, Abbie turned an amused smile his way. "See, those pretty eyes are useful. I told you."

A stack of papers was delivered and Abbie began to read. Just a few minutes later, Jaron was brought in, looking haggard and terrified. A bright bruise bloomed over his cheek.

Abbie held her hand up to stay Marcus. She addressed the guard, "Please unshackle the prisoner before you leave."

"Ms. Haws, this one's been charged with murder."

"Yes, I know. You can have a guard stand outside the room but there's no reason to keep him shackled." She lowered her voice. "You know that, James."

The guard, James apparently, nodded and removed the bonds from Jaron's wrists and waist.

Once the guard left, Marcus rushed to hug his son, and then Roman did as well. Jaron felt insubstantial in Roman's arms. So unlike his own sons, who were so hale and braw.

He wanted to use his power to walk out of the building with

Jaron right then. Considered it. He was Roman Lyons, after all. Not abusing his power had never been so hard.

As if Abbie sensed it, she touched Jaron's shoulder. "Sit down, Jaron. I'm Abbie and I'm here to help you. Let's start at the beginning. Tell me everything so I can get you out of here."

Jaron took a deep breath and began to speak.

Chapter 9

$\mathscr{A}$fter leaving the lockup, Abbie headed back to her office and worked for the rest of the day and into the evening. When she finally got home, she slumped into the shower and stumbled over to lay on her couch while she considered if she had the energy to get up and prepare herself something to eat.

A soft tapping at her door pulled her from near sleep. She knew it was him before she looked out the viewer.

He stepped inside and closed the door, locking it before looking back at her. "I can't stay away." When he touched her, she arched into his hold. He drew a fingertip down from the hollow of her throat, slowly over the curve of her breast bone, between her breasts, until he reached the tie of her robe. "Are you naked under there?"

"I can't remember." She couldn't even remember her address

right then. The heat blasted from the front of him, he was so close each time he breathed in, the barest brush of his body against hers brought gooseflesh over her skin.

He laughed and she gave in, sliding her palms up his sides. He felt good, substantial, and it pleased her more than it should that he was there.

"You shouldn't be here," she murmured as she kissed the spot on his neck she uncovered when she unbuttoned his shirt. "But I'm glad you are."

"I love the way you feel against me, Abbie. So small but so strong. I'm going to unbind your hair."

"It's probably still a bit wet. I braid it so . . . ohhh." Rough shivers went through her when he tugged on it. Not to the point of pain but he got her attention, bringing her nerves to life.

"Did you like that? Mmm, you smell good. You have such beautiful hair, Abbie. Why do you keep it up in that knot instead of letting it free?"

"Yes, I liked it. I can't very well have it loose at work, it would be in my face all day. And no one takes me seriously when I leave it down. You're very tall and I'm getting a pain in my neck looking at you. Come and sit or lay or something."

He grinned momentarily and sat, bringing her down atop him. She straddled his body and went back for a kiss.

"I can feel how hot your cunt is through my pants. Take off the robe for me, Abbie."

She shrugged off the robe, letting it slide from her skin like a whispered caress. Her nipples hardened into dark points under his gaze and she realized they'd never been totally naked with each other.

"You're beautiful. Sexy." He brought his hands up to take the weight of her breasts, thumbs sliding lazily back and forth over her nipples until she began to squirm.

"I want to see you."

"Soon enough, Abbie. Right now, it's about you. You and your pretty thighs, your bare cunt, glistening with juice just for me." He looked up into her face a moment and she looked back—without judgment; in fact, rather with pleasure at his words.

They stayed like that, locked together for long moments, until he seemed to make some sort of decision and surged to his feet. She held on, surprised and amused that he held her so easily.

"Do you have a mirror in your bedroom?"

She nodded, speechless at whatever he might have in mind.

Still wrapped around him, she kissed and licked the outer shell of his ear as he took the quick trip into her bedroom. Which was currently a total mess, with clothes everywhere.

"Ah, right at the foot of your bed. Well, that's handy then." He sat. "Get up for a moment, please."

She scrambled off, quickly lighting some candles she'd had in votive holders on her walls but hadn't used in a very long time. A golden glow licked over the walls.

When she turned back to him, he'd gotten naked. "Hey! I wanted to do that."

"Next time I'll let you undress me. For now, I have plans and I'm impatient."

She walked around him, taking in his body from hard, well-defined calves, up muscled thighs, the very impressive cock jutting out proudly, the flat belly, the lightly furred chest, and up to that face. She wanted to sigh wistfully but just barely held back.

"If you're done looking me over like a prized bull, sit on my lap. Facing the mirror."

He'd scooted back enough so she could straddle him, her knees on the bed. He was much taller than she, so she could easily see his face in their reflection in the mirror.

She smiled.

"I do like the placement of that mirror."

"Do you like to watch, Roman? Watch yourself fucking a woman?"

"Yes. Does that bother you?"

"No. Why should it?" She slid her hands up her body to hold her breasts, pinching her nipples, liking the way his eyes widened and then went half-lidded. "Your desires are nothing to be ashamed of."

He leaned in to kiss her shoulder and then hesitated. When his eyes met hers in the mirror she moved one hand to her pussy, spreading herself open before she touched her clit, just a small pat, before pressing two fingers inside.

As she'd thought, he forgot about her scars, the three lines, faint by now, from the lower part of her shoulder blade up to the top of her shoulder near her neck. Instead, his gaze homed in on her hand. "Are you hot and wet?" He spoke into her ear, sending shivers down her spine.

She nodded, an urgency building within her. She liked to come. A lot. But at the same time, she wanted to let it roll through her, lure him in, seduce him as he'd done her.

"You make me hungry for your cunt. I don't want to share it with anyone. Not even you." He leaned forward and reached around, sliding two fingers into her.

She was very full but didn't remove her own fingers just yet. She left them there as he slid his own in and out. Her inner walls clutched at the invasion, slickening in response.

"You're so slick. Slick and snug and perfect inside."

His wife had been a lucky woman to have had this in her bed all those years. He was forty now, but Abbie was pretty sure he'd been just as hot ten and fifteen years before. She envied that. Wondered what such a bond would be like.

"Don't close your eyes, Abbie. I want to see your face when you come all over my hand."

An unwilling moan broke from her lips as a rush of pleasure flooded through her.

"You want to move, don't you? Do it. Fuck my hand."

She had to move. Had to come. He'd made it inevitable. Freeing her fingers, she braced her hands on his knees and rose and fell, grinding herself against him to get more.

"That's it. Take it, Abbie."

She struggled to keep her eyes open and her head up, but he wouldn't give on that. His gaze held hers implacably. A man used to being obeyed.

He watched as she took her pleasure without apology. Her honey rained over his hand, the scent of her making him hard, making him want her even more.

He'd tried to stay away but couldn't. Just watching her that morning with Jaron had been too much. Her mixture of strength and tenderness went straight to his cock. And his heart. Abigail Haws got under his skin and being with her seemed as necessary as breathing. Touching her, the need to feel her against him, was a deep craving.

Her cry as she came, the way her body clutched his fingers, the way a flush worked up her pretty, pale skin, it all made him nearly mad with the need to be inside her.

But she scrambled up and out of his reach before he could angle himself to fuck her. That shower of hair, dark and lush, hanging nearly to her ass, shimmered around her like a cloak.

"I want to suck your cock, Roman."

How could he refuse such an offer? He'd only imagined her mouth on him just about every waking moment since he met her.

He scooted up her bed and she climbed up between his thighs. Her hair, cool and soft, trailed over his legs as she kissed her way from his knee to his cock, just barely breathing a kiss over it, and then back down to the other knee.

He groaned, wanting to tell her what he liked but also worried he'd scare her off. She'd been with him so far, something he'd never really thought he'd have.

The heat of her mouth sent little shocks of sensation skittering through him. She moved up high enough to firmly grab the base of his cock in one hand and, while watching his face, slowly licked over the head.

She did something to him. Uncoiled the things in his gut he never gave voice to. It was disarming as well as frightening. No one should be able to get to him that way. He was a controlled man, because losing control in his position could be disastrous.

"Tell me what you want." Her tongue swirled over the head, spreading the liquid pearled at the tip. The sensation of it nearly brought him off the bed. The words, given permission, loosed from him in a hot rush.

"Hold me like that. Yeah. Keep me wet and swallow my cock as far as you can."

She shivered, her pretty, round ass up high in the air, swaying a bit as she kept him juicy and slowly took all she could into her mouth.

"So good, Abbie. Your mouth on my cock is so good. If I could, I'd keep you in bed, naked and ready for me at any time. Maybe in my office. Mmm. Yes, that's the way. In my office to drop to your knees and suck me off any time I needed it."

She hummed her amusement around him and he smiled. Sexy and a sense of humor, too. If she was Ranked, he'd have staked a very public claim by this point. Damn it all. It didn't bear thought just then. All he wanted to think about was her and being with her for whatever stolen moments they had.

She pulled off with a soft pop and licked down the length of him, her tongue leaving warm trails along the ultrasensitive skin of his balls. He hissed when she pressed the pads of her fingers into the space behind his sac, making his cock jump with pleasure.

"I'm not ready to come yet," he murmured, sifting her hair through his fingertips. "Keep it slow."

She worshiped him with her mouth, made him feel totally desired. Totally masculine. He relished it—just being Roman and Abbie. A man and a woman, finding some refuge with each other in the quiet spaces in daily life.

His balls drew close as orgasm hinted at the edges of his consciousness. "Abbie, enough. Come up here and ride my cock."

No one needed to tell her twice. Abbie let go of his cock with a parting kiss and moved up his body, positioning herself over his groin. Pleased to look down at such a beautiful man in her bed, she ran her nails down his sides, just shy of hard.

"I like that. I like that you take what pleases you."

She reached around, grabbed his cock to position it and sank down on him in one hard movement. Insanely intense pleasure coursed through her from the point where they were joined.

"Gods that's good." She rolled her neck, loosening her muscles as she set a pace, undulating her hips more than riding him in and out of her body. "And Roman, life is far too short to not enjoy something like this. You're handsome, clever, sexy, you're good with your equipment. Why shouldn't I give in and run my nails down your sides? Or"—she scraped her nails this time over his nipples, liking the way he groaned—"over your nipples?"

He remained quiet for some time as she rocked over him, keeping him deep. After a while he said, "You're right. There's no reason why we shouldn't give in and enjoy each other."

Did he mean more than just then?

"Spread your pussy for me. I want access to your clit."

She smiled slowly. "I love your mouth. I love how the moment the door is closed, the most delightfully naughty things come from you. It's so. . . " She paused, trying to think on just exactly the right word. "Unexpected. Deliciously unexpected. Like a secret."

He grinned as his fingertip began to dance, ever so lightly, over her clit. "I'm glad you enjoy it. I . . . well, it's not something I've done often."

She lost track of what she'd planned to say in response as he squeezed her clit between slippery fingers, just so.

She began to teeter on the edge of climax. Abbie sped up her pace, rising up and coming back down on him with a little swivel of her hips. She tightened herself around him, liking how he grunted in response.

"Inside you're so soft and wet as you hug me. Gods, there's nothing like your cunt, Abbie. So juicy. And look at your thighs. I never would have imagined such fine thighs hiding under your skirts. I do like stockings. Very much."

Words flittered away from her as orgasm settled into her cells. Filled her physically, and deeper. Her eyes closed so she could revel in the feeling, in the way it felt to come with his cock lodged inside her, of his scent, their scent, hanging in the air.

"That's the way. I love to watch you come nearly as much as I love to feel you coming around my cock. Now it's my turn," he managed to gasp out before strong hands moved to her hips to hold her down as he pressed up and came.

She fell to the side and couldn't resist a lick over his left nipple. He tasted good. She said so.

He laughed, drawing his fingertips up her spine. "I happen to think you taste pretty good yourself. In fact," he said as he eased up on his side, head on his hand, "I think after I regain feeling in my legs, I'm going to taste you nice and thoroughly."

"Do you need feeling in your legs for that?" she asked, tossing an arm over her head and laughing. He snuggled up to her side and pulled her close, kissing the side of her breast.

"For someone so small, you pack a lot of punch. I was impressed by you today."

"Well, the brain isn't hindered by my size. I'm a powerhouse when I can fight with my wits." She snorted, wishing she didn't know the difference.

"There's a story there." He toyed with her hair.

"Everyone has stories. What's yours?"

"Ah, evasion. I raised two boys to manhood. I do know about evasion."

A surge of tenderness rocketed through her. "It must have been hard. Being on your own like that with them. Tell me about her."

He drew circles on her breast, around the nipple, which perked up at the attention, and then upward until he reached the top of her shoulder. He tapped it and looked into her eyes.

"I'll tell you about Lindy if you tell me about the scars."

Something cold washed through her. She didn't want to talk about the attack. Not then with their scent heavy in the air. "They're scars. Do they horrify you?"

Anger darkened his features. "Do you think so little of me?

They're scars. A small imperfection on so much beauty is of no consequence to the whole. In fact, it makes the whole more appealing for the flaw. But what is of consequence is how they got there."

"It's also not something I want to talk about." When was the appropriate time to share such a horrible story? She didn't know him well enough to rip her past open that way.

Her face closed off and he knew well enough to back away from the topic. For then. "All right. Lindy and I were seventeen standard when we were married. So young." He laughed at the memory. "She got pregnant with Dem right away, and a year later, Corrin came along. Having the boys so close together was hard on her. I don't think she was ever the same. She died twelve years ago now."

Abbie moved to face him, leaning in to kiss the space above his heart. "I'm sorry. It must be hard without her. How did she die? If you don't mind my asking."

"Okay, at least tell me about the spectacles if I tell you."

She rolled her eyes. "Fine."

"She'd been sick for years after Corrin. She was so gentle, but always sort of melancholy. She got an infection, in her blood. We don't know how. But it just slowly ate away at her. We tried everything but she just slipped away."

She'd faded like a ghost. Had given up and left them. He wasn't sure if he blamed himself for wanting heirs or her for not wanting them enough to fight to stay with them to be their mother.

"That's terrible. You must have loved her so very much to have married so young."

He laughed ruefully. "My father was very ill. I needed to step in to run the Family, and they felt if I was married and had heirs, I'd be able to hold the position with more authority. My father has no brothers but he does have a cousin, and his sisters are married. It was imperative I take over and show a healthy, strong face for the Lyons. Lindy's Family, the Kerrigans, needed the alliance, and we cemented power here on Ravena. I got her out of her house, Saul Kerrigan's house, and she gave me the facade of adulthood so I could take over."

"That evil bastard is your father-in-law?"

He laughed but it was without humor. "Yes. He shows little to no interest in the boys, other than as his key to power, and I'm grateful. Lindy was nothing like him. You know, she used to talk about her governess. I looked into it and Gretel Mortan . . . well I want to help with funds if they're needed. I'm putting pressure on Saul to drop it, even if I pay her retirement."

"You'd do that?"

"Not all the Ranked are Saul Kerrigan, Abbie. Just like not all unranked are like whoever gave you those scars."

Her smile disappeared. "Those scars were not from an unranked person. And I know you're not all the same. I have spectacles because the problem that causes my bad vision can be fixed with surgery but if it's not addressed by the age of five, it's permanent. My father . . . we lived in the outback for many years. He's a teacher and he taught at a rural school. There were no surgical med centers out there, and by the time we came back here, it was too late. But I'm not that bad off. I just need them when I'm working and reading."

"Your father didn't come to the city to get his child's vision repaired?"

"I'm not blind. I can see with spectacles. It's not like I would have died or anything. The children in the school needed him more than I needed surgery. This conversation is going in a direction far away from your mouth on my pussy."

She flopped on her back and he loomed over her. "I'm sorry if I offended you." Still, he was a father, too, and he'd never dream of not doing what it took to get medical help for his children. The surgeries were free for those who couldn't pay. There was no reason for her to have suffered.

Not that he'd let that stop him from tasting her again. They'd argue later as they learned more about each other. He hesitated . . . However that happened. Their situation was beyond complicated but for the moment, he had a task.

*A*bbie sighed as he settled between her thighs and spread her labia, exposing her to his mouth. Long, slow licks, nuzzles, quick flicks of his tongue—he played her cunt like a beautiful symphony and she closed her eyes and let him.

Having had a few orgasms already, her clit was incredibly sensitive and he knew it, taking great care to not overstimulate her. He worked slowly but thoroughly until she began to writhe, needing more from him.

Two fingers slid into her, stretching her just a bit, while his pinky stroked over her back passage in an unexpected and rather pleasant way. She'd let him fuck her in the ass. A man like him would totally work the taboo of it to its fullest extent.

She'd be at his mercy, stuffed full of him, fingers digging in the blankets, and he'd be over her, talking in her ear.

She huffed out an aroused sound and he sucked her clit between his teeth just lightly, but it was enough to rocket her into orgasm. A great, rolling, deep-to-her-bones orgasm that left her utterly spent after it held her for long moments.

The kiss he gave her tasted of her and of him as well and she moaned at how delicious it was. How delicious *he* was.

"Can I sleep here?" he asked softly.

It would be so nice not to wake up alone. But inadvisable, and he had to know that. "Are you sure that's okay with you? If you're seen leaving here in the morning, you'll have a lot of explaining to do."

He sighed. "You're right. I don't have a change of clothes so I'd be very conspicuous." He got up and she followed.

"Would you like to shower first? I'm sure you need to be scrubbed all clean. You're very dirty." And how she loved that.

"How could I resist such a fine offer?"

*E*ven after the shower he smelled her on his skin.

"Are you hungry? Do you want something to eat before you leave?" She bustled around her apartment while he watched, strangely content.

"I'm sated." He looked her up and down and knew that was a lie. "But a mug of something warm, perhaps?" Just a little while longer with her.

She laughed and put a pot on to boil. "I have some tea one of my father's old students makes. It's very nice."

They sat companionably together for some time, sipping the tea. At last he knew he had to get going or risk being seen. He didn't want gossip swirling around her and he didn't need the problem himself. He didn't want to leave. The moment he did, he'd miss her.

He stood to go.

"Thank you. For, well, for tonight and also for what you did for Jaron and Marcus." Because he couldn't resist, he touched her hair. His reward was a smile he was fairly certain she didn't show many.

She saw him to the door. "You don't have to thank me for the sex part. You showed your appreciation. Four times, as a matter of fact. As for Jaron, he's got several hearings over the next few days. I'm hoping to get him out prior to trial. Marcus knows to comm me any time if he needs me."

He nodded, his hand on the door but not opening it. "So, yes. Well. I looked over your proposal. I'm meeting with Dem tomorrow to talk about it. He'll be taking over for me. I think he's going to be bringing some other Family in with him. He'll contact you."

Understanding lit her eyes and she took a step back. "Okay then. Thank you. I guess I'll be seeing you on the vids."

He left, but it ripped part of him away to do so.

Chapter 10

"*I*'d like you to get in touch with Comandante Ellis and have him do a check of Abigail Haws's background."

Marcus looked up at him as Roman left his office to head for a General Council meeting. Surprise etched his forehead. "Why?"

"Because, she's very involved in our lives at this point, don't you think? Shouldn't I know what her background is? I'm sending Deimos in with his group to examine this whole adjunct governance structure. What if I back her and she has something bad in her history?"

Marcus took a deep breath. "Roman, really. You think that's the case? After spending any amount of time with Abbie, you think she's hiding something horrible? Like what? Do you think she's a weapons runner in her three breaths' worth of free time every day?"

"Marcus, be real. Everyone has something to hide. Anyway, Saul and my brother are trying to harm her. Perhaps I can help." He shrugged. "What is it going to hurt?"

"Fine, but if she finds out, she's not going to be happy. I'd suggest you just ask her, but the two of you seem to be going out of your way to pretend you don't want to see each other and yet, you're always talking about each other." Marcus waved his hand, annoyed. "Never mind. You're both as stubborn as the other. I won't be here when you get back, by the way. I'm going down to the justice administration building. Jaron has a hearing and I want to be there. I've arranged coverage for you for the time I'll be out."

Roman squeezed his friend's shoulder. "It's going to be all right."

"I know . . . I do. I trust Abbie. She's been so good to me. She's been to my house three times now. She brings the paperwork, goes over it with me step by step. Explains all the complicated stuff. She's so good before the adjudicator. She made sure I could get in to see Jaron and got him moved to a cell by himself. She's gentle with him, patient and kind. He's so frightened. Hells, *I'm* frightened, but she just makes me feel better. I'll never be able to repay her for all she's done."

A stab of something hit Roman. Jealousy, perhaps? Not that Abbie would sleep with Marcus. Or maybe she would, but he doubted it. But that Marcus had seen her. Multiple times. He'd been with her and Roman hadn't, no matter how much he'd wanted to. He hadn't seen her in nearly two weeks, and each day that passed without her made him even more miserable.

"Do you need credits? I've been meaning to give you a rise in your pay."

Marcus sniffed. "I'll always take more credits but I'm fine. I have credits saved and her agency only charges a percentage of the actual defense costs. What means so much to me is your support. You've been . . . I don't know if I'd have been able to keep my head when I first got the news if you hadn't been there for me."

"You know I'm here for you. You're my friend, and I know Jaron is innocent. We'll get him out of there soon. I know Abbie will do it." If not, Roman would use his power to get the boy out of lockup, no matter what. There were places Jaron could go where no one would ask a single question. It lay unspoken between himself and Marcus, but it comforted nonetheless.

There wasn't much evidence, but Jaron had been in the wrong place when a fight broke out. Two men were killed and several injured severely. The crowd in the bar, a low establishment, hadn't been able to pin anyone specifically. The evidence against Jaron was vague but he'd given them a target for their grief.

"You should give things with Abbie a chance," Marcus murmured as Roman began to leave to attend a Council meeting.

He paused, wanting to reply, but instead, he kept walking.

"*H*ow long are we supposed to wait? Abbie, he's stringing you along. The Council is running scared with this attack on you and your license. You weren't raised to run from a fight. The time to move is now. On the streets!" Abbie's father spoke from his seat at the table. The assembled members of the MRD had been bickering for the better part of Abbie's break from work.

"She's not *running* from anything," Georges argued back. "It's so easy for you to say. She's doing her job. You know, the one she's paid to do? The one she makes a difference with every day? And then she's doing the work of the MRD on top of that."

"You either care about democracy or you don't! You're too comfortable and the minute you get threatened, you want to back off," another one of the members, one not so supportive of peaceful means, shot back.

Abbie gripped the edge of the table as the furor rose. "This is getting us nowhere, and I have a hearing to get to. We have some people at very high levels willing to listen to us. We've never had that before. It's absurd to be patient all this time and suddenly get so impatient that we lose everything we've gained. I'm not advising we run." She shot a look at her father. "I'm advising we let this process play out before we jump to conclusions about whether it's working or not. Georges and I have met with Deimos Lyons and one of Proctor Feist's grandsons. They are open to us, it would be disastrous to not be *patient* here."

"How successful can you be, Abbie? Roman Lyons isn't even attending the meetings anymore." Robin smirked.

Abbie would not let them goad her into quitting. This would work if they just gave it time. If it didn't, they'd at least have a reason to be upset and agitate for something meaningful. "He's the head of the Council. He's got a lot more pressing business than sitting through a task force meeting. He's sent his son, his heir to House Lyons, and that's more than you or Jonas or anyone else has done. This is a process. It takes time. This is moving in the direction we want it to, but if we rush, we'll lose everything we've worked for. Use your damned heads. The streets? Who would do that? You, Robin and four other people? The unranked are nervous and upset. You might get a damned riot or two out of it and then we'd never get an advisory council."

"Abbie is right. Robin, shut up. Dai, you're not giving Abbie enough respect here for all she's done," Georges spoke up again.

Abbie looked at her brother, grateful for his support.

She stood. "I've got to go. Hold it together and be professional. We have the weight of the unranked behind us, but let's take care with it and not squander or betray it. I'll see the rest of you at the next meeting. I'll keep you apprised of any changes."

Sweeping out of the room she headed toward the justice administration building. She had a hearing for Jaron and wanted to catch Marcus to reassure him before it started.

Though she wished it didn't, it shook her more than she wanted to admit that her father wasn't more supportive of her. It wasn't a crime to try and balance her life with the MRD. She still ran it more than efficiently. And yes, it shook her up that someone was trying to harm her and remove her livelihood. She wasn't going to apologize for that.

And now she had to deal with another administrative hearing for Jaron. Several things had slowed down the process. First, murder wasn't overly common in Ravena, so there were more layers of hearings and administrative process before they even got to the point where she could get him out until trial. And then, there was the fact that he was the son of an unranked man who'd worked for the Lyons for some time. In light of the situation with Family members working with the Imperialists, the extra scrutiny weighed against quick actions. No one was inclined to give Jaron a break at this point.

She was grumpy. She'd seen Roman on the vids the night before and it only made her miss him more. Worse, the commentators hinted he was prime marriage material. Something that'd been hinted at many times before. But he hadn't been in her bed then. It didn't bear thinking on but she couldn't get it out of her head.

Marcus paced just outside the front doors to the building and came toward her quickly as she approached. Time to stop being mopey, moony-eyed Abbie and to start being hard-assed Abigail Haws, barrister who made the inquisitor on the other side fear her.

She liked that thought. In fact, it would definitely make her feel better to make someone quake in fear. *Hmpf.*

The hearing was long and nearly pointless but she did feel better that she made the inquisitor jump. Twice! She was not one of Abbie's favorite people and was being obstructive on purpose. Just because she had the power to be. But Abbie hoped the next hearing would be one where she could argue to free Jaron until his trial.

Marcus was able to visit with his son while Abbie dealt with several of her other clients, and when she swung back through lockup, he was ready to go back to work.

"I wanted to thank you for all you're doing for Jaron. He told me your mother brought him sweet cakes yesterday. He . . . *we* appreciate that so much, I can't even begin to tell you."

He was so kind and caring. Such a good father. Why couldn't she be attracted to him instead of his totally unattainable boss?

"My mother runs a bakery. She loves to bake and she does it to relax. I told her about Jaron and she thought he'd appreciate a little bit of home. She said she thought he was a very well-mannered young man. I'm glad it gave him some comfort and I'm quite sure she'll be back with more goodies for him. It's who she is." Abbie laughed. Her mother was a good-hearted woman. One of the best people she'd ever known. It made her happy to know some of that rubbed off and brightened Jaron's day.

"Roman said your sister has a café? And your mother has a bakery? Your kitchen must have been a fun place growing up." Marcus smiled as they walked outside.

She turned up the collar of her coat. It was definitely getting cooler. "My mother and sister share a space. The bakery is in one part and the café in the other. Mainly the café is open at midday and the evenings and the bakery first thing. If you like good local food you should give the place a try." Gods help her, she was pleased that Roman had shared that information with Marcus.

"Will you let me buy you a meal just now? I don't have to be back to the office for a bit of time, and Roman is at a Council meeting, so he probably won't be back until much later." He stopped, putting a hand on her arm. "I know your type. I bet you haven't eaten in hours."

"All right. Sounds good. My sister's place is just across the plaza there." She pointed.

They walked in companionable silence and Nyna sat them near the front windows, placed a pot of steaming tea on the table along with a basket of bread and hustled off to bring them the special offering of the day.

"Your sister is a beautiful woman. Older? Younger?" Marcus poured the tea, trying to look nonchalant.

"She's younger. My brothers are bookends. Daniel is the oldest, Georges is the youngest. I'm the second oldest and Nyna is just younger than me by a little bit over a term. My mother was with child for pretty much five standard years. We're all very close in age."

"Although completely different." Nyna put plates before each of them. "Stew to warm your bones. Fruit and cheese in a bit. I'll keep the bread coming. Mai is going to be disappointed she went home and missed seeing you."

"Sit with us, Nyna. If you're not too busy." Abbie patted a chair and tried not to smile at Marcus's reaction.

"Not too busy to sit with my sister and her handsome friend."

She winked at Marcus, who'd recovered enough to laugh and look at her through his lashes.

"Nyna, Marcus is Jaron's father. He's the boy they're pursuing on murder charges."

Nyna shook her head and patted Marcus's arm. "My mother thinks your son is wonderful. I'm sorry you're both having to go through this but Abbie will get him out. She's the best."

Marcus smiled and looked back at Abbie. "She is. Jaron and I are in her debt. And your mother's, too."

"I'm obviously biased, but I think Abbie has one of the best legal minds in the 'Verse. She can be quite scary for someone so small. She gets it from my mother, who's even shorter than Abbie is."

Abbie thwacked her sister with the napkin before she went back to her stew. She liked seeing Nyna flirting with Marcus. It was good for both of them.

"And so pretty. Don't think Roman hasn't noticed. But then you know that." Marcus raised a brow in Abbie's direction.

"Doesn't matter, Marcus. He and I are not . . . It wouldn't work. He's a nice man. A good man who needs to know a heck of a lot more about the people he governs. But he is not for me." Abbie blushed furiously.

"Only if he's an idiot." Nyna huffed an annoyed breath. Abbie had shared every last detail of the situation with her sister and Abbie knew Nyna wouldn't let anything slip but she still kicked her shin under the table for good measure.

"He's got a lot on his mind. With the first treason trial beginning, it puts him in a difficult place. He's being pulled among many constituencies. It's not that he's opposed to your group as much as he doesn't know how to even think about it and having the other, more hard-line Families pushing, fighting amongst themselves for power, well it just makes things even more complicated." Marcus hummed his satisfaction. "Nyna this is delicious. I can't believe this café has been here three standard and I've never eaten here before."

Nyna leaned in and took a piece of his bread. "Well, now you know, so you can remedy that."

Abbie wisely held back a laugh. She'd have to give Nyna all the details about Marcus later on, but until then, she'd let Nyna and Marcus forge their own path. At least they could.

Bitterness made the tangy mouthful of stew go to ashes. She sighed and pretended to be carefree as they shared a meal. All the while, she was not able to stop thinking about whatever Roman happened to be doing at that moment.

Chapter 11

Roman trudged into the foyer of his home far after dark had settled. He'd argued with the faction calling for sanctions against the MRD for most of the day. Ridiculous.

At a point when they should be banding together, Roman had to squander his time on this petty bullshit and it made him angry. All this small stuff when their world was being turned upside down. It was a waste.

He couldn't quite recall when he'd last been so angry. Perhaps in the time after Lindy had died and he'd been alone with two young sons. The futility of her death had enraged him, frustrated him, made him want to hit someone.

But, this silliness was, well, it was bullying. It was quite definitely what the unranked activists had been painting them all to be. It was Ranked people punishing those who dared to question the system.

The hard-line Families and Associate Families had been calling for Abbie's job. They'd wanted to have her charged for sedition. Saul Kerrigan had even called for Gretel Mortan to be placed back in lockup! Roman was a fair-minded man, he took leadership seriously, and the behavior he'd witnessed that day offended him to the core.

He sighed heavily and sat to remove his shoes.

The faint tinkling of the keys of the piano in the back of the house wafted through the air. Corrin, most likely. Roman stood to go to the one constant in his life.

The large music room held a massive piano that had been in the Lyons Family for generations. Roman loved it and had been thrilled when his mother gave it to him when he took over the Family. Corrin and Deimos were musical and both had mastered several instruments and had good singing voices. The latter they owed to their mother. Corrin was the more artistic of the two, pursuing music and sculpting and starting an interesting career. Roman was very proud of both of his sons.

As he stood in the arched doorway, he looked on at Deimos's dark head bent down over a sheaf of papers, his feet up on a stool while Corrin laughed with a friend, his fingertips idly playing across the keys.

They'd sustained him a very long time, his boys. But the loneliness that'd been drawing him in of late—since he'd first met Abbie Haws, he'd realized—ate at him. He was more than someone's father. He wanted to have a connection to a woman again. Wanted to share that part of himself with someone. That need had awakened and the loss of Abbie's presence, once he'd tasted it, brought an ache.

He'd been so lonely he'd considered pursuing some of the unattached women in his circle. Had even gone to several social events to do so. But not too long into a conversation, all he could think was how much these women were nothing like Abbie. Nothing like the one woman he could not stop thinking about.

"Dai." Deimos looked up at him with a smile. "You look tired. I heard some reports about the Council meeting. Was it as bad as the rumors say?"

Mercy, their cook and the woman who had been their governess while the boys grew up, must have known he'd come home because she entered the room with a tray and placed some food out for him, along with a steaming mug of tea. The look she sent him dared him to not sit down and begin to eat. Because he was hungry and knew how much this woman cared for him and his family, he sat and began to spoon up the warm soup.

"Thank you, Mercy."

She waved over her shoulder as she walked out, taking Corrin's empty mug and chiding him about picking up the shoes he'd left under the piano.

"If by bad you mean did I come close to punching your grandfather Kerrigan in the face and throwing him out onto his large and lazy ass? Yes, it was bad."

"Uncle Alexander was there, too, I hear. Dai, his heart is in the right place. He just doesn't go about it right."

Roman shrugged. "It's my job to lead, even when things are difficult. Your uncle—" Roman paused, looking for the right words. He didn't believe Alexander was a bad person. But he had been raised as the spare, and so where Roman had been pushed and trained and molded into a responsible man from birth, Alexander had played. And it showed. He was selfish and irresponsible and frequently incapable of self-reflection of any kind.

"I know." Deimos got up to bring a packet of papers to him.

"Marcus sent this over earlier today. Dai, this is information about Abbie Haws. Why would you have her investigated? I've been working with her for a while now. She seems like a good woman. Hells, I wish she liked younger men. Gods know I've hinted at a romantic interlude a few times only to have her ignore me." His son grinned and Roman wanted to pop him one for even *thinking* about Abbie that way.

But then he saw Deimos had been poking fun at him. Had he been so transparent?

"She's working with my son, the heir to House Lyons. Of course I'm going to have her looked into." He jammed some food into his mouth, grabbed his mug and made a hasty retreat to read that file.

The stone stairs absorbed the soft sound of his ascent up toward the master suite. The enormous room overlooked the innermost ring of the city and a wall of windows faced out over the parapets and balconies beyond, giving him refuge when he needed time alone.

Now, the light from the stars and the far-off rising moon gave the space a pale, cool glow as he tugged off his work clothing and headed in to run a bath in the adjoining bathroom.

Laughing, Abbie waved at her siblings as she entered her building, her arms filled with bags from their day of shopping and a lovely dinner with her parents. The tension between Abbie and her father had continued, but for once, her mother had absolutely refused to tolerate it and had browbeaten her father into behaving.

So she had leftovers enough to last several days, as well as a new set of sheets for her bed and a new sweater to beat back the chill in the air. Georges had brought a friend by to introduce to her. The effort was so transparent it had amused her. And it was time to move on, so she'd accepted the rather sweet dinner invitation. She had nothing to lose. She had to stop mooning over Roman Lyons.

But there he stood, leaning against her door, head down, a bag at his feet. Roman Lyons, a man not really tall, about a head or so above her own, but so big it felt as if he stole all the air in the hallway.

She stopped, unable to not take him in with something fairly close to wonder that someone so masculine and sexy actually existed and that he'd been naked in her arms.

When he looked up, those eyes of his locked onto hers just before a long, slow perusal of her body. There was something in his gaze, hot, predatory, something else . . . Anger, perhaps?

"I didn't expect—um, how long have you been waiting for me?"

She bustled past, trying to balance her keys to unlock the door. He growled low in his throat and took them from her, unlocking her door and opening it so she could get inside with all her things.

The click of the tumblers sounded, tugging deep, as if he unmoored something within her as he locked the door to the outside.

She put her things into the cold box and then turned to face him. "Why are you here acting all broody and silent? If you're angry at me, I deserve to know why."

"I can't stay away," he said simply, voice taut.

"And that makes you angry? Because I have to tell you something: That you'd be angry because you're attracted to me, that makes *me* angry!" She threw her hands up. What did he want from her? And why did he have to smell so good?

"I need a drink." He dropped the bag he'd brought in and scrubbed his hands through his hair.

"What the seven hells is wrong with you?" She approached him, looking up into his face. "Are you all right?"

The heat in his eyes flowed into something else. Anguish? Sadness? "I don't know how to ask this and I can't keep myself away."

She froze, her fingers still sifting through his hair. "What is it? You can talk to me. You're really beginning to worry me."

He began to speak but then shook his head. Before she knew it, he'd wrapped her in his arms and pulled her to him, bringing his mouth down to crush over hers.

His taste raced through her, chasing away her doubts like smoke, intoxicated her, blurred everything around the edges.

He made her forget everything, made it difficult to recall just what their differences were. It was dangerously erotic.

He ripped his mouth from hers, panting. His eyes flashed, filling her with an edgy pleasure/fear. Not fear that he'd harm her physically but that she had no idea where this was headed. It probably wasn't good and yet she had no intention of stopping.

"I want you. Abbie, can I have you?"

Words flitted from her brain, leaving her able to only nod in response. He made a sound, low in his throat, all sex and need. It rode her spine, flowed into her body until she could do nothing but writhe against him as he moved a bit back, awaiting her answer.

Once she'd agreed, he was on her again, body pressed against hers, his hands holding her upper arms as his lips descended and claimed her mouth. His stubble, pale and gold in the low light of the room, brushed against the skin of her chin as his taste slithered through her system again. Hard-edged and yet deep. Yearning, so much yearning. Stoking her own need again.

She gave as much as she took, her arms moving up to encircle his neck. His teeth nipped her bottom lip, dragging a moan from her.

His tongue swept into her mouth, sliding along hers and she sucked on it, causing him to arch into her harder and move his hands down to her ass, squeezing. The movement caused a slight bit of friction in her pussy. Just enough to build her pleasure but not quite enough to come.

Stretched up on her tiptoes, she kissed down to his chin and over the line of his jaw, over the thundering pulse just below his ear. Greedy hands ripped open the buttons on his shirt, and she stepped back to look at him.

His eyes had deepened in color, his mouth was swollen from kisses, lips wet and slightly parted. He watched her with a gaze that brought a shiver.

"Did you bring that bag so you could stay the night?" she asked, slightly breathless.

"Yes. If I'm welcome?"

"You know the risks, Roman." She wanted it, but she wanted him to do it knowing what might happen if he got caught leaving the next morning.

"I do, but I don't care. I want to wake up with you."

She nodded, more touched than she could afford to be by his comment, and pulled her shirt up and over her head, tossing it behind her. His pupils enlarged and he shrugged out of his own shirt, letting it fall to the floor.

Reaching out, he popped the catch between her breasts and her bra fell open and down her arms. "Have I told you how much I love your breasts? Full, gorgeous. The stuff a man's dreams are made of." He took their weight, sliding his thumbs back and forth across her nipples.

All sorts of witticisms raced through her head but none made their way to her mouth. The heat rose from his bare torso, sliding against her skin along with his scent. She slid her palms all over his chest, drawing his nipples between her thumb and forefinger, squeezing until his hips jutted forward. She breathed him in, her mouth hovering over his heart, wanting to simply touch every part of him while she had him in her possession.

Suddenly, the bizarre situation, the way two grown people had to hide their involvement, the utter impossibility of it all, seemed hilarious. What else could she do but enjoy him and this thing they shared?

Laughing, she fell to her knees. Her hands went to his pants, unbuckling his belt and popping open the row of buttons lining the stalk of his cock. Plain white underwear shielded his erection as it strained against the soft fabric.

Shoving the pants and underwear down his legs, she then pushed him back so he was sitting on her couch. She settled between his thighs and looked up at him as she took him into her mouth.

He hissed. "I've been thinking of this every day since I saw you last. It seems too long ago. I nearly forgot what your mouth around my prick felt like."

She let her mouth remind him. Her hair began to tumble down from the knot it had been pinned in as he'd unmoored it. His taste, the heady scent of him, seduced her. He may have nearly forgotten what her mouth felt like but she'd remembered what his cock felt like. He was fat, wide, delicious. His veins throbbed against her tongue as she swirled it around him. His balls rested in her palm and drew up, tighter against his body.

"Oh, so fucking good. Yes, just like that." His voice was a low growl, strung with tension as she drove him up.

She flicked her tongue hard against the underside of the head and he groaned. She did it again. And again each time she pulled back up off him until he brought his hands to her shoulders and pushed her back.

"Sweet Abigail," he breathed out. "Wait. Wait. I don't want to come yet. I want to fuck you. Stand up. Let's go to your bedroom. I want to spread you out while I eat you."

Oh, that was good. Once he let go, the man was a fucking genius with the sex talk.

He tasted good and she loved the power there on her knees before him. Slowly, she gave him a parting lick before allowing him to help her up.

"You're so beautiful." He trailed his fingers along her scars, not breaking his gaze with hers and she wondered if he knew but quickly pushed it from her mind. "Walk ahead of me. You have the sexiest sway, and your ass is a masterpiece."

Even when he was drop-dead sexy, he still brought something carefree to their sexual interaction. She laughed and obliged him, putting an extra bit of hip action into her walk just for his amusement.

Once in her bedroom he stopped her, moving to strip her of her skirt and shoes, humming his satisfaction when he caught sight of the stockings. "Keep those on." He ran his palms up and down her legs and the material of the stockings. One quick movement and he drew his fingertips over the dampened crotch of her panties, bringing a gasp from her. "I do love the way these frame your pussy."

The warm, thigh-high stockings had just been a guard against the cold air with her business-style skirt, but suddenly she felt very sexy in them.

He stalked her until she backed up to the bed, falling against the mattress. He smiled, slow and sexy, and she gave over to the rapid beat of her heart. He was a predator. Even with a perfect haircut and soft hands, he was the master of his universe, hells of all the 'Verses,

and he knew how to stay that way. It made him alluring and mysterious, strong and very, very powerful.

Above and beyond all that, he was a man, a beautifully masculine one, and Abbie wasn't even sure what to look at first. He stood
naked above her, his body hard and mouthwatering. Her gaze slid
down his body, snagging on his cock, which was so hard it tapped
his stomach. Her pussy clenched at the sight. *She* made him that
way.

Using her elbows, she pulled herself up a bit and he got on the
bed after her. Tracking her movements with his own.

"Hands above your head."

Swallowing hard, she put her arms above her head, grabbing the
headboard. Skimming his palms up her legs, he pulled her panties
down and off. "Pretty." He tossed the dark blue scrap of lace over
his shoulder, never taking his eyes from her.

He was the one completely naked but the two thick stockings
covering her legs didn't protect her from feeling totally exposed by
his gaze. She felt more than just naked. There was nowhere to hide
from him, and so she didn't try. There were enough secrets. Things
he couldn't know. But that wasn't all of what she was, and so she gave
him everything else.

His breath hitched a moment before he leaned over her on all
fours and took her lips again. Soft hands, big and powerful, swept
over her skin, up her arms. "So beautiful," he murmured as his lips
skated down the column of her neck and across her collarbone. She
tightened her grip on the spines of the wrought iron headboard as
she arched up into his touch.

Kissing down her body, he stopped at each nipple. His mouth
drove her crazy as she writhed beneath him. The edge of his teeth

applied just the right amount of pressure over the sensitive point, tongue coming behind to lave the sting.

"Oh, please," she whispered, needing more of him.

He rolled his eyes up to look into her face. "Please what, Abbie?"

He meant to make her beg. Wanted to hear her, hear the need in her voice to know he wasn't alone in it. Roman wanted her so badly his hands shook. It weakened him. He didn't like it but at the same time, he accepted there was a deep need for her and he would fill himself with her presence.

"Please make me come. I need you."

"With my hands?" The tip of his tongue swirled around her nipple teasingly.

She shook her head.

"Tell me what you want."

Closing her eyes, she exhaled before opening them again and focusing on him. "I want you to go down on me."

"My mouth on your cunt? Two fingers deep inside you? Maybe three? My tongue sliding through each fold and up over your clit the way you like? Hard and then soft? Over and over until you come and your hot, sticky honey coats my lips and tongue and your taste burns itself into my memory?" Gods, he'd meant every word. He wanted to be indelible.

She shivered. "Yes."

"You sure you want that?" He trailed his fingers down her stomach and teased around her clit with an idle fingertip.

She gasped, rolling her hips up, arching to get more contact. "Yes. Damn you!"

Pulling his hand back he tsked at her. "Oh! Manners, sweetheart. Manners." He scooted down her body and spread her open, blowing over the heated, wet flesh of her pussy.

"Please, please," she burst out.

"Much better." Dipping his head, he tasted of her, using his tongue to touch every part of her he could. He slid two fingers deep and hooked them, stroking over her sweet spot as he took a leisurely tour of her cunt with his mouth. Wet and hot, her inner walls hugged his invading fingers.

Oh, how he'd missed her! Hadn't wanted to. Tried not to. But when he'd seen that folder with all that information on her, when he'd read the polis reports about her attack, he couldn't resist her any further. He'd had to see her.

Seeing her walk down the hall toward him, her hair beginning to come loose from that bun of hers, her cheeks pinked from the cold and her arms full of packages, he knew he was jumping into something with both feet. But how could he resist her? Knowing he'd licked every inch of her skin brought it roaring back with a vengeance. When he was like this with her, there were no secrets. No class difference. No failure to communicate. Here, with the flat of his tongue pushing hard over her clit the way he knew drove her crazy—here they connected. He knew her. She knew him. Knew him in a way no one else bothered to.

She was so fucking wet. Hot and slick and juicy. He brought her off then by sucking her clit into his mouth, lightly abrading it with his teeth. A low, guttural moan ripped from her lips as her back bowed off the bed.

Waiting until she'd stopped spasming around the fingers still deep within her, he pulled out and moved up her body. He kissed her deeply and then painted a nipple with her juices and licked at it until she made that low moan that made him want to shove his cock into her as fast as he could. In fact, that was a fine idea.

"Abbie, I'd like you on your hands and knees." His voice was low as he watched her, taut as she looked over her shoulder at him and got to her knees.

"Shall I grab the headboard?" She leaned to grab it and thrust her ass back at him. He nearly lost his mind.

"I am a lucky man."

She quirked up one corner of that mouth of hers and spread her thighs, exposing her pussy to him, opening for him.

He scrambled up, kneeling behind her, and guided himself to her sex. Grabbing her waist, he rolled his hips and thrust, hilting in one stroke. He halted, just letting himself feel the glory in the way she welcomed him, the way her body felt as if it were made for him and him alone.

Each time they'd been together it had been even better than the last. Abbie could get used to this on a regular basis. "Yes. Oh, you feel so good." She moaned, feeling him throb deep within her. Wet sounds of sex filled the room as he set to work, fucking into her body with deep, feral digs of that fat cock. She locked her elbows, really feeling the last bit of every thrust he made into her body.

"Make yourself come, Abbie. I want to feel you come around me." It wasn't a request, at least not one she planned to ignore.

Carefully letting go of the headboard with one hand, she reached down to where they were joined. Gathering her honey, she brought her fingers to her clit and touched herself the way she liked.

He continued to fuck her while she brought herself closer and closer to orgasm. Grabbing her hair and wrapping it around his fist, he moved her head so he could lean in and kiss her.

"I'm going to come any minute. Don't make me do it alone," he said, lips just above hers. "I know you're close, clit swollen and hard under your fingertips. I can still taste you on my lips. Your scent is in my nose. Come on, sweetheart, come for me. You know you want to."

Her eyes closed and rolled back as orgasm claimed her with a sharp crack of pleasure. It shot down her spine and straight to her cunt and she was sure, his cock, as the sensations rolled through her in wave after wave of blinding intensity.

"Yesssss," he hissed, and she felt his cock jerk as he came. The fingers on the hand still holding her hip dug into her flesh, keeping her there as he pressed as deeply as he could. The other held her head so he could plunder her mouth.

After long moments he sighed softly and gently pulled out. He rolled out of bed and returned shortly, climbing under the sheets she'd pulled back in his absence.

She snuggled into his body and listened to his heartbeat as they lay in companionable silence for long minutes.

Chapter 12

"So, this thing between us." He hesitated, watching her move gracefully around her small kitchen, wrapped in a thick robe, her hair loose. It was late, but after another bout of sex, hunger had driven them into the kitchen. "I don't want it to stop. But I don't know how to keep it going without making you feel like a secret." He sighed. "I can't, we can't. You know that. Gods, this is complicated. Maybe we need to stay away from each other."

She placed the teapot between them on the table with two mugs and then sat. "You can't what? Be seen squiring me around? I know." She sliced into a loaf of something that smelled better than most anything he'd smelled in a while. "We're not just from two different worlds, we're from two different realities. I'm not looking to marry you. We both know it's not possible for us to be a real couple in any sense. As it happens I enjoy you. And your lovely dick."

"A lovely dick?" He couldn't stop the smile her words evoked.

"Cock. Penis. You know, your tool of manly deeds and stuff."

Lindy would have never uttered that sentence. Never.

He reached out and grabbed the piece of the cake she'd sliced. Spice burst through him when he took a bite. "I'm glad you find it lovely. This is delicious, by the way." He sipped the tea; it was warm and sweet and it hit the spot. "I enjoy your company. I like you. If things were different . . ." He shrugged.

"But they aren't. So what do you want? We can end it right here. Chances are I won't see you often anyway." She didn't say it in a harsh way, but it felt harsh. He'd been without her and he didn't want that.

"I wish you understood just what I was up against."

She made a sour face and waved the comment away. "Show me. I'm not a dullard. I can learn things, you know. Show me and I'll do the same."

"What do you mean?"

She took his hand, kissing the palm. "I mean, let me show you a bit of my world. The world of the unranked. I think we can keep you incognito. I have a source for some nifty disguise gear. You can tell me about your world, about your life. I can't just traipse around in your life, you know that; not as easily as you can in mine. But you can share with me. We can learn from each other. And in doing so, we can see each other. Until it's time not to."

He didn't like the sound of her last sentence but it was inevitable. So until then, he could enjoy her and her friendship. Friendship was something he could keep after they had to end the sexual relationship part. Somehow he felt she would always be part of his life. Which seemed sort of silly, given that they'd only known each other for about eight standard weeks. But still.

"Does this lesson include lots of sex?" He grinned and she laughed.

"There are some things that do not change from Ranked to un-ranked. If you'd like, I'm going out tomorrow to interview some of the people who were with Jaron the night of the murder. We can go and do that and then how about you come dancing with me?"

"Investigation and dancing? How can I refuse such an offer?"

"I have a few more offers to make, if you're up for it."

How was he going to let this woman go? he wondered as he took in her face, the way she smiled, the shimmer of her hair as she tossed it over her shoulder.

"What in particular brought you to me tonight?" Her brows rose in a charming way. An unexpected tenderness sliced through him. And then guilt.

He hesitated and decided to wait for her to tell him the truth about her past. "Just hearing Marcus talk about you so much made me crave you." He shrugged. "Now, I'm nicely energized from our snack, so I say we work it off in your bed. I have nowhere to be at all for the next day."

Chapter 13

*F*unny how even walking through the streets of the outermost edges of the second ring of the capital, Roman still radiated power. Daniel had come by, dropped off a duffel filled with clothing and some items to disguise Roman's appearance, and had delivered a clipped lecture about safety and the cost of getting caught.

Roman assured Daniel it was all right, that he'd been trained in self-defense and was quite capable of not only protecting himself but Abbie, too. To which Daniel had replied, "If my sister is injured in any way, I will show you just how defenseless you are," and left.

His hair was darker and he wore lenses that made his green eyes dark brown. He'd taken a pill that had darkened his skin a bit, and his usually dressy clothing had been replaced by casual pants and a nice snug sweater. He looked tasty, and he'd garnered plenty of looks as they'd walked from the tram they'd taken from the center near her building.

"What the seven hells would Jaron be doing all the way out here?" Roman voiced the same question Abbie had been asking herself since she'd read the original charging papers.

The third ring, at this outermost edge, wasn't a place a boy with nice manners and a good home should have been. While it wasn't as lawless and chaotic as the fourth ring where Abbie's family had lived when they came back to the capital from the outback, it was a place where you watched your wallet and jewelry. It certainly wasn't the kind of place where you hung out in bars with people you didn't know.

"I don't know. I asked him and he said he'd met up with some acquaintances from his time in the corps. He didn't know them very well but they'd all seemed a nice enough sort and he was happy to see them."

She kept her voice low as they moved through the narrow streets. Her posture appeared relaxed but she was ready to run or fight at a moment's notice. After the attack, she'd gotten training from Daniel's friends. It was her way of taking her life back.

"It's hard to believe any adult male could be so naïve. Marcus is going to have to have a long talk with his son when he gets out of this," Roman grumbled as they jumped over a suspicious puddle. "If he does."

"He will. There is no way I'm going to let him go down for this. There's not enough evidence to send him away for life. I just hope to hells I can get him out totally. He doesn't deserve even a disorderly and a few months in lockup for this. From all my contact with Jaron, I've found him to be sweet and so very soft. I can see him unable to understand how stupid it was to come out here. I mean, he wasn't raised to have to be so very aware of the dangers in this world, you know? I just need to find these others." She looked up and saw the numbers she'd been looking for. "Here. Now listen. Stay quiet unless I tell you otherwise, all right?"

The way he pursed his lips, wanting to argue, charmed her but she hardened herself to it. He had to let her lead.

He finally nodded.

The scent in the hallways made her think of that tiny flat her family had crammed into from when she was fourteen until she was just a season away from turning eighteen standard, the age of majority. She had left it behind for a slot with a barrister to serve as his protégé and a space at the university, far away in the center's innermost circle.

Spices, cleaning fluids from the families who scrubbed their tiny homes with great pride, alcohol from those who had less pride every day, and beneath all of it, the hint of just barely getting by. It wasn't as bad here, but it hung in the air like a ghost.

"One more floor." Thank goodness both of them were in good shape.

She knocked and rang the bell, heard the sounds inside and the slide of a viewport being opened. Abbie looked straight into it, letting the person behind the door see her face.

"I'm Abigail Haws, here to speak with Fane Albert regarding the murder charges against Jaron Mach." She held up her government-issued identification card and after a time, the locks slid open and the door breached a crack.

"I'm Fane's mum. What do you want with him?"

"Do you want me to do this in the hallway?" Abbie leaned in so the older woman could hear her.

"And who's he then?" Fane's mother nodded in Roman's direction.

"This is my assistant. So? Shall I ask my questions out here?"

With a heaving sigh, the woman opened the door and let them in.

Roman watched, frankly amazed at what a hard-ass Abigail Haws could be. She'd zeroed in on Fane Albert, who sat sullenly on the couch, letting his mother answer the door and hide him from the public. At first the youth had tried to suck up, flattering her, and then he'd gotten rude. All throughout, Abbie had simply stuck to the subject, taking notes and following up. Roman had been impressed by her mind, by the way she'd stayed on task while seeming to wander around and keep Fane unsure as to what she wanted. Somehow a ruthless woman existed beneath that tiny exterior and Roman got off on it.

Abbie acted nonchalant as they left, but her walk was flavored with purpose. She obviously had a destination in mind. Roman didn't like the neighborhood, the way people watched them through curtains and down alleyways. It made him nervous as they moved to the next place, but she didn't seem bothered. So far, her little experiment to teach him about the world of the unranked hadn't given him many positives.

"Fuck, that's him," she said as she began to run. "You! Cris Balow, stop your ass right there!"

For a small woman she moved amazingly fast. He would have lost her if his legs hadn't been so much longer than hers.

This Cris person didn't have Roman's legs or his luck. Abbie pushed her way through a group of boys, ran straight up to Cris and poked her finger in his chest. "You made me run. I hate to run," she snarled. She grabbed his ear and pulled him out of the crowd and toward a café on a nearby corner. Roman looked on, amazed the kid didn't hit her or try to stop her in some way.

"Hey, lady, let go of me! Who do you think you are?" Cris whined.

"I know your sister, Jasmine. She would knock you out if she had any idea the crowd you were running with. What are you *thinking*? Those boys are nothing but trouble. Now you tell me everything about that night in the Two Moons and you tell me right now. Or I'm making a comm to Jasmine."

The youth's eyes widened and he looked around furtively.

"They can't hear. They scattered because they think I'm either corps or the polis. Either way, you're fine. Unless you don't tell me."

"I don't know much, I swear. Fane's cousin Mikel had just come back from Borran where he'd been training in the corps. He saw some soft, inner-circle guy he knew. Said we could count on him for a night of free drinks and food." Cris shrugged. "Who am I to argue? The guy seemed really out of his element, you know? Nice. I felt bad. You can ask the others, I tried to get him to leave a few times, and when he didn't get it, I tried to run interference along with another guy to keep the softie safe. There were women, way too fast for the likes of me, much less this Jaron kid. A fight broke out. You know, women, a few guys with credits, too much alcohol. I don't know what happened, I don't know who started what, but this Jaron, he'd been at a table with me. The action was near the bar."

"Did you tell the polis this?"

"Are you kidding me? I ran out of there, trying to drag him with me, but he got caught up in it. I have a few priors on my record. If I go into lockup, there won't be anyone to help my mom and Jasmine. How did you find me?"

Abbie sighed and closed her notebook. "Jaron told me your name and the names of people he could remember. I've just been to Fane's and his mother helped him remember pretty much the same story you've given. Now, I'm entering this into my evidence. I'm trying to get Jaron out of lockup, trying to get the charges dropped. I may need you to come and give your statement in person. I know you won't want to, but you can't possibly be related to Jasmine if you'd let someone rot in lockup when you know he's not guilty."

Cris hung his head and nodded. "I guess you know where I live anyway."

"And where you work. So don't even think of running. I'll find you and then have you tossed in lockup until trial. It won't be pretty, and your mom and Jasmine will miss the income."

"Why you gotta be so mean?"

"Mean? You listen here, Cris. Jaron Mach is a good, honest man. A person you were content to use for his credits, although I do believe you tried to help him in that bar. Mean is letting him stay in lockup. You know what it's like in there. Now, you imagine a softie like him in there. Yeah, I see you get the point. I'm not mean at all. I'm not having you thrown into lockup just in case you might run. *That* would be mean. You should be ashamed of yourself. Now go on home, and if you remember anything else, you call my office. Your mom and sister both know how to contact me."

Cris ran off without another word, and Roman chuckled. "Well now, that ear twist thing is a handy move."

She laughed. "I imagine you've had to use it yourself a few times. Or did you never have any trouble with your boys?"

"Deimos was relatively easy but Corrin was more problematic. Missed his mother, I expect. My sister lived with us for several standard, helped with them. She's a second mother more than an aunt. She had the ear twist down to a science. That and the guilt thing you did at the end there."

"That was nothing. My mother is an artist. She had to be, really, with four kids. It wasn't so bad in the outback, not a whole lot to get into trouble over. Just miles of empty space. But when we came back here—" Her eyes lost focus and her words wandered off. She came back to herself moments later. "Anyway, my mom is pretty darned good at it."

He stood and held a hand out. "Come on. Let's go back to get changed. You promised me dancing."

"I did, didn't I? Well okay. We need to stop near the tram entrance. There's a sweet shop there that carries the nut pralines my sister loves. I need to grab some for her. Her birthday is coming up."

They walked, his arm around her shoulders, as the afternoon settled in around them. Street vendors hawked their wares from the sidewalks and she stopped here and there, chatting and buying odds and ends she tucked into her bag. The time was deliriously normal. Something he'd rarely experienced in his life, even more rarely with a woman at his side.

The sweet shop Abbie directed them to had steamed windows and when they entered, the scent made his mouth water. Rosewater and lavender, honey and vanilla, purri fruit and all the different smells of his childhood.

A tiny, birdlike woman came out from behind the counter and enveloped Abbie in a hug. "Abigail! It's been a long time. It must be Nyna's birthday coming up."

"Mrs. Pike, it's nice to see you. Your memory is scary. Yes, it's Nyna's birthday soon. I was here and thought I'd stop in to get some of your famous pralines. While you're at it, the honey bites and some of that rosewater candy my mother likes, too, please."

"Here, you look like you could use a bit of something sweet.

Other than our lovely Abigail, that is." Mrs. Pike handed Roman a small bundle. "Caramels? My ancestors brought these recipes through from Earth. This shop has been here in one form or another since Ravena was settled."

"Mrs. Pike, this is my friend Roman. Roman, this is Mrs. Pike. When I was in school, we would often come down here to this very shop to load up on sweets. Then she and my mother became thick as thieves."

She'd not introduced him by name back when she was interviewing people, but now he was Roman. This Mrs. Pike must be someone he could trust, at least with his name. He liked her, liked the pride she showed in her shop and her candy. He popped a piece in his mouth. Perfect, a hint of sweet, a hint of smoke, soft and delicious. Sort of like Abbie.

"It's a pleasure to meet you, ma'am. This is the best caramel I've ever tasted."

"Of course it is. I made it myself." Mrs. Pike puffed out her bony chest and dared him to argue. He wouldn't even if she had been wrong.

Being with Abbie this way, the scent of the shop making him think about his youth, walking side by side with a woman he'd grown to enjoy, it made him feel truly happy, carefree, for the first time in years.

Mrs. Pike wrapped the candies up with a pretty bow and Abbie tucked them into her bag before she and Roman hustled off to catch the next tram.

The tram ride was short enough when they took the express back to the center. She did everything with an efficiency of movement and effort, and he admired that a lot. She was so self-sufficient. Powerful in a way he had to admit he saw only rarely. Women in

Families weren't raised to be independent. She was alien in the most refreshing sort of way.

The breeze was cold as it came in through the partially opened windows of the tram. He realized he rarely used the public trams for travel. This one was comfortable and well maintained. The neighborhoods became brighter, cleaner and safer-looking as they traveled toward the center. But all he could really think on was how good it felt to have her against his side, her hair brushing against his cheek, the softness of her body against his.

The walk to her place was quick and when they got inside safely, he had nothing on his mind but kissing her. So he did.

Roman was so full of surprises. His mouth covered hers and she gave in easily, wanting the contact after a day with him at her side. He'd kept quiet when she told him to and, it seemed, had even enjoyed being someone else for the day.

The kiss was mellow, slow and sweet, another surprise from the always surprising Roman Lyons. He took his time, tasting, teasing, meandering through her defenses and obliterating each one. Not with force, but with seduction.

Every time he touched her, all she wanted was him. Her need for him was relentless. It never left her. Part of her thrilled at that. No one had ever made her feel this way. On the other hand, it scared her to react so deeply to someone.

He pulled back and looked into her eyes. "I've wanted to do that all day. How long until you sweep me off to go dancing?"

"Not very. We have reservations shortly." She slid a hand into his pants and grabbed his cock. "Enough time for me to take care of this though."

"On your knees, then. You know how I like it."

No hesitation in his tone. He owned it and it brought a shiver to her. Abbie loved how he was finally at ease enough with her that he could just say it instead of working around to it or using half measures. The man liked it hard and dirty. What was wrong with that?

She sank to her knees, rubbing her face down his belly, over the soft material of his sweater, her fingers nimbly loosing his cock from his pants on the way.

"Lovely." She looked at his cock for long moments before licking around the head while holding the length of it tight, just how he preferred. He hummed his satisfaction and the low sound echoed straight to her clit.

"Not as lovely as what I'm seeing. So very pretty you are, Abbie. Your mouth wrapped around me, sucking me just right."

His fingers wove through her hair after he'd taken it down. It never seemed to stay up long around him. She smiled inwardly as she took him into her mouth over and over. The taste of him changed as the surface of his cock changed. His skin was electric, hard. His hips canted forward as he thrust into her mouth. Not too hard, but he wanted her to suck him deeper and he made that clear with his body.

Breathing steadily through her nose, she concentrated on the way she knew she made him feel. There was power on her knees, his cock in her mouth, and she reveled in it. Never had any man been so alluring to her and each moan she wrenched from him made her feel potent, sexy, beautiful.

"I'm going to come in your mouth. I love that. I love that you'd do that for me."

His fingers tightened as his pace quickened. He hissed a breath and his entire body went taut. A groan echoed through him as he filled her with his taste. Behind her closed eyes, she saw bursts of color as she fell along with him, knowing she'd made him come, knowing he'd trusted her to let his defenses down.

When his grip relaxed and his movements had smoothed into a gentle stroke instead of a frenzied grasp, she licked the head of him, tucked his cock back inside his pants and stood.

"How long do we have?" He pulled her tight to him and kissed her neck, just below her ear.

"I have to change clothes. We don't have time for reciprocation. I'll collect later." She winked at him.

"I can't stay tonight, unfortunately. My sister is coming to stay with us for a few days. She's here to see the boys and probably the rest of my family." He scowled and she wanted to laugh at his expression—like a tot who'd been refused sweets.

"Are you sure you have time for dinner and dancing? We can do this another day." She didn't want him to say no.

He spun her, pulling her back to his front and grabbed her breasts. "I have time. I'd rather fuck you senseless, but seeing you dance won't be a hardship."

"All right then. There are clothes for you on my bed."

She leaned back, let him kiss her forehead and moved to the bedroom to get changed. There were no his and hers dressing areas in her flat. It was nice. Years and years of saving and her position as a barrister had enabled her to apply for and secure a place in this block. Close enough to a vent so it wasn't terribly cold during the chilly parts of the annum. Safe. Secure. It was small but home.

Abbie wondered what his house would be like. What the house of the most powerful and influential man in all the Known Universes looked like. Warm she was sure. Abbie bet he had all the hot water he wanted and more. Palatial, most likely. She pulled on a bright, flowing skirt shot with silver threads. Her blouse was as vibrant but in a complementary color scheme to the skirt.

Abbie might have to wear muted colors to work but when she went out, she loved to wear bright colors and flowing skirts. The feel of the breeze on her legs as she moved, the way the fabric swirled and flared as she danced made her happy. It was a chance to be something other than a barrister or an activist. She got to be a woman, plain and simple.

Once she'd secured the front of her hair back with pretty silver clips, she dabbed on some lipstain and put on some earrings before heading back into the living room where Roman was on a comm.

"Deimos, it's Dai. I'm just calling to check in. Is everything okay?"

She smiled. Here he was, making sure his grown sons were all right. She liked Deimos Lyons a lot. He was intelligent and well-spoken, and he understood the world was more than just his small part of it. Men like Deimos gave her hope for the future.

Men like Deimos, who were most likely the way they were because of how they were raised.

Roman's gaze found her and took a leisurely trip from her toes to the top of her head. She saw his gaze flare as he took in the more feminine outfit, the way her hair was down and her lips were glossy and red. She knew she looked pretty, but his eyes spoke of need. She craved it, craved his regard and attraction. It ate at her edges, made her want more.

"All right then. Abbie and I are going out now. No, no one will recognize me. Hells, son, I barely recognize me. I'll have to show you this getup sometime. Yes, yes keep it quiet. I will. And yes, I love you, too." He disconnected and smiled. "You look beautiful." He stood, moving to her, circling her.

She liked him in all black. In fact, she was sure he'd look even better in all black with his pale hair and his green eyes. Whatever he wore, she'd take him any way she could get him, and in the black button-down shirt tucked into black trousers with black boots was quite the way to have him.

"Thank you. You don't do so bad yourself. I'm used to you looking dressed up and professional. But this look is very nice, too. Your ass looks better in these pants, I must say." She patted his butt and he laughed, putting his arm about her waist.

"Deimos says to tell you hello."

"He knows then? About us?"

Roman nodded. "I wouldn't be hiding it at all if I could, you know that. He's my son. I trust him. And he likes you. In fact, I had to tell him this because he said he'd flirted with you several times and you steered him away from it. I can't believe I'm competing with my son for a woman."

She laughed. "He's a boy, Roman. A good one. You've done a job you should be proud of. But a boy. I prefer the man."

"Very good answer. Now come on before I rip that blouse from you to feast on your nipples. The color makes your skin look . . . well, I want to lick you. All over."

She shivered. "I'll cash in on that later."

The place she took him was on the edge of the first circle. The capital buildings and complex occupied the center, or inner circle. The Families also lived there. It was the most heavily guarded and considered the safest of anyplace to live or be in the capital. The first circle was where Abbie far preferred to be. It was filled with a wide array of people, Ranked and non-, from all walks of life. Mostly professional because the housing was more costly, and closer to the vents that provided heat and energy to the housing and commercial units. Littered with wonderful cafés, shops, parks and social halls like the one they were on their way to.

Social halls usually had a theme of some kind or another. Either a type of food or dance music, sometimes a particular neighborhood culture. This one, called The First Circle, was one of the latter.

The bright lights and the sound of music spilled out of the doors as they approached. Daniel and Georges had met them not too far from Abbie's building and they'd all made their way there. The evening had been brisk but the mood was light. Abbie was relieved her brothers seemed to like Roman although Daniel remained a bit wary. She couldn't blame him. She was sure his siblings would have been the same given different circumstances. Sadly, Alexander Lyons seemed to want to destroy her but she didn't know much about his sister Sophia other than she'd helped raised Deimos and Corrin and appeared to be one of those exceptionally beautiful, sheltered Family females who were petite, protected and coddled. But she'd done the right thing and helped her family, and that meant a lot in Abbie's opinion.

Roman liked Daniel Haws. Abbie's older brother was very strong and smart. Most importantly, he was obviously protective of his sister. In fact, Daniel had been the one to find Abbie after her attack. He'd fought off the others and had ended up having to go into the corps early to avoid lockup. His records, though locked to prying eyes on the outside, had shown a man with a great deal of courage and inventiveness in the service of the Federated Universes. He worked on one of Comandante Ellis's special teams, but they didn't speak of it.

Georges was a lot like Abbie, vivid, lively, gregarious even. He didn't walk; he seemed to eat up the path with great, galloping steps. His smile was infectious, and he and Abbie seemed to feed off one another. It was so interesting to Roman that both siblings were far more professional and calm when doing anything dealing with the MRD. They both believed in what they worked for, which was a very powerful motivator. Roman understood that. It also made a huge difference to Roman, to his overall feelings about their proposals.

The social club was a riot of color and scents. The moment they'd taken their seats, great heaping plates of food and pitchers of fermented juice were placed before them. Roman dug in, loving the taste of nearly everything he tried. Funny how he'd never eaten so many of the things before him. He'd been born and raised in Ravena, here in the capital, and yet, he'd never experienced a social hall or eaten the spiced bread he used to sop up the juices of a rice and vegetable dish.

It wasn't that his world didn't have moments of fun. He laughed all the time with his boys. But he'd never been to any place like this one. He'd never seen this sort of dancing and singing, servers wending through the crowd like dancers themselves, avoiding dropping the trays held high above their heads.

"I told you it's not all like what you saw out in the edge of the second circle today. Even out there you'd have seen social halls similar to this one. Although more like the one Jaron went to the night of the killing."

He leaned in, speaking into her ear, "Next lesson you can be naked and then tell me about how it all works between circles. I

mean, I know the basics, obviously, but there are things you understand better than I do. I want you to share that with me. I need your
insight."

"All right." Her voice was lower, clearly affected by his comment
about her being naked but also pleased. He liked that he'd made her
happy.

"Come and dance with me." He stood and she took his hand,
laughing.

Out on the floor, the heat of the crowd melded with the libation
and the scent of Abbie's skin. There was no one out there but the
two of them. She moved like she was made for dancing. The music
caught her and she let it flow through her like breath. He simply
stood near her, swaying, and watched.

Her hair flowed around like a dark river. Roman scented her
soap as she moved close. Her eyes went half-lidded, her lips carried
a secret smile. She was magic there on the floor, fey, like a little pixie.
He wanted her to alight on his hand and never leave.

The club filled up with laughter. With celebration and music.
These were his people in a very real sense but he was convinced he'd
never seen them more clearly than he had right then. Smiling, in
love, a bit drunk, out with friends, everyday citizens enjoying their
lives just as he did. Although he was fairly convinced the unranked
knew how to enjoy themselves far more than the Ranked. He'd
never seen anyone kick up their heels like this with such utter abandon. He'd seen hired dancers and the mistresses his brethren brought
around. But this was different.

And quickly, that elation fell away as he realized he'd never have
this with her as Roman. The thought of it felled him and he had to
have her. He had to bury himself inside her to know he was real. To
know *they* were real, even if fleeting.

"I need you, Abbie. Can we go? I have to go back home in the early hours and I want every moment I can get with you. Please."

She looked up, standing on her toes and kissed him. She gave him what he needed and didn't ask for anything in return. She could be using him right now for her MRD goals but she wanted him to see it himself. No one in any 'Verse was like her.

"Come on, then. If we hurry we can get a tram." She pulled him through the crowd. They said their good-byes and hustled through the crowd, many of whom called out to her, and she smiled and waved as they slipped out into the night beyond the hall.

Chapter 14

The cool air outside was welcome as they half ran, laughing, holding hands, to the nearby tram stop and jumped on.

She climbed into his lap. The tram was empty, the night rushed through his hair but it was all her. Her scent wrapped around him as she ground herself down on him.

She caught his surprise. "You've never done anything like this." A statement. A true one.

He shook his head slowly, caught in the honey of her.

"Shall I stop?" She tilted his head, her lips hovered just above his. Her hair had slid forward, screening their faces.

In answer, he stretched up just that breath away, meeting her lips, feeling them curve into a smile.

"Let me give you this memory. Something that's only yours and mine. Touch me."

He found the waist of her shirt and caressed the soft skin of her bare belly beneath, warm against his hand. Her nipple beaded against his palm, hardened further when he peeled the material of her bra back and pinched it between thumb and forefinger.

"No one knows it's you," she whispered in his ear, ending on a gasp.

She was right. He was anonymous. He could do the things he'd always wanted to but couldn't because he was the face of House Lyons. The freedom in anonymity hardened him, brought a rush of pleasure through his system.

He bit her neck and she arched with a small, hushed sound of arousal in his ear. The scent of her pussy reached his nose, sticky sweet and ready. His free hand made its way under her skirt and found her bare to his touch.

She laughed, knowing he'd be surprised.

But her laughter died away as he thrummed against her clit, his fingertips sliding through the slick folds of her cunt. Instead, she whispered, "Yes."

The natural rocking of the tram as it moved through the city brought friction against her pussy.

The world passed them by, flickering, wafting through the windows as he worked her pussy, fingering her until her breath against his neck quickened.

"I'm going to make you come. Right here, right now when anyone can see." As he said it, he pinched her nipple and her clit.

"Yes, you are," she said, right before biting into his shoulder. Her cunt clasped around his fingers as she came in a hot rush against him.

"That's right, give it to me. I love the way you feel, Abbie. Hot and wet, just waiting for my cock."

She lifted up. "Fuck me right here, then."

Could he? Could he be as bold as the woman in his lap, offering to let him fuck her on a public tram?

"We're four stops away. Can you do it in time?" She let her head fall back, her hair falling away, exposing the line of her body to him, to anyone who might be looking on from the windows they passed by.

It felt like someone else's hands undoing his pants, like someone else's hand holding his cock but definitely her pussy welcoming him, soft and inferno-hot. She held onto the seat behind his head and rode him with utter abandon.

It was as if he watched two other people fucking. Something so intimate and rare, so beautiful it made him ache deep inside. Silly really. It wasn't their first time together, or, gods willing, their last. It wasn't excessively carnal; in fact, the way her skirt sat on his lap, none of their skin was actually exposed.

But it was the act, the act of being inside her, fucking her in public as they moved toward their stop. The inexorable reality of coming deep within her cunt before they stopped, the way he knew people looking out their windows could see them and might wonder if indeed he was fucking the beautiful brunette woman on his lap—these things made his pleasure sharp and nearly unbearably good. Made them special in a way he'd hold close forever.

She sat up, looking into his eyes, a smile on her lips as she gave herself to him, as she took at the same time. "You're close."

He nodded, for once, words not on the tip of his tongue, rather buried in a place he couldn't seem to let go of.

"Fill me."

Arching up, holding her down on him, he did.

* * *

They nearly ran from the stop back to her building, arms wrapped around each other's waists, happy. His humor slipped away as they got inside.

"I have to go soon." It felt as if the words ripped him in half.

He caught the way she blinked back tears. "Why don't you shower? It'll get rid of the color in your hair. The color contacts are disposable according to Daniel. He says the skin-darkening effects of the pill should wear off by morning. Would you like me to scrub your back?"

"Yes, please."

She laid out fluffy towels and turned on the water, which heated quite quickly.

"Pretty good. My water isn't even this fast to heat."

She blushed. "This is my big vice. Don't tell anyone." She pushed him into the stall and crowded in behind him.

"What? Showers with men?"

She snorted and he lost track of his words for long moments when she began scrubbing his back, her fingers digging into his knotted muscles.

"No, water. I got a rise in credits recently and I think it all goes on water fines. I can't help it. I love long, hot showers. I've defended so many of the family members of the people who own and run the building and my siblings' buildings, they often look the other way."

He scrubbed the color from his hair, grinning. "My oh my. Until this point I had the feeling you were perfect in every way. Defender of the downtrodden, a childhood in the outback, taking care of your family and those who needed you. A social conscience that brings you to the brink of losing your license to practice the law, even. But here it is, your dark secret. Abigail Haws is a water criminal."

She slapped his ass with the washing cloth and slathered her soapy hands all over his reviving cock.

"A girl needs a bad habit or two."

He turned, rubbing his soap-slick body against hers for the pleasure of contact. "I can be three, can't I?"

"You're much more than a bad habit, Roman Lyons." Her voice lost some of its amusement and he knew what she meant.

"There's no reason to even think about that now. How's my hair?"

She looked up. "You got it all. Give it one last wash and rinse and use that cream there to soften it. The chemicals will strip it of moisture. I'd offer to help but I can't reach."

"You are awfully short." He kissed her nose. "Do I look like the sort of man who'd worry about how soft his hair was?"

She laughed. "Yes, as a matter of fact, you do. It's actually quite attractive I must say."

He worked on holding back a smile but he couldn't. Instead he made sure she saw him work the cream into his hair, liking quite a bit that he would smell like her for a while at least.

"Would you like some tea before you go?" she asked as she got out. He liked the way her breasts swayed as she handed a towel his way.

"I should probably just go. It's already very late. Sophia will be arriving or have arrived already. I'll need to be smart about how I leave." He got dressed in his regular clothes, putting Roman Lyons back on as he did.

She nodded. "Right. Well, take the back lift. It leads to an alley. Follow it to the end and cut behind the next few buildings. Keep the hat on and your coat collar up. You will end up down near the blue tram line. You'll be fine from there."

He bent and kissed her. "I wish I didn't have to go."

She nodded. "I know. But you do. Comm me when you can. Thank you for coming with me today, and for tonight. Not just the dancing and dinner but the tram. I've always wanted to do that."

"Me, too. Obviously I don't get around to fucking in public much."

She smiled and he felt better for having put the smile on her face.

He kissed her again, needing to have her taste in his mouth. "You gave me a gift today. All of it. I'll come to you soon. It's your turn to learn about my world next."

"I can't wait." She winked and looked out into the hallway. "All clear. Be well."

He left quickly, not wanting to prolong his departure or he'd never go.

He followed her directions and found his way around, quietly and quickly. Once he got back out into the plaza near the administration building, he was far enough from her place that no connection would be made. Still, even among the people out walking, he was just another person to not bump into. He cherished this last bit of anonymity, not knowing when he'd get it again.

Once back at home, he checked in with his staff, looked in at his sleeping sons and went into his room after leaving a note for his sister. His muscles were pleasantly sore after the many hours of sex he'd enjoyed in Abbie's company. She challenged him in a way he'd never been before. No one had dared to, he supposed. But she also made him comfortable. Made him forget about the trappings of who he was. With her he was simply Roman. Not anything but a man who wanted her and that simple thing made being with her sweeter than anything he'd experienced before.

Chapter 15

"*J*ust what exactly do you think you're doing, Abbie?" Daniel sat down on her couch with a glare in her direction.

"I'm fixing a button that fell off my sweater."

He raised one brow in her direction.

She sighed because he saw right through her. "Fine. I'm not doing anything. It's just a thing. Between me and him. It has nothing to do with anyone else. Leave it."

"I can't leave it. You are going to get hurt here. This can't go anywhere, you know that. He can't be with you. You can't be with him. You can't plan to be his mistress!"

"Of course not!" She sent him the same glare right back. "I'm annoyed you'd even suggest such a thing."

"People do all sorts of crazy and ill-advised things for love, Abbie. You know that as well as I do. Look at our parents. Do you really think Dad is good enough for Mom?"

"He has a good heart. He just doesn't know how to—"

"How to be a father? How to be a husband?"

"He did the best he could. He's helped so many people, Daniel. People who needed it. We had Mai, those other kids didn't have even that. He was it for them."

Daniel sighed, flicking a piece of imaginary lint from his pants. As if real lint would dare to alight there. "Why do you make excuses for him? After all you've suffered? You would have no need for spectacles if he'd been a decent father! You'd not have been attacked and savaged in the streets if he'd had a safe place for us to live. Instead he worried more about his causes than his family and you nearly died. Nyna hides behind her food. Georges rarely takes anything seriously unless you do."

"What about you, Daniel?" she asked in a soft voice, hating the pain she heard in him.

"I turned into a killer, Abbie. Every face I saw was that Ranked bastard and his buddies who raped you. I killed them over and over because I couldn't kill the real thing. I'm angry all the time because I failed you. And now I see you in this thing with him and you will end up hurt. There's no way around it. I see how he looks at you, I'm not saying this is one-sided. But he can walk away. What about you?"

She swallowed hard, knowing if she cried, it would only make him feel worse. Instead, she placed her mending to the side and sat next to him on the couch, putting her head on his shoulder.

"In those days after the attack, when I woke up and I was broken—" She had to swallow again and blink back tears. "You were there every day. By my bedside, holding my hand. You went to therapy with me and made me do those exercises I hated. But I can use my left arm and hand because of that. Because of you. You stopped it, Daniel, and then you had to go off and pay the price. You didn't fail me. The system failed us both. But we survived. I'm happy. I truly am. I know I can't have him. He's meant for a Ranked woman who will most likely bear more children for him. I'm meant for a rabble-rousing unranked man and I'll bear him children and I'll love him. This will be something I can look back on fondly because I know it can't be anything more than it is. I love you. I love that you worry about me. But I'm fine and, Daniel, so are you."

He put his cheek to her hair and relaxed. "You're not broken. They hurt you, they took something from you, but not the spark within that makes you who you are. You're bigger than that. Better than that."

"And you're not a killer. You went into the corps and you did what they trained you to do. I'm glad you did it well because that means you're alive here with me. As for Dai? What can we do at this point? Should I cry because I have to wear spectacles? Or because he never remembers birthdays? He's never going to change. And so I accept him for what he is and take the good things for an example and know I'd never do the bad. I can be someone fighting for what is right without losing sight of the everyday things that are important. He's wrong about how I'm going about this whole thing. I know that. I'm convinced of it. But he cannot know about me and Roman. He wouldn't understand why I don't cross lines."

"But I do, and so your secret is safe with me and Georges. And Nyna, too, of course. She and Marcus Mach have been building quite the friendship lately."

"He's a good man. I like him."

"Me, too. All right, enough gooey talk. Feed me, woman."

She got up and squeezed the hand he held out to her. He was her touchstone, the person she knew she could count on no matter what.

"Because you're old I'll let you get away with that. Anyway, Nyna sent over food earlier today so I don't have to work very hard."

They sat at her table to eat and he got his serious face back. "Be careful with him. Already many people know. They're all people who care about you, of course, but the more people who know, the bigger the risk."

She knew. She understood it every time she had to deal with this ridiculous business about her license to practice. Saul Kerrigan did not like to lose. She had made him lose face over Gretel Mortan and since it became known that Gretel had a hand in raising Lindy Lyons, he'd had to drop his complaint against her. Abbie had the feeling Roman paid Gretel's stipend but whatever the case, Kerrigan could not be pleased.

She also knew four of the five adjudicators on the licensing panel were squarely on her side. Her license was safe but it still scared her that anyone wanted to harm her. It brought back memories of a lesser member of House Kerrigan who felt thwarted by her not wanting any part of him and who'd nearly killed her instead.

"I know. I don't know how often I'll be seeing him anyway. His sister has been in the capital for six days. I haven't seen him in all that time although he did comm me a few times to check in. But we're careful." Even though she missed Roman more than she could afford to, they'd both been careful.

Daniel looked at her gravely. "These Ranked are dangerous people when they sense you're trying to take something they believe is theirs. Watch your back. And when you can't, I will."

*D*aniel walked her back to her office where she finished up some work and took the long way home again. She wanted time to think.

She had lost something back when she was seventeen. It had taken her ten standard years before she could really think of herself as healthy, as feeling attractive and wanting attention from a man. The attack hadn't stolen her soul and with Logan, and really with Roman, she realized they hadn't stolen her sexual identity either. She could love sex, love her sexuality, and not connect it to one horrible event she experienced nearly fifteen years before.

And she could pursue her dreams of shared governance and still want to lick Roman Lyons from head to toe. She *could* keep her business and professional lives totally separate.

Being with Roman had taught her a few things about herself. Big, important things. But right then, all she wanted to do was have him buried inside her, looming over her as he showered her with kisses and stoked her desire with that deep, dirty voice of his.

Chapter 16

"Ms. Haws, I'd like to speak with you, if I may."

Abbie turned around to face Alexander Lyons. He looked very much like Roman, only Alexander's eyes were darker and he was taller. But the look on his face was nothing she'd seen on Roman before. Entitlement. Superiority.

"And you are?" she asked, knowing the answer but wanting to make a point about manners.

"Oh I do apologize. I assumed you'd know. I'm Alexander Lyons of House Lyons."

"Ah, the man trying to have my license revoked. What can I do for you, Mr. Lyons?" She had a few ideas. She was on her way to a meeting with Deimos to talk about shared governance. She'd also just appeared before the licensing committee and presented her rebuttal of the charges against her.

"Saul said you thought yourself above your station. I see he was correct."

"I'm on my way to a meeting. If we're to stand here, you being acerbically amusing and me pretending to be abashed, let's just get it over with. My *station* is that of a barrister who did her job and was assaulted in a public hallway by Saul Kerrigan. Because an old woman was let out of lockup until her trial. And because of that, he seeks to remove my ability to make a living and to do my job."

"Interesting. Well, I'm here because I wanted your side of the story. My brother seems to hold you in high esteem. My nephew says your group is not trying to rip our system apart. You seem very defensive."

She laughed and he jerked back. "Mr. Lyons, what do you feel the proper reaction would be? That's a genuine question."

The crowd moved around them, some gawking openly. Anger licked at her insides. Who did he think he was? He was judging her reactions to this whole thing?

"Well, I don't know. I can't say because I've never put myself in that position."

"It would seem we need a lot more time than a hallway discussion leaves us, Mr. Lyons. At the moment, as I said, I'm on my way to a meeting. If you'd like to call my assistant," she handed him her data card, "she can set up a meeting and I can explain to you that the overwhelming majority of Ravena's citizenry has to put themselves in a position of this sort all the time. Your not having to is a luxury." She took a step back, amused by the confusion on his face. "Enjoy your day."

She stalked off, holding in a smile.

* * *

$\mathcal{D}$eimos looked up when she entered, along with Georges. "I apologize for being late. I was delayed on my way over." She moved to sit.

"Not a problem. Abbie, I've spoken with several other members of the Auxiliary Council and we'd like you to address our group at the next meeting. As you know, the AC is where the heirs and secondary House leaders are seated. It's a younger crowd, less, well, less entitled let's say. Many of them are open to the idea of an advisory council where representatives of the unranked citizenry of Ravena are seated. Some will never be swayed. But many can be. Can you do that?"

She laughed. "Can I talk people into things? Deimos Lyons, I do it all day every day. And I would be honored to have the chance to address the AC on behalf of the MRD."

"All right then. You have a week." He grinned at her and she blinked.

"Good gods! I'll be ready. I just won't sleep in the meantime." She grinned back.

"Oh, do us a favor, Abbie. You can do this stuff in your sleep and you know it." Georges turned to Deimos. "Thank you. I know this wouldn't be happening if you weren't advocating on our behalf."

"My father and I believe you have something important to say that the Houses should hear." Deimos shrugged but she caught his blush. Sweet. He was a good young man, a credit to his Family.

They continued to speak for a while, talking about the different members of the AC and what their different perspectives were. It gave Abbie a big advantage when it would come time for her to address them.

On the way out, Deimos stopped her. "When is Jaron's next hearing?"

"I'm on my way now. I'm hoping we can get him released into his father's custody until his trial. You're welcome to come along if you like. He'd like that. He speaks of you often."

"I will, if you don't mind."

They began to walk. She debated on speaking to him about his uncle and decided against it. Abbie didn't want to put him in the middle.

"Oh and here." He handed her an envelope. "You'll need this, but don't worry about it until you're at home."

It must be from his father. Her heart sped at the thought. She put it in her bag. "All right. Thank you."

When they turned the corner toward the courtroom, her breath caught. Roman stood with Marcus, both speaking quietly. Roman's hand was on Marcus's shoulder. She went all squishy inside at the sight.

"Marcus, it's good to see you." She approached and took his hand. "Mr. Lyons, it's an unexpected pleasure. I'm sure Jaron will be glad of the support."

"Ms. Haws, it's a delight to see you." Roman bowed to her and clapped his son on the back.

He didn't touch her, which was good. Instead, she pulled herself together and they went into the hearing room. "Marcus and I are going up front, but you two can sit here in this row. We should be early on in the schedule."

She went to the front table and sat, looking through her papers. Marcus was right behind her in the first row. He shifted as Jaron was brought in from lockup. The guard unshackled him and he sat next to his father. Abbie knew those moments enabled Jaron to make it just a while longer in lockup. Father and son clearly loved and needed each other.

*R*oman watched her, needing to shift his folder over his lap to hide just what she did to him. Her spectacles perched on the tip of her nose only made her sexier. He wondered if she had any idea.

All he wanted was to ease her back to the table she sat at and peel off her clothes, kissing every bare bit of her he exposed.

She stood and made her case to the adjudicator and he sat back to watch. Admittedly, he knew his presence in the room would affect the proceedings, but he loved Marcus and Jaron and he knew the boy was innocent. He wasn't above helping in a small way.

Abbie parried with the inquisitor who argued to keep Jaron in lockup. The woman was a complete idiot whose main argument seemed to be that Jaron was already in lockup so his lack of a history shouldn't matter because murder was bad.

"Sir, I beg to differ from my honorable colleague's view of this case. Even the most cursory examination of Jaron Mach's record will show a boy who has been an exemplary citizen. He's never been in trouble before. He served his time in the corps honorably. He has secure employment. His father has been employed with House Lyons for his entire adult life. Jaron Mach is not a risk for flight. He is not a violent person. His father and his father's employer have put up a bond to ensure Jaron's appearance at his trial. Keeping him in lockup provides no service at all. It simply takes up credits to house him when he could be at home with his father." Abbie's voice remained calm through the entire speech. Roman saw Marcus sit up straighter, squeezing the arm he held around Jaron's shoulder.

"Sir, this is not a minor crime. This is *murder*, a high crime, and it should be treated that way." The inquisitor's delivery was *not* calm. Abbie had gotten under the woman's skin for some reason. Roman found it fascinating to watch.

"We don't claim this isn't a murder charge. This hearing is to decide whether or not Jaron Mach should be remanded back to lockup or be allowed to be home until his trial. I am quite sure Ms. Proctor knows the multitude of examples of the accused being free until trial, including those charged with murder. We will most definitely refute the murder charges. *At trial.* For now, I can't see that we're serving justice by trying to get off track." Abbie's voice had a slight edge, but nothing too obvious. The inquisitor, however, stood up and stomped over to the dais where the adjudicator sat.

"This is a murder charge! I demand this boy be kept in lockup. This boy is trying to use his connections to House Lyons to get away with killing someone. We cannot allow that to happen."

"Ms. Proctor, we are aware of the charges." The adjudicator didn't appear to be impressed by the inquisitor either. In fact, her little tantrum seemed to annoy him. "Step back. Your demand is declined. After reviewing the briefs in this matter and the boy's lack of a criminal history, I'm inclined to agree with the defense. Jaron Mach is free under the custody of his father until the outcome of his trial or unless he violates the terms and conditions of the agreement."

Before Ms. Proctor could argue, the adjudicator slammed his gavel and the next case came before him. Abbie smiled at her opponent then turned back to Marcus, who hugged Jaron before a guard took him back through the door he had entered just minutes before.

Abbie ushered the rest of them out into the hallway. "They're going to process him out of lockup." She looked to Marcus. "Go on over there. They'll take him through the back way here. You'll need to sign the agreement and be sure he obeys it to the letter. The closer he stays to home until trial, the better."

Marcus hugged her and she blushed.

"Abbie, thank you so much. I'm in your debt. I'll keep him home or with me at all times. I swear to you." Marcus turned and let Roman and Deimos hug him as well. "I'm going to run over there. I don't want him to have to wait for me."

"I'll come with you. I have to interview a client there anyway." She turned to Deimos. "Thank you for today." And then to Roman. "Thank you for coming. I know it meant a lot to Marcus and it couldn't have hurt having you there in support either."

He watched her walk away. Wanting to stop her. Wanting to tell her how much she impressed him. Wanting to touch her. But he couldn't.

"She's amazing at her job." Deimos smiled and they began to stroll down the hall.

"She is very impressive, yes. Come on, let's go home and have Mercy make a big welcome dinner for Jaron."

Chapter 17

How in the 'Verse she'd let herself get talked into this, she didn't know. But Nyna wanted her to go because she was Marcus's date. Jaron had given her those big eyes of his and Marcus had done nothing but smile and look on the verge of tears every moment since Jaron had walked out of lockup, so she couldn't say no.

Even as she approached the monumentally huge front gates of House Lyons, the actual house, and wanted to vomit, she was glad she came when Nyna squeezed her hand and then looked over at Marcus with eyes that told Abbie just how much her sister felt for him.

"Now listen, he's a good man. He invited you, we invited you, don't be nervous," Marcus whispered in her ear.

She'd run home to change before this dinner celebration and before she'd done anything else, she'd torn open the note Deimos had given her.

Abbie,

*How I've missed you all these days. I've thought of you often,
wanted to consult you on different things as they came up but my sister
was here and Alexander as well quite often so I couldn't.*

*We will have time soon. If I have to move heavens and every
'Verse, I'll be touching you, holding you soon.*

R

She'd held the paper to her mouth like a silly girl. A love letter.
She'd never received one. Or a lover's letter, she should say. It made
her happy with a sort of sharp pang of pleasure, bittersweet but
sweet nonetheless.

And now she was on his doorstep. Or on the seemingly endless
parade of stairs leading up to doors several heads tall. Massive.
Classically ornate. Not overdone but impressive. Power lived here.
Glory lived here.

He opened his own door with a smile. "Come in! I'm so glad
you're here." Roman ushered them all in and his hand brushed the
small of her back, sending shivers through her. She bit her lip, hard,
to stay focused. She'd only stay a short time, just long enough for
Nyna to feel comfortable and then she'd make her excuses.

Roman handed her a glass of mulled wine. She inhaled the spice
of it, letting the heat ride through her palms into her body. The air
was colder now. Soon there would be snow and the capital would be
lit with beautiful colored lights because the days would be short.

A staff passed around trays with delicious little bites of everything imaginable and she found herself near a large piano and Roman stood so close she smelled his skin and wanted to rub against
him.

"You were amazing today. Congratulations on getting Jaron

home where he belongs." He smiled, his eyes holding something private, just for her. Pride.

She had been happy he'd seen her work and knowing he was impressed by her made her flush inside.

"Thank you. I'm relieved everything went well."

"What is the story between you and the very disgruntled Ms. Proctor?"

"She fucked my fiancé. I caught them and dragged her out of our flat by her hair. She was naked at the time. She holds a grudge. So do I." She kept her voice low but it was impossible not to get angry every time she saw Marcala Proctor. The memory of her naked, in Abbie and Logan's bed, with Logan pumping away, never ceased to make her feel like a fool. She'd tossed him out that day, too.

It had taken years before she could bring herself to speak to him again much less be friends. But Logan was broken in some sense. She'd never take him back but he was good in bed, safe for what he was and she got lonely sometimes. In truth, he'd been a very good friend in the time since she'd let him back in her life and she did believe he was truly remorseful for what he did. So she forgave, but she didn't forget.

Roman laughed. Gods how she loved the sound. Her cunt actually spasmed, wanting him. She squeezed her thighs together.

"And what did you do to him?"

"I threw him out, too. And then I set fire to his suits. It wasn't nice, but I felt a lot better afterward."

"You're very vicious. It's an attractive quality," he added quietly. "Did he slink off to another 'Verse? He's not still with her?"

"Gods no! His taste in side bits was very bad but he was smart enough to know what Marcala was and wasn't. I never should have said yes when he proposed. In fact, I believe he never cheated on me until he proposed to me. It was his self-destruct button. He's a good man in his own way. An excellent barrister but a horrible fiancé. I shudder to think about the poor woman who marries him."

"Barrister?"

"Yes. Logan, you met him I think, a while back."

His mouth tightened a moment and then he relaxed. *Was that jealousy?*

"Ah yes. He did seem the sort to throw away a wonderful woman for momentary pleasure."

She laughed. "Very nice answer, Mr. Lyons. Now I see why they talk about you on the vids in those breathless voices. Wondering which woman will snap you up."

He rolled his eyes and she realized how pleasant it was to have just a normal moment with him. It would have been more pleasant to be naked and alone with him in her bed of course, but normalcy was something she hadn't expected from him. In the midst of his huge manor, it seemed a funny word to choose, but it was.

"I should go." She looked up into his eyes and wanted to kiss him so badly her lips felt the phantom touch of his.

"I wish you wouldn't. After all, Jaron wants you here. You're quite welcome. We're pleased to have you after all you've done for Marcus and his son. At some point, I'd like to speak with you on a business matter. Deimos tells me you're addressing the AC, which I endorse. Perhaps we can discuss that at some point?" He cocked his head in a particularly charming way and she nearly sighed. Gods, she was losing three years of maturity every second she stood with him. Soon she'd start twirling her hair and thrusting out her chest at him.

She swallowed and licked her lips nervously. His pupils widened and she wanted to groan. The two of them were volatile, the chemistry between them was bigger than the room and she felt caught in it, like swaying sea grass.

"I can, yes." She'd meant to tell him to comm her so she could set up an appointment or a vid conference.

"Can I give you a tour of the greenhouse? We grow all our own fruits and vegetables here on the grounds. They're the original from when we came through and set up the colony here."

She loved the pride in his voice.

"I would be honored."

They strolled together down a long hallway, side by side but not touching. The sounds of the room where the food and people were dimmed as they drew away. He pointed out the art on the walls and she nodded, half listening. Her body grew heavy in his presence.

She wasn't sure what she'd expected when he said greenhouse, but it wasn't what she stood looking at.

"I'm at a loss for words." The greenhouse was gargantuan, which, given the overall scale of the house and complex itself, made sense. Huge stands of fruit trees lined a central walk and on either side and hanging from the rafters just beneath the glass ceiling, plants abounded. Vegetables, fruits, berries and flowers exploded in her vision. The scent overwhelmed, heady and fecund.

"When we first came through the portal and began to build a colony, House Lyons built this greenhouse and planted the seedlings and seeds they brought through. We fed our people then from this ground." He bent and sifted dark, rich soil through his fingertips.

She got it then as she stood there in his greenhouse. Leadership wasn't just a job he held because he was born first. He took being the ruler of House Lyons seriously. He took conservatorship of the people of Ravena and the associated 'Verses under Lyons' control seriously.

He was House Lyons in a way she hadn't understood until that very moment as he held the earth responsible for nourishing his people.

"I don't think you're a bad man," she said quietly, bending down with him. "I believe you have done an excellent job. Ravena is prosperous. Our literacy rate is the highest of all the Federated 'Verses. Quality of life is high. I'm not doing this because I think you're mismanaging your people. I want to share the burden, not add to it."

"There are things I'd like to talk with you about. Things you should know but I can't just now." His voice was the barest sound and it alarmed her.

"All right."

"Can I come to you? Tonight?"

"Yes." Was he kidding? She'd craved him every day since she'd seen him last and there was the look in his eyes just then. It worried her.

He straightened and brushed his hands off. The scent of the rich soil drifted to her as she stood.

"It's beautiful here."

"What I love about this place is how generations of Lyons children played here. How this soil has fed our people. How our 'Verse grew from this spot. From breadbasket to factories. It started here. In my home. I'm proud of that, Abbie."

"You should be, Roman. It's something to be very proud of. It would be a terrible invasion of your private life but people should know about this place. It should be part of the history of this 'Verse. What do you do with all this food?"

"We feed the household with it. Set aside for the cold months. Mercy makes jams and sauces, she preserves things. We also donate to a program in the fourth ring. A boarding school for children who've lost parents to lockup or death."

"Martinson School." She knew it. It wasn't too far away from where they'd lived when they first came back to the capital. "That's wonderful, Roman. It's a good program. Nyna and my mother participate, and several restaurants in the capital send food there on a regular basis as well."

He smiled. A genuine smile. She liked him unguarded. "That's good to hear. It alarms me that the population there has grown in the last years. I'm working with some on the Council to enroll the older ones in different apprenticeship programs so they have a place to go after they do their time in the corps."

"If you only knew how all this do-gooder stuff made me feel." She laughed and he joined her. They walked the path and turned to go back. He wasn't just some isolated, out-of-touch despot. Roman Lyons was a man who cared about his people. It only made her want him more.

"Ah, there you are, Roman. And look who you're with. A secret assignation, perhaps?" Alexander stood at the top of the steps leading back into the main room where the party was.

Thank goodness they hadn't even risked touching.

"Abigail Haws, this is my brother, Alexander. I apologize for his sense of humor. He believes vulgar is the height of hilarity." Roman's mouth arranged itself into a semblance of a smile but it was automatic, not real.

"I met him today at the Justice Administration building. He informed me I was defensive. I informed him he had a great deal to learn."

Roman looked toward Abbie, alarmed his brother had sought her out. Protectiveness surged through him. No one would hurt her. Period.

"Is that so? And what were you doing so far away from your club?" Roman placed himself between them slightly.

"If you two will excuse me? I need to say my farewells to my sister and Marcus. Mr. Lyons." Abbie nodded curtly at Alexander. "Thank you for your hospitality, Roman. Please do consider what I said about the greenhouse and placing it in historical context. I know I found it fascinating to see such an important part of our history right here."

He bowed slightly. "Of course. Thank you for all you've done for Marcus and Jaron." He wanted to walk her out. Wanted to touch her to make sure she was all right; her back was so straight it looked as though she'd shatter.

She left and Alexander stared at her a little too long for Roman's comfort.

"What are you doing here, Alexander?"

"I stopped over to see Corrin. I wanted to hear how he did with his last exams."

One thing Roman could not fault his brother on was his attention and affection toward Deimos and Corrin. He might have been a cad in his personal life but when it came to his nephews, he was attentive and a fine uncle. Roman's boys understood their uncle less than perfect, but Deimos in particular had taken on reforming his uncle as a sort of holy mission. It seemed to amuse Alexander and it certainly gave Roman a chuckle to watch.

"He placed in the top three in the program." Roman smiled.

"Of course he did. Boy is a natural. Despite our differences on political matters, you've done a fine job with them."

"Thank you." Nice, but Alexander could have commed about it. "Why are you here, Alexander? Really?"

"I met the rather fetching but quite angry little barrister today. She's trouble, just as Saul says. But Dem seems to think she's got a point. I tried to speak to her but she told me she had more to say to me than she could in a hallway between meetings. She told me to call her assistant to set up a meeting and walked away. Really, the unranked these days have quite the attitude. Here I am, a member of House Lyons, and she walked away from me."

"Because she was on her way to meet with me."

Alexander turned to see Deimos approach. "You'd better not mess with her, Alex. She's no pushover, and she's not a doormat. She's not going to fall into bed with her thighs open for you either."

Roman only barely stifled a harrumph at the very idea that Abbie would do anything of the sort. Well, with anyone but him.

"She's addressing the AC in a week. You're not going to win your silly battle to take her license. Why don't you step back and let it go? She didn't do anything wrong. I tell you, she's a good citizen. And she protected the woman who raised my mother and she got Jaron out of lockup today and you know he didn't hurt anyone." Deimos used the big eyes on his uncle and Roman wanted to laugh when he saw it work.

Alexander was such a contrast! Roman had tried to figure his brother out from childhood but he never could. Yes, part of it was being born second and having all the emphasis put on Roman. But Roman took over House Lyons when Alexander was just ten years old. He had a lot of time to be something but he had sort of wandered around. Other second sons worked hard and ran Family projects and businesses.

But he wasn't all bad either. He was a good uncle and he loved their sister, Sophia. Alexander took care of their mother as well, squiring her to her meetings and luncheons.

Still, he treated most other women horribly and Roman had had to pull him out of many different potential scrapes because of it. There was a fund of sorts to deal with the messes Alexander left behind with his women. Unpaid bills, disgruntled women with flats and rent due, that sort of thing.

"I admire Abbie Haws greatly, Alexander. She's intelligent and works hard and she is strong. What she wants isn't so very bad." Roman was torn between this discussion and wanting to sneak off to be with her.

"Right now? With things the way they are? Any slight upheaval could be disastrous. How can you even consider her plan, Roman? It's madness." At least Alexander was concerned in some sense. Roman had to give him that.

"This has nothing to do with any problems with the Imperialists. In fact, we could actually alleviate some of our internal problems if the unranked felt listened to." Deimos was on to something. Roman and he had discussed the subject just that morning. "Come with me to our next meeting with her. Or take her up on her offer to meet with you and hear her out. She's a very intelligent woman, informed, well-spoken. Give her a chance, a real one, and don't be an idiot." Deimos laughed and Roman wanted to groan.

"You'd go against your grandfather in this, Dem?" Alexander asked.

"Saul Kerrigan is my grandfather only because he contributed genetic material to make my mother. He's not part of my life in any sense and I am fortunate to not share any of his traits. My father believes Abbie has something meaningful to say, as do I. That's what's important, Alex."

Roman was very proud of his boy just then. And proud that his brother actually seemed to listen.

Chapter 18

He tapped quietly on her door, anticipation thrumming through his veins. She opened, wearing a soft robe, her hair loose like he preferred. He stepped inside and everything felt right again.

"I'm sorry. I wanted to get away earlier but Alexander wanted to talk. And talk some more. I escaped as soon as I could. Is it too late?"

She cupped his cheek. "I've missed you. I'll take whatever of you I can get."

He moved into her arms because it was where he was supposed to be. She was warm and soft and felt like home.

His clothes melted away, their hands working together to make him naked, as naked as his heart was.

Her bed was ready, the blankets pulled back, and he laid her gently down, opening the front of her robe. Her body revealed to him and him alone. Rain pelted her windows, scattering sound through the room as he pressed a kiss between her breasts, breathing her in.

She caressed his neck, kneading the knotted muscles there. He unfurled in her presence. Relaxed, calmed and left all the other context weighing him down at her door.

"There, now you're here with me," she murmured, kissing his shoulder. "All you need to think about is right here. Leave the rest of it until later. For now, lose yourself in me."

She wrapped a thigh around his waist and her pussy made contact with his cock. "Gods, you feel so good," he said as he kissed down her neck.

She sighed and arched as he reached a nipple and tugged it with his teeth. Responsive, vital, Abbie Haws responded to his touch with all her being. She threw herself into sex like she seemed to do everything else.

"I want you to lick me, please."

He looked up into her face. Gods, she was exciting. "I think I can do that. I like it when you ask me for what you want." The satin of her belly met his lips as the scent of her body seduced him.

Her pussy opened to him as he bent his head and took the first long lick through her. He loved putting his mouth on a woman's sex. Loved the taste of her, the scent. His wife had not been very enthusiastic about it, sadly. They'd been young and she'd been raised with negative feelings about it.

But Abbie widened her thighs and rolled her hips, seeking more of him. He'd been with women since Lindy's death. He'd enjoyed sex with them. But he hadn't matched so closely with a partner the way he did with her. It was liberating to him to be able to be himself without any judgment on her part. She accepted all of him, not just accepted but encouraged.

Her breath caught when he pressed the flat of his tongue over her clit. Her heels dug into the muscle of his shoulders and back.

"Mmm, yes. Like that." She breathed out.

"This?" He repeated the slide of his tongue over her clit. "Or this?" He sucked it slowly, abrading it with his teeth just slightly.

She laughed, her fingers digging into his hair as she urged him on. "Either. Both. Whatever."

He hummed against her clit, loving the way she squirmed in response. Salty-sweet, her taste slithered through him and he couldn't get enough. He used his palms to press her thighs flat against the bed and moved his mouth, lips and tongue back and forth over her pussy.

Her words melted away until all that was left were soft, begging sounds that wrapped around his cock, his gut, his heart.

A gasp, a sigh, a strangled moan, and she came when he pressed two fingers deep into her gate.

Pleasure rushed through her, white noise in her ears as she held him tight to her. His hair was soft against her fingers, something that always surprised her. Smooth and cool. Unexpected and, yet, totally like him in many ways.

When she opened her eyes he was smiling at her, his lips glistening with her honey. "You're beautiful. Now on top. I want to watch you fuck me."

He rolled, taking her with him and she scrambled up to position herself over his cock. "I'd really rather suck your cock."

He thrust up and into her body, filling her. "I'd really rather be inside your pussy. I've been thinking about little else for days and days."

"So very used to getting your way, House Lyons."

"Leadership means I get many benefits."

Laughing while having sex wasn't something she did often and she wouldn't have expected it of him. But he had such a love for it, such an appetite for her body, it made her giddy and lighthearted.

And she'd never admit it but he was just right-sized. Not hugely tall, so big he made her feel small and in fear of being crushed or trampled. But just tall enough she felt overpowered in a sexy sense and not a fearful one. It wasn't often she liked feeling small, but with him, it worked.

She ground herself down on him, rubbing her clit on his pubic bone. Her hands were braced on his hips to hold herself steady as she rode him.

"I love this trail of hair here," she said, tracing her finger from belly button to the spot the hair disappeared where they were joined. "And your belly is so flat and hard. Not the body of a man who sits behind a desk all day."

He laughed, sending little shocks of pleasure through her as he moved. "I go from meeting to meeting all day long, love. I walk everywhere. I heft files. I try to keep up with the boys. I fuck beautiful barristers. I need to be in shape for that. Wouldn't want it to get out that I'm too old for this game."

She pulled a single hair on his belly and he hissed in pain even as he laughed. "Vicious!"

"Mmm-hmm. Don't forget it." She tightened her muscles around him and he moaned.

"With a pussy like that, how can I?" He cupped her breasts. "These are so very fine. Nipples so dark and pretty. I love seeing you in your suits, knowing what's beneath. Knowing I've touched them, licked them. Knowing I'm going to come on them soon." Another hiss. "Well now, that works for you, doesn't it? Nearly as much as it works for me."

Instead of speaking, she slid her hand down her belly and watched him watch her idly play with her clit.

"You're so sexy. I've never met anyone like you."

And she never wanted him to again. Selfishly, even though she knew she couldn't have him, she wanted to be indelible. She wanted to be the woman who marked him forever. Gods knew he'd marked her. She'd forever measure every man she ever met against him and they'd all end up paling in comparison.

"I love to come with you inside me."

"I love to watch you come when I'm inside you. We're a perfect match." His smile lost its edge and she knew what he felt. She did too.

Stupid rules. Stupid, stupid Family rules.

Instead of lamenting, she concentrated on what she had right then. Him in her bed, in her body, his hands on her, his gaze devouring her as she made herself come.

When it came, it hit faster than she'd expected it to. It raced up her spine, dizzying her. She drove herself down on his cock over and over, hearing the *slap, slap, slap* of wet flesh each time.

"Keep your eyes open, Abbie. I want you to see when I come. See how you make me feel."

She dragged her eyelids up and locked her gaze with his. His grip on her hips tightened, his fingers digging into her muscles. He exhaled hard and his eyes lost focus as she felt him pour into her body.

He held her there, down on his cock, until he finally softened. Carefully, he carried her into her bathroom and they showered without a word. He put his hands all over her body. Soaping, caressing, rinsing and she let him minister to her, loving it all the while.

* * *

Roman never expected the depth of feeling she drew from him. She reached deep inside him and touched places he'd walled off years and years before. But she laid him bare, and while he felt exposed, he also felt safe.

He dried her off and they headed back to her bed to snuggle under the thick coverings.

"It's cold in here. Come closer and let me warm you up."

She obeyed, pressing herself to him. That she let him take care of her like this was nearly as good as fucking her. He took care of people every day, all day. But this was different. This was not caretaking, this wasn't her needing something, this was his woman and he wanted to show her what she meant.

"Why isn't the heat up?" he asked, kissing the top of her head as she nestled it under his chin.

"It is. This is as warm as it gets." She laughed. "I warmed up some sweet cakes my mother sent over just before you got here. That's why it wasn't cold when you arrived. This building has two hundred units, that's a great deal of steam. We can't all live in an enormous mansion that sits on steam vents." She said it sleepily, without any anger.

"Are you this cold the entire season?" It angered him to even contemplate her not being comfortable at all times.

She turned to look into his face. "Are you angry?"

"I'm—yes, I'm angry! I don't want you to be cold. I'll have the building owner fix the problem immediately. It's unacceptable, Abbie. Warmth is—should be—a right of all my citizens."

She kissed the tip of his nose. "Roman, that's very sweet. It really is. But the flat we lived in when we came to the capital? The walls were very thin. My mother stuffed sweaters and blankets around doors and windows to keep us warm. This isn't bad. This is a nice building, as it happens. It's not painfully cold. I sleep with nice, thick blankets and I'm comfortable. Many people have less. You have to know that. You're not naïve." She put two fingers over his lips. "And you can't fix everything either. The farther people live from the vents, the less immediate heat they have. That's a reality and that's why most people settled in the inner circle and the first two rings. The resources are here. Poorer people live further out and that's a reality, too. People with more credits live more comfortably." She shrugged.

He sighed. "I hate to think about you cold. I want you to be in my house. In my bed. Where it's warm and bright."

Her eyes filled with unshed tears. "We can never have that. Reality, Roman."

He sat up and pushed the hair from her face, cupping her cheeks. "I hate that. I hate having to hide this. I want to touch you in public. I want to kiss you when the mood strikes me. I want you to be warm and taken care of."

A tear broke and slid down her cheek and he thumbed it away.

"Don't make this harder than it is. Do you think I want to wait here alone? Knowing you're off somewhere living a life without me in it?"

So complicated. He sighed. "You're in it. Even when I'm not with you, you own my thoughts." Settling back down, she eased against him once more.

"Don't you have to get back home?"

"I do. But I don't want to. I want to be here with you. I want to sleep here."

She sighed. "Roman, as much as I love having you here, tomorrow is a work day. The paths and walkways will be filled with people. You will be recognized. I want you, but I don't want to destroy you. Do you understand? You risk a great deal to be here. You could, of course, pass it off that you're just getting a little taste of an un-ranked woman before you settle down. But that's not who I am and you are not allowed to think on a woman like me in a serious fash-ion."

"Why do you have to be so good? Can't you be selfish?" he teased.

"I'm so very selfish." She laughed without humor. "I want what I cannot have. Each time you come to me you risk yourself. And yet, I want you here."

"A less principled woman would use this to get her way on the advisory council issue. What would your parents do if they knew?"

"My mother would be worried about my heart getting broken." She shrugged before her face got very serious. "But my father cannot know. Listen to me carefully. If my father had any idea, he would use you. He would manipulate us both to get what he wants."

Roman did not like the pain he heard in her voice. "Why would any father harm his child?"

"You don't understand. He is committed to many things, his causes are chief in his life. First it was the school and in recent years it's been the MRD, which I actually organized and started. He loses all his logic when his causes are at issue. He's not evil, but he would see using this to his advantage as the greater good."

He snorted. "My father shoved a seventeen-year-old boy into the leadership of House Lyons, married him off to a total stranger and nagged, using his health as a cudgel, until he had grandchil-dren. I do understand the greater good parenting excuse. I just don't believe in it."

"You tell me something, then. If you were ill tomorrow, thought you were going to die, would you give House Lyons to Alexander or would you give it to Deimos? Knowing he'd have to give up his youth to lead? Millions upon millions of lives at stake. You and I both know Alexander would not rule well. He does not care for soil, for earth and seeds and steam heat for citizens."

"Why must you be insightful? Can't you be but a pretty piece of fluff waiting for me in my bed each night?" He hugged her tight and she squeezed him hard in return.

"You said you needed to tell me something earlier. What is it?" Her words were slightly slurred. He remembered his presence robbed her of sleep.

"What are your plans for your days off?"

"I have none. I usually work or spend time with my family."

"I want to have three days with you. Just you and me. Alone. Marcus knows about you and me, I'll have him schedule something, make arrangements. Can you get away?"

"Yes. Yes, I'd love to spend the time with you."

He got up, pressing a kiss to her forehead. "Stay beneath the blankets. I'll let myself out. Marcus will be in touch."

"Be careful, Roman. I'll wait to hear from Marcus."

He carried her scent on his hands as he quietly left through the back lift and into the city.

Chapter 19

Abbie stared at the house on the shores of Lake Alessandre. Marcus had described it as a cabin, but like everything else about Roman, this "little cabin" was a grand home.

She'd taken the train out of the capital and had traveled due south for a large part of her morning. Instead of taking a stack of work, she looked out the windows and read a book. Leisure time wasn't something she got much of, so she thought that for those days she had with Roman, she would take them.

The train moved past the outer rings and toward the mountains in the far distance. At the station nearest the lake, she'd detrained and headed, according to Marcus's directions, up a small hill and through a lovely wooded path.

Because it was the off-season, there were few people, and she enjoyed the silence and time alone as she made her way to the cabin.

And now she stared at the two-story manse and laughed, breaking the silence.

Roman poked his head around a line of hedges, his face softening when he saw it was her. "You're here!" He came forward quickly to take her small bag. "I'm sorry you had to carry this all the way from the station. I wanted to pick you up but Marcus gave me a lecture about being seen."

She stood on tiptoes and kissed him soundly. "Hello to you as well. Thank you for carrying my not very heavy bag, and Marcus is right."

Sliding his arm around her shoulders, they walked through the lovely garden at the rear of the house.

"This is, um, pretty impressive. And also? I'll be taking you to a cabin one day, just to show you this is *not* one. This is a manse."

"Come inside. It's cold out here. I've built a fire and dinner is nearly done. And this is not a manse. It's a large house." He snorted and led the way through the large double-glassed doors and into the house.

"If you say so." She turned a circle, looking up at the beautiful wood and metalwork. "It's beautiful, Roman. Truly."

He dropped the bag and pulled her against his body. "I'm glad you're here. I have you all to myself for three days. Whatever shall I do with you?"

She grabbed his cock, already hard and poking into her belly. "I have no idea at all."

"Hmm." He looked around and reached for a pillow from a nearby chair, tossing it on the floor. "You can suck my cock while we think then."

"What an original idea." She dropped to her knees, the pillow softening her fall.

Abbie just wanted to fade into him. To be absorbed into his body and soul. She rubbed her cheek over his cock through the soft material of his pants and smiled as she felt him unpin her hair. She would have worn it down on a normal nonwork day but she knew he took pleasure in unbinding it, so she put it up just for him to take down.

How lovely it was to know that about him.

She unfastened his pants and slowly pulled the waistband of his underwear down with her teeth. Given the sound he made, he heartily approved, and she made a mental note to do it again in the future.

The heat of him flowed against her face as she inhaled his scent. Man, musk, sex, power. Roman Lyons was a walking aphrodisiac.

The slit of his cock seeped a bead of semen. The salty taste of him entranced her as she ran her tongue through it. Swirling the tip of her tongue round and round the head, she sank into the rhythm of pleasing him. She let herself listen to his body, to remember and learn what he liked, what made him moan and hiss, what brought his hips forward unexpectedly.

She angled him so she could suck him into her mouth, her hand gripping at the base. Her other hand palmed his balls, massaging but not squeezing too hard. He liked a bit of rough handling, but it took a lot of trust to let her down there with his cock in her mouth and his sac in her hand, so she took it slow, built up gradually and took care of him.

His fingers slid through her hair until he cradled her skull. She rocked, forward and back, sucking him in and pulling off, keeping him nice and wet.

Abbie licked down the column of his cock, down around his

balls and he gave a low, deep sound of need and pleasure, so sharp
her cunt clutched and her clit bloomed. She was wet, so wet she
knew her panties would be wet. She could smell her longing, the
tang of it hardening her nipples in response.

"Fuck." He nearly growled as she took his balls into her mouth,
first one and then the other. "Abbie, gods, that's so good."

She urged his thighs wider and then, reaching between her
thighs, she got her fingers wet with her own lube and brought them
back to him, just past his balls and against the pucker of his ass.

He tensed up as she circled her slick middle finger there, against
the sensitive, nerve-laden skin. She pulled back and looked up at
him. "Roman, has anyone ever played with your ass?"

He blushed. This dirty-talking man actually blushed. She caught
her bottom lip between her teeth and pressed a bit.

"I'm going to put my fingers in there. I'll stroke a spot inside you
so good you'll wonder why a lover never did it before. But not while
you're standing. Later when you're on the bed."

He exhaled and relaxed, moaning slightly as she continued to
circle that pucker.

She went back to sucking him, in and out, harder and faster, as
the time passed until his grip in her hair went tight, tight enough
tears stung her eyes and he came, filling her mouth with his taste.

Abbie had barely finished when he dragged her up the front of
his body and kissed her, his tongue invading her mouth, owning her
and she let him because she was his.

Utterly and totally.

"Abbie, you're so damned sexy. The things I have planned for us,
well—" He sent her a wicked grin. "You'll need to get your rest
when you can. You'll need your strength."

She laughed. "Feed me, then. I'm starved and it's been a very long day."

*R*oman looked at her as she sat across from him at the small table. Her feet were tucked beneath her and she enjoyed every bite of the dinner he'd prepared. Or rather, of the dinner Nyna had prepared and he'd brought with him.

"My sister is an amazing cook, isn't she?" Abbie winked at him. "What? You think I wouldn't know?"

"She offered. Through Marcus. I can manage the basics, I'm not completely helpless, you know. But I'm better at heating things up than preparing them."

She laughed and he loved the sound. He'd lit candles and the golden light made her appear luminous. Abbie was so very pretty. Petite and lovely. Big brown eyes, full lips, skin pale and creamy. She did everything with zeal, listened with interest, spoke with passion and fucked like no one he'd ever met. And she was there in his home. Gods, he enjoyed her.

"What?" She tucked her hair behind her left ear.

"Nothing. I just like looking at you."

"Oh. Well, thank you."

"And now I want to lick your cunt."

The flush on her face made her even lovelier.

"Come with me. I have a surprise."

She took his hand and he led her upstairs to the bath attached to the master suite of rooms. As he'd expected, she froze in the doorway at the sight of the magnificent bathing tub.

"There's a hotspring. The water here comes directly from it.

Undress and I'll run us a bath. I know a few people with some influence, I think I can avoid the water fine."

"You're officially my favorite person ever." She tossed off her sweater and shimmied out of her shoes, tights and pants.

"No underpants and a see-through, shiny bra? You're officially *my* favorite person ever." She removed the bra with a flourish and stood before him naked and gorgeous. "Correction. *Now* you're my favorite person ever."

Laughing, she stepped into the deep tub and sighed happily. Lindy needed constant praise, big, expensive presents all the time. And here Abbie was, happy about a big bath.

"Now you should be naked so I can look at you and have lust in my heart," she called out gaily as she quickly twisted her hair into a makeshift knot.

He got rid of his clothes and stepped in, sinking into the water with her. "Naked, wet and willing."

"Don't tell anyone. It would ruin my reputation as a tough barrister. By the way, I'm being interviewed on the vids right after the appearance before the AC." She delivered this bit of information as she settled back against him.

"Abbie," he warned.

"Don't you *Abbie* me, Roman. I have a job to do. People want to know what's happening and I'm going to tell them. I hope I can assure them we're being listened to. But if we aren't, I'll say so. I may enjoy this thing between us, but your cock isn't so magical I've lost my sense of direction."

He didn't want to be amused. She had no idea of how grave things had become since this whole debacle with the Walker Family involvement in treason. If the Imperialists found a weakness they'd exploit it. Still, he was amused because she had an unwavering commitment to her dreams, and even while she sat naked and cradled against his reviving cock, she stuck to her convictions.

"You're a pain in my ass."

"I was a pain in the ass long before I met you, Roman. Don't take it personally."

"On the edge of the tub then. Show me that ass. I want to eat you from behind. I'm going to lick your clit until you come."

She turned slowly, sending the water around them. "I love your filthy mouth."

"Knees on that step there. You can watch in the mirror. Let's see if I can't make you love my mouth a bit more, shall we?" As she knelt and then bent forward, her top half braced out of the tub, he drew his fingertip down her spine, over the cheeks of her very fine ass and unerringly found her gate.

"I'm pretty fond of your fingers just about now."

He laughed before he bent forward to bite her ass cheek. She squealed, laughing, and water sloshed up. He made a small wave, moving his hand back and forth so the water caressed her pussy. Her laughter melted into a sigh.

When she started to squirm, needing more, he spread her wide, exposing the pink folds of her pussy to his mouth and hands.

He slid his tongue through her, briefly dipping into her gate and moaning at her taste. She thrust back against him and he gripped her tight, wanting her where *he* wanted her.

He lapped at her, suckling her clit softly, abrading it with his chin because it made her gasp so prettily. He slid his thumb back and forth over the pucker of her ass, a new curiosity in him after she'd played with his.

Roman had fucked a few women that way in his time, mainly to mix things up and keep from getting bored, but he'd never engaged

in any ass play himself. Her fingers on him earlier had felt unbeliev-
ably good, and more than that, he liked the level of trust it represented. At his age, there weren't many first times left sexwise, and
he liked that she would be the first he tried it with.

Needy whimpers floated through the air as he ate her cunt. Gods,
she tasted fine and right. The heat of the water made her soft, pliant,
and all he wanted was to rub himself all over her, licking every inch.

He recognized the catch in her moan, the hitch in her breath,
and she came in a scalding rush.

Before she'd even opened her eyes he'd picked her up and impaled
her down on his cock, driving her into another orgasm. She braced
her hands against the wall in front of where he'd knelt, one foot in
the tub, the other on the edge, and held on as he fucked into her
body. Her fingers curled against the smooth, cool tile on the wall.

"When my mouth is on your pussy, all I can think of is ramming
my cock into you over and over," he said at her back. "Your cunt
welcomes me every time."

She nodded eagerly. Oh yes, she wanted him buried in her as
much as he wanted to be there.

Her ass partially rested on one of his thighs and she felt the flex
and play of his muscles as he thrust.

Abbie was relaxed and open for him. The way he'd licked her to
orgasm, coupled with the warm air and water, the lovely meal and
the glass of wine, had transformed her into a woman primed to receive pleasure, to open up and let a man take from her all he could
in return.

The angle of his thrusts brushed the head of his cock across her
sweet spot deep within her, over and over with exquisite, torturous
sensation. She smelled his body as the scent rose on the heat buffet-

ing her back. The wiry hair on his thighs abraded her skin just enough to add to the experience, to remind her it was a man back there working. In a society that featured more smooth men than those with body hair, his mat of chest hair and the hair on his legs made him even sexier to her eyes.

"I love to take you this way. Pinning you while I fuck you so hard your tits jiggle." He leaned in and nipped her shoulder, hard enough to sting, and then laved over it. Shivers erupted in the wake of that small violence and tenderness.

He swiveled a bit, circling his hips, creating friction against her clit. Gods, she was going to come again. She leaned her head back against his shoulder and let it happen, let it take her, pull her under. Her orgasm was deep, warm, rolling waves of pleasure, over and over.

He groaned, and within her she felt the telltale jerk and jump of his cock as he came, filling her up.

She stood there while he rinsed her off, drained out the water and poured more over her, keeping her warm. The heat was nearly as luxurious as three orgasms in a row in a giant bathing tub the size of her office.

"Now, let's dry you off and I think a nap is in order. What do you think?"

She dragged her eyes open as he wrapped a towel around her and he laughed.

"I think that's my answer. We don't have to be anywhere or do anything for some time. Come and sleep with me in my bed."

She let him lead her into the master suite. She wasn't that surprised that his bed was gargantuan, but the softness of the bedding and the weight of the blankets were a nice greeting as she slid in.

He settled in right behind her, his arm over her waist. Right before she dropped off she admonished herself to not get used to it. He was a fleeting luxury, a gift from the universe, but she couldn't keep him and it wouldn't do to get attached.

Chapter 20

He awoke to the sound of ice against the glass. The room faced the water and he realized it was snowing. The soft *tink* of icy snow drifted into the heavy silence of big, white flakes.

He lay there for some time just watching. The moons above were enough to see, even through the clouds, and the snow began to reflect the light back, giving that beautifully muffled glow only a snowy evening could provide.

Abbie stretched and opened her eyes, following his gaze. Roman wasn't sure he could describe the joy in his heart at the sight of wonder on her face. She threw the blankets back and scampered to the window to look out.

"Snow!"

As he had when he'd taken her from behind and the other times they'd been naked long enough for him to see all of her, he noted the scars on her shoulder and back. Anger rose in him, bitter and ugly, and he wanted to do violence to anyone who'd mar her physically and, he could guess, emotionally, too.

But when she turned back to him, the light in her eyes dancing with her pleasure at seeing the snow, the anger faded.

"I have warm wraps." He got out of bed and went to his wardrobe to hand her one. She hummed her pleasure as she put it on. "How about a fire and something warm to drink? And then sex. Yes, more sex."

She burst out laughing and tossed her hair behind her shoulder. He caught her upraised brow and knew she'd done it for his benefit.

"Let's go, then."

He wrapped an arm around her, happy he could touch her as much as he wanted while they were there. "Sit on the couch. The blanket on the back there is nice and warm if you need it."

She watched while he made a fire, her eyes occasionally wandering to the wall of windows where she took in the falling snow.

Once the fire crackled on the hearth he turned back to her, loving the way she looked, her feet tucked beneath her, totally relaxed. Roman would wager this wasn't a side of Abbie she allowed herself to show very often. So busy and active, his woman.

He moved to sit next to her, reaching out to caress her thigh because he could. "So, tell me about yourself. What made you decide to be a barrister?"

She looked at him for a very long time without speaking. So long he began to get uncomfortable, but he let her work through whatever internal war he saw raging on her features.

Finally she took a deep breath. "It's a long story. Are you sure you want to hear it?"

Ah, she was ready to tell him then. He nodded. "I want to know about you. All of it."

"Do you have alcohol?"

"I was just going to suggest either something warm or a glass of something that would warm us up."

"Oh, very nice."

He kissed her forehead as he made to get up. "You know, you don't have to tell me if it's too painful. I want you to share with me but I don't want you to hurt."

She rested her hand against his chest, over his breastbone. She didn't speak, but he sensed the upswell of emotion within her. She simply kissed him right over his heart. "It's a memory, it happened a long time ago. The hurt is mostly gone."

He kissed her again and went into the kitchen to grab a very fine bottle of mash liquor his cousin made in small batches on Borran, one of the 'Verses House Lyons held. He also brought a bowl of candied nuts his sister was partial to, so they were always on hand.

"Oh, I do love these," she said after she took a bracing few sips of the mash and spied the bowl of nuts.

He wondered if she'd changed her mind, she was quiet so long but finally she looked from the scene outside back to him.

"When I was nearly fifteen, we came back to the capital. The heat was very hard on my mother and Nyna and finally Daniel told our father that it was either we all come back or Daniel would simply bring us back and my father would be alone." She sighed. "My father—he's not a bad person, Roman. But he's stunted. He's not—complete. He totally lacks any real ability to self-reflect or accept responsibility for the basic things in life. It wasn't so much that he didn't care about my mother, but that he cared about his students so much we were an afterthought really.

"Anyway, we came back and he got a job fairly quickly, teaching again, in the fourth circle. My mother's health had gotten pretty bad at that point and she couldn't work, so we lived pretty much where the students were. It wasn't a pretty place to live. It was hard, so far from the vents. People out there live very difficult lives. In the outback, it's rural. People farm, they work the land, but the poverty there is just different than in an urban environment."

She looked at him and blushed. "I'm giving you the long version. I should just give you the notes." Her laugh was forced and he took her hand, kissing it.

"You should tell me the whole story. Let it go. Let me share your burden."

She swallowed hard and he hated the hesitancy on her face.

"To help out, I took a job cleaning the tram station and some of the local government office space. It was decent pay and I made friends and started thinking about the future, what I'd do my apprenticeship in once I turned eighteen. But there was one man who"— she wet her lips—"was very interested in me. It wasn't right. I knew it and I stayed away from him as much as I could. But he found out where I lived and began to show up on our street. He'd follow me, try to get me alone."

Her hands shook as she took three more swallows and drained the glass. He refilled it.

"I got out. I began to travel to the second ring for some classes, legal history classes, as it happened. My teacher was a senior barrister who'd come up from the fourth ring. He gave me a job filing his papers, organizing his schedule. The credits were better than my cleaning job and it enabled me to latch on to a possible future and to get the seven hells away from *him*."

"But he didn't like that." Roman said it flatly.

She shook her head. "I didn't know at first. It was after about a year I realized he'd still been looking around for me, had come by our home. My mother had sent him off but he'd begun threatening to evict them."

"He's Ranked." Most building owners and landlords were Ranked.

She nodded. "So I was walking home from the tram when he and several of his friends stopped me. There was this abandoned field, it's got a housing block there now. Anyway, they circled me. He—" Her voice caught but she shook her head, hard, when Roman began to move to her.

"He told me I could just fuck him and get it over with or he'd toss my family out. His friends would also get a turn, of course. I'm ashamed to say I considered it. He had this metal hook, the kind they use in the factories out there. He kept swinging it at me. I thought if I just let him fuck me, I could get away. The hook—I thought he'd kill me. But I took too long, apparently, and they all set on me like wild beasts. Tore my clothes. He—he used that hook to hold me, used it on my back. Impaled me on it like a fish or a piece of meat." Her jaw was clenched and she put her glass down.

Roman took her hands, wanting to kill the bastard who'd harmed her. The file had been purged, even for him, of the identities of her attackers. He knew enough to understand it had to be someone Ranked. No one else would have the ability to scrub the record.

"You don't have to say any more." He tried very hard to keep his voice even, to keep his emotion from bleeding into it. He didn't want her to feel shame or to make herself responsible for how he felt just then.

"I do! Damn it! They raped me in that field. I screamed and screamed and no one came. He used a hook on me, tore my back open so severely that they didn't think I'd be able to use my left arm again. But someone did finally come. Daniel. Daniel had a pipe and he nearly killed two of them. The polis finally arrived and they took me to a med center. They didn't arrest Daniel but he was in trouble for harming a Family member."

"Who was it, Abbie?"

"Bentan Kerrigan."

A House affiliated with his. Lindy's cousin. He'd been sent to the Edge for several years. Had a substance abuse problem. Drank too much and liked to hurt women. Roman would make sure he never did again. "All right."

She looked at him and he waited to see if she'd tell him to leave Bentan alone. She didn't and he liked her even more for it.

"So getting back to why I became a barrister. I was in a coma for several weeks. I had swelling on my brain and internal bleeding. They used nanites on me to help the healing process. At the time they were still fairly experimental, but I'm alive today because of them. Daniel stayed at my side the entire time but like I said, he was in trouble. My mentor made a deal for Daniel to go into the corps early, to do an extra two standard years and avoid lockup and charges. And he offered me an apprenticeship. I agreed and never looked back."

She poured herself another drink and he wanted to laugh at how intoxicated she'd be in a few more minutes.

"So there you have it. I became a barrister first and foremost because it gave me a vocation and a way out of the fourth ring and shitty little rental flat like the ones I lived in growing up. It's not noble, Roman. But I also do good work. I help people, and when Josef, my mentor, heard the defense agency was looking for entry-level barristers six years ago, he told me and I jumped at the chance."

"Because you were so honest with me, I'll be that way with you, too. I knew. About the attack. Not all the details but some. Not who, or that it was the catalyst for you to become a barrister. Oh gods, I'm fucking this all up. I just didn't want any secrets between us."

She snorted. "I should have known you'd poke around. You're not a man who likes not knowing things. Does it make a difference?" The shy way she asked twisted his gut.

"Only in that I think you're amazing. Well, more amazing. Thank you for trusting me with that story. You've survived a lot. You're very strong."

"I still have to take pills sometimes, to sleep without nightmares. And stupid stuff triggers me and I start to get panicked. I'm not that strong."

He remembered the panic on her face when Saul Kerrigan attacked her in that hallway and wanted to smash his fist into his former father-in-law's face.

"You nearly died, Abbie. Having to take a pill sometimes seems to me a small thing in comparison to that."

Her eyes drooped a bit and she sort of went sideways, leaning into him. "And you're going to be very drunk shortly. That mash is very strong."

"Mmm. Yes. I think so."

He held her as she dozed there in his arms. He didn't want her to wake and he certainly didn't want to let go of her.

Several things were completely clear to him. First, that he loved Abbie Haws fiercely. Second, that he couldn't have her. That made his chest constrict and his gut burn at the unfairness of it. He was rethinking the idea of having a mistress, of simply never remarrying and keeping her that way, but he knew she wanted children, knew she would never want to be merely a mistress. And he couldn't have children with her if they didn't share the same legal status as Deimos and Corrin did. Sure he'd officially recognize any children she bore as heirs, but the system allowed it at the whim of the Family member and he knew she wouldn't want that sort of dependence on anyone.

He'd take all he could get and be with her until he couldn't be any longer. He'd take care of her and she would not complain or refuse, and that would start with a flat in a building closer to the vent so she could be warm the entire cold season, and one with a higher water capacity so she could shower and bathe to her heart's content without a fine.

He disliked her father severely. He disliked how she made excuses for him, too, but Roman knew all about messed-up fathers and making excuses for them, so who was he to judge? He would take care of Bentan when he returned, as well as Saul, who, as the leader of House Kerrigan, would have to have known about the attack when he manhandled her in that hallway.

As she slept, he planned and watched the snow.

Chapter 21

Abbie loved the snow. Because the core of the capital sat on steam vents, she didn't see much snow sticking in the first circle and never in the outback where it was all high temperatures and unrelenting sunshine. But out here they were away from the heat of the capital's inner core and there weren't a lot of buildings and houses to raise the overall temp. Really, Abbie thought this place was absolutely perfect. The house was nice and warm, heated from the hot springs. Plus, she had Roman all to herself.

Here she could play to her heart's content and no one cared. She didn't have to be at work. The snow wasn't dirty and she wasn't freezing like the old days in the fourth circle. No, she had a good, warm coat, fuzzy mittens and a hat. The perfect tools for packing snowballs and hurling them toward Roman, who clearly had enough experience tossing snowballs himself.

"Hey!" he yelped when she managed to score a direct hit to his head, knocking his hat askew.

"Don't be a crybaby!" She laughed as she dodged his return volley.

"If I promise to make you come a few times, can we go inside? I'm hungry!"

She sent him a theatrical sigh and then nodded his way. "All right then. You're very demanding."

He laughed as he caught up to her, picking her up and spinning in a circle as he dropped a kiss on her lips. Abbie liked this side of Roman. Carefree, affectionate, not laden down with being the face of House Lyons.

"So," he said as he dried his hands after slicing up some fruit, "what do you think you'll be saying to the vids next week?" The carefree Roman had gone, replaced with the face of House Lyons.

She sighed. "I thought we were having sex. I don't want to talk business."

"We can't avoid it. Anyway, we can fuck later." She slid a piece of fruit between his lips and he groaned.

"Fine. I'm going to do my job. I'll tell them the truth."

"Like what?"

"What do you mean like what? Do you want me to send your office a copy of my comments before I go live or something?" She frowned at him.

"That would be good. Then we could talk about it first." Roman smiled like he wasn't the biggest idiot in the 'Verse.

"You're joking, right?"

"Well, no. Why can't you meet me halfway on this? If the Council sees you helping me out, if I can tell them you're vetting things through my office, they'll be pleased."

"Roman, I will not ever vet my comments about something having nothing to do with you through your office."

"Why the fuck not? Why are you making this so hard for me? Don't you want me to help?"

"Oh, look at you, Mr. I've-Never-Been-Told-No! What do you mean 'why the fuck not'? I'm not your employee. I'm not beholden to you because your son is allowing me to speak before the AC, and I am sure as the seven hells not beholden to you because you fuck me. No matter how good a job you do." She moved away from him and began to pace. He pushed his chair back and she spun.

"Don't you move. I'm not done. I am not making this hard for you. This has nothing to do with you. I'm making a presentation. I don't know what my comments will be until I see what sort of reception I receive. There will be no comments written out ahead of time to send you because how can I know what I'm saying until I say it?"

"You don't know what I'm dealing with here, Abbie. I'm offended you'd assume I asked because you owed me for having sex with you."

She sighed at the genuine hurt and confusion in his voice. "Would you ask Georges for this information? You're asking me because I'm here, in your house. Because we have this intimate relationship. You're asking me because of that. I shouldn't have said fucking, that wasn't fair."

"You're making this more complicated than it is, and it's already ridiculously so." He pulled his bottom lip the way he did when he was tired and annoyed. It made her smile that she knew his habits that way. He frowned at her. "Why are you smiling? We're in the middle of a fight."

"Didn't you ever fight with her? With your wife? It's a fight, not the end of the 'Verse." She propped a hip against the counter and watched the light filter through the window, over the soft gold of his hair.

"No. We didn't fight. She—" He shook his head. "Back to the subject please."

"You're saying it's complicated. Tell me how. Tell me what you're facing."

"You know there are factions within the Families on the Governance Council?"

"I've assumed. There are many 'Verses and many ways of seeing the world." She shrugged. "You're certainly not House Licht or even your brother."

Roman made a face. "We'll talk about *that* in a bit. My brother is an entirely different subject. Right now, as you might imagine, things are tumultuous. Some of the Families want to crack down until things calm a bit."

"Crack down? On who?" A chill went through her.

"On anyone and anything they feel threatens the way things are."

"Like the MRD."

"Yes. We don't all feel that way of course. But the Council is irritable, reactionary in some quarters, the Associated Families more so because they are closer to the unranked than most of us are. House Kerrigan is most troublesome."

"Troublesome." She crossed her arms over her chest

"Abbie, all of this detail is supposed to be a secret. Everything that goes on in the Council chambers is protected. I shouldn't even be telling you this right now."

"I think we've crossed all sorts of lines already, Roman. Don't you?" She sighed. "Look. I get it to a certain extent. You're in a tough spot because the hard liners think the rabble is making trouble. I'm the rabble and you want me to try and keep it reined in so your opposition doesn't have anything to use against me and you as well. Yes?"

"I don't think you're rabble."

"But they do. And, I will be honest with you, I'm dealing with some internal issues of my own. I am the head of the MRD but there are other voices, and some of them are sick of waiting. So far I'm keeping things calm, but people won't wait forever. The whole scandal with Families working with the Imperialists really affected overall perceptions of Family Rule."

He exhaled sharply. "Your father and his little protégé, Robin Moreland?"

"How do you know that?"

"I'm Roman Lyons, holder of House Lyons. Chair of the Governing Council of the Federation Universes. It's my business to know these things." His back was rigid and she chewed her lip, thinking on her response.

She wasn't offended, not really. She got as much information on him as she could as well. It was simply good strategy to know what your opposition was up to. But he could be such an arrogant prick sometimes.

Roman also knew Abbie's father was having an affair with his protégé but kept that to himself. That part wasn't his business. That the man had been watching Abbie so very closely was. And the way he'd been meeting with the MRD whenever Abbie wasn't around was also a problem.

"Abbie, please don't be angry. I have to check these things out," he said gently.

She waved it away. "I know. Gods, you are so new at this fight thing, aren't you? What are your parents like? Didn't they ever discuss politics? Didn't they argue from time to time?"

Gods, the woman confused him. One moment she was angry and out for his balls and the next she was asking about his parents.

"My parents aren't very close. My father has a mistress but he's too old and frail to do much of anything with anyone. He's been on the verge of dying since I was in my teens. People don't argue with him. He's a great and respected figure."

She snorted. "No disrespect intended, Roman, but arrogant men always need a woman who's willing to kick them in the ass when they get out of line."

Figures that's what her opinion would be. She wasn't of the quiet helpmate school of wifery, he was damned sure.

"Did your parents argue a lot?"

"At first, when we were young, they argued and laughed, and then they went into their bedroom for hours." She smiled. "But over time, she got sick and he just checked out. He lives in her house, she does everything it takes to keep it all going, but they don't share passion anymore on important things. I don't think I've seen them have a political discussion in about fifteen years, maybe longer." She moved to Roman, straddling him to sit on his lap and putting her arms around his shoulders. "It's really too bad you and I can't be together. You need a woman like me to keep your arrogance in check."

He kissed her. She tasted like snow and laughter—and regret. "You're a puzzle, Abigail. Are you angry? Sad? Happy? Do you like fighting with me?"

"I'm angry that the Council is messing with me when I'm trying to do something basic and right. But I understand why. People don't like change, they don't like what's different and it's a threat to share what's yours, what's been your sole possession for all this time." She caught his bottom lip between her teeth and pulled until he moaned.

"I'm happy to be with you and to be sharing this thing we both believe in so much. We're not that different, you and me. We approach it in different ways, but we both want what's best for Ravena and her people. I don't like fighting with you, but I'm not afraid of it. I fight with you in your kitchen because I trust you. I trust that you're doing this from your heart and you won't harm me, at least not with what you know about me as Abbie.

"And I'm sad because people in power are stingy and they would rather threaten me and mine than open their damned eyes and realize the biggest threat is a disgruntled and betrayed populace who do not have a voice and who are tired of it." She massaged his shoulders. "And because I can't be with you and that's really what I want."

She touched him in a way he'd never been touched before. Boldly, but with great care and thought. She gave herself to him knowing they couldn't be together but it gave him courage to enjoy her fully as well and not to hide behind any *just sex* notions. He felt for her and she for him. That's what made it all the more sweet, and painful.

"Take off your sweater. It's time for the fucking. We can continue to argue afterward if you like."

She crisscrossed her arms and yanked the thick sweater off, exposing a soft tank top underneath with no bra to shield very hard nipples.

"What can I say? I can't hide how pleased I am to be here, half naked, on your lap, about to be ravished."

He stood, sitting her on the edge of the table, and removed his clothes. She leaned back on one arm and watched as he did, that smile on her face. The smile that told him she knew he'd fuck her and soon and that she'd enjoy every moment of it.

He pulled off her boots, her socks and the soft pants she wore, humming his pleasure when he noted she had no panties on. "I do like this trend of no panties."

"When I'm with you, it seems rather pointless."

"I completely agree," he murmured, whipping the tank off and moving his mouth to her nipple and latching on. He stepped in between her thighs and thrust into her pussy, which was already soaking for him.

He thrust until the bowl of fruit on the table fell off, until her breasts bounced ever so delightfully, until he nearly came and then he pulled out and stepped back.

Holding a hand out, he pulled her upright. "Come to the couch. Ride me and look into my face as you come. I want to look into your eyes."

Roman Lyons was an experience she'd never regret or forget. Abbie watched the muscles of his body flex and bunch as he moved and then sat. The man was spectacularly beautiful. And hers for the time being.

She never took her gaze from his as she straddled his thighs. Reaching around her body, she grabbed the slick root of his cock and guided him true before sliding down his body with her own. He stretched her, filled her, sent shockwaves of sensation flowing outward from the center of her.

Abbie loved this position with him. Looking at his face, at his body while she rose and fell on his cock, the sensory pleasure of it was the perfect addition to the physical pleasure.

He pressed a palm against her lower stomach while she moved on him. The broad, fat head of his cock brushed against her sweet spot with delicious agony. Right on the point of pain over and over, hovering but never falling. Shivers of delight and intense sensation rode her flesh.

"Yes, that's the way. Inside you feel so right, hot and so tight. It's the best thing I've ever felt, your cunt wrapped around my cock this way, your body right here for me to wonder over, to look at and never forget."

His hands slid up her stomach, over her ribs and to her breasts. He took their weight, those big, soft thumbs of his flicking over the distended nipples slowly. Each pass sent little sensations to her clit. She needed more purchase so she gripped the couch behind his head, her arms bracketing his shoulders so she could increase her speed as she rode him.

"Some days I'm at work, sitting at my desk or in a meeting and I can't get you out of my head. The feel of your pussy sucking my cock back into your body, not wanting to let me go on the upstroke. The feel of the vee of your thighs, hot and wet when you fuck yourself onto me like this. The long line of your body as you rise above me, arching back. Your spine, each and every beautiful bump. The way your tits move as I fuck you from behind. The *O* your mouth makes right before you come, like you're surprised. The look in your eyes as you give yourself to me, even knowing this will end. You're written into me so deep, Abbie. Indelible."

She couldn't stop the gasp his words evoked or the swell of emotion in their wake.

"I carry this thing between us, like a weight. A good weight, in my pocket. I reach out and hold it from time to time like a wonderful secret. I will always have that. I will never feel this way about another woman, ever. My heart will be yours forever, no matter who shares your bed, no matter whose children you bear. I'm here." He tapped her chest. "And you're here." He tapped his own.

Touched beyond words, she leaned in and kissed him softly against his temple. "You mean so very much to me, Roman. In so many ways, on so many levels. You're important in my life. I wish things were different."

The sun set against her back in a riot of reds and purples as she undulated on him. The light was brilliant as it reflected off the lake, off the snow, and refracted from millions of beads of water. Their union was magic at that moment, a gift she'd never wish away. She gave and he received. He gave and she received.

For the longest time they traded sweet and heady kisses until he reached down and slowly circled her clit, ramping her up steadily until she broke around him and dragged him down with her.

"I love you," she murmured as she came.

"Oh gods, Abbie, me, too. How can I give you up?"

She curled into him, her face in the crook of his neck. "You don't have to yet. Let's not think about it for now."

Chapter 22

The sound of the snow crunching under her boots still echoed in her ears as she walked down the hallway. She'd left Roman two days before, after three of the most remarkable days of her entire life.

When she'd returned home, she'd buckled down and continued to prepare for her presentation. She knew it backward and forward at that point, had done a few practice runs with her sister and brothers as her audience and they'd responded well.

Now it was time for the real thing.

Ever since her first time before an adjudicator, Abbie hadn't been nervous. Once she'd entered the room anyway. Until the point where the door closed behind her and she focused on presenting her case, she was a mess of nerves.

But she'd already thrown up in the bathroom down the hall and had brushed her teeth and freshened up. Nerves rode her, but with each step closer to those larger double doors ahead, she began to fall into that place, that place where her brain simply took over and did all the work.

That Abigail Haws loved the challenge. Loved the way she could sway an audience with her words. The power of it was intoxicating, and she wasn't above admitting to herself that it was a huge ego boost.

She'd been allowed to bring one person with her, and at her side stood Josef Sheen, her first mentor, a respected barrister, a feared adjudicator and her biggest fan. He was a Walker on his mother's side, a powerfully connected man. That he'd be her support on such an important day meant the 'Verse to Abbie.

"I have every confidence I will not have to yell at you until you cry after this is over," he said shortly before the doors opened.

She'd never been inside such a grand chamber, and this was just the Auxiliary Council. High ceilings covered in majestic carvings rose above them, high into the air. There were carvings featuring lions, the symbol of not only House Lyons, but of Family Rule. Big windows cast light against the pale stone columns supporting that grand ceiling.

And at the head of the room, a large table that looked as if it were carved from a single tree. And she knew it was. The table was millennia old and had come through with the Lyons from Earth. This was the little brother to the one in the Council chambers.

An ombudsman stood, waiting just inside.

"Barrister Haws? Please do have a seat just here." He looked to Josef and bowed deeply. "Mr. Sheen, it is my pleasure to have you in our chambers."

Josef nodded once and made a gruff sound. That was all the ombudsman would get. Josef was a man of very few words, and the few he parted with were mostly critical anyway. She held her smile back and simply let herself fall into the place she needed to be.

$\mathcal{R}$oman sat behind the frieze, just above the chamber floor. There was a small viewing space where guests, or spies originally, could sit and watch the proceedings. He intended to see just how Abbie did.

She looked hard and determined. He recognized Josef from the pictures and vids. He'd met the man once or twice at larger Council functions. Back when Roman had to take the mandatory classes on Family and 'Verse history, Josef taught three of them each term. He'd made Roman stutter a few times; no one else had ever managed that feat. If he was Abbie's observer, things were going well for her already. Josef was a revered man, respected and trusted.

Deimos came in with the rest of the AC. Roman smiled. His son was a man, and he wasn't sure just exactly when it had happened. It seemed like it was just months before when Dem had taken his first steps, had gone to school, begun to date. And here he was leading the AC, readying himself, along with the rest of those assembled, to take over the next generation of leadership of the Federation 'Verses.

Marcus settled in beside Roman and handed him a mug of kava.

Abbie looked up, standing when the AC filed in. Deimos looked quite handsome in his long, wine-colored robes. A lion decorated each lapel.

"My brothers, today we have a guest speaker, Barrister Abigail Haws. She's going to present a petition regarding an advisory council. I will let her explain it to you. Please hold your questions until the end of the presentation when there will be an open question period." Deimos looked down the room at Abbie and nodded to her. "Barrister Haws, please approach the podium and address the Auxiliary Council."

She was within it by then, sliding calmly through the current of her power as she walked to the podium. She took a sip of water, adjusted the microphone and began to speak.

"Esteemed members of the Auxiliary Council, I'm here today because I was invited. If I hadn't been, I wouldn't have even been allowed in this building, much less this chamber. I'm Abigail Haws, I'm thirty-two standard years old, I've been a barrister for six years. I was mentored and apprenticed by one of the finest legal minds in the Known Universes and I was born right here in Ravena.

"And yet, I couldn't have addressed the very people responsible for the governance of my home 'Verse without a note from one of them." She moved away from the podium and began to pace. Very slowly.

"My organization, the Movement for Representative Democracy, was started four years ago, right here in the capital. By me. Because I care about my 'Verse and I care about her people. Ranked and unranked. We've spent a great deal of time attempting to address our concerns to our Family representatives and for four years we've been put off, ignored, fobbed off on assistants who promised a comm or a meeting and nothing happened.

"Nothing until recently and you all know why. But I'm not going to use that right now. I'm going to tell you honestly that I believe every single member at that table of yours, every Family rep who sits on the Governing Council, should know what the opinions, the experiences and the perspectives of the people he or she is governing are. The unranked have no voice other than what the Ranked choose to give them, and that is wrong. It is outdated and undemocratic, and it is part of your problem right now. Because after a while, the unresponsiveness you see will turn into something else. Now you can turn it into passion and involvement by the creation of an advisory council, a council of popularly elected unranked representatives with one or two seats at this table and one at the GC, or it can be a negative one. But a change is coming one way or another and ignoring it will not make it disappear."

She spoke to them in her smoothest voice, in the voice Josef hounded her into using until she sounded like one of them and did it without effort. Right then, she wasn't an unranked person asking for a handout; she was speaking in their voice. A professional woman asking to be heard and telling them the hard truths they knew but didn't want to face. But she did it with a motherly smile.

She continued on until her time was nearly up, going over, very briefly, a basic timetable and some ideas for how an unranked advisory council might look. And then she stood back, bowed and moved to the podium to await her questions.

oman and Marcus watched her, openmouthed.

"Gods, she's amazing. Look at them listen to her," Marcus said very quietly in Roman's ear.

Roman had noticed that himself. Had noticed the way the body language of the assembled group had gone from hostile to wary to actually engaged. He hadn't heard the voice she now used with them. Her accent was totally smoothed out, soothing, cultured. Abbie was a canny woman and she knew her audience.

The questions were predictable and none too hostile. She clearly had opposition to her plan, but Roman was pleased to note more than one head nodding as she spoke. Deimos already supported her proposal, Roman knew that much. His son understood times were different now than they were even just a generation ago. He believed Deimos and Corrin would lead House Lyons into a new era, maybe even one where everyone had a voice.

"Shit," Marcus whispered. Roman snapped to attention and saw, with growing horror, Saul Kerrigan walking in with Bentan at his side.

Roman stood. "That bastard. Marcus, get the guard and do it now. I want Bentan Kerrigan removed from this chamber immediately and put in lockup. Under my direct order. Do you understand?"

Marcus moved quickly, speaking into his personal comm and then turned back to Roman. They took the stairs toward the chamber.

"Roman, what is it? What's with Bentan that has you so upset?"

"I'm sure you read the information you had gathered on Abbie. Bentan is the man who attacked her." And Saul knew it. Had brought her rapist here to shake her. Roman would not let this stand.

*A*bbie turned and with dawning horror, realized who stood right behind that asshole Saul Kerrigan.

Deimos rapped a gavel in the background, the sound echoing in her ears. Her hearing had gone funny, like she was under water.

Josef's face was livid with fury. He stomped right up to Saul and Bentan and used his walking stick to halt their advance to her. Roman burst out of a side door with Marcus. Chaos erupted and guards came into the chamber.

Saul began to yell and Abbie straightened her suit jacket, marched up to the microphone and spoke into it.

"Let Mr. Kerrigan speak."

Roman drew up short but she nodded when he indicated he was having Bentan removed. Josef knew Bentan was under lockup orders should he return to Ravena and Abbie trusted he'd get that information to the guards.

But she would handle Saul Kerrigan right then because he could not be allowed to get away with what he'd just done. She would not allow it.

"You should ask yourselves why this unranked woman has just caused this upset!" Saul yelled as he approached the table.

"Why, Mr. Kerrigan, I believe it was your nephew the rapist who caused the upset." She wasn't sure how she kept her voice so calm.

Saul looked shocked and she sent him just the slightest smile. He would not break her.

Abbie turned her attention back to the AC. "Yes, that's right. When I was seventeen, Bentan Kerrigan and five other men, some affiliated, attacked me. Beat me, raped me and left me in a coma for weeks. Bentan was found guilty and the Kerrigans sent him to the Edge as part of an agreement. One he just broke. Perhaps the question is, why did Mr. Kerrigan bring Bentan here today knowing I'd be addressing this body?"

"You have no say! You're just an unranked bitch not good enough to service Bentan. I brought him here to show this body just what a threat you are. If you don't get your way, you manipulate to use the system to harm Ranked citizens. She did it with Bentan and she'll do it with you."

"You are out of order, Saul." Deimos stood, his face tight with anger. "Ms. Haws, thank you for your presentation today. We will

take it under advisement and there will be discussion and a recom-
mendation before our next session." He'd dismissed her and she
understood. She had to go to let them deal with this privately.

She nodded. "Thank you." Then turned and stalked out of the
room, Josef on her heels.

In the hallway outside guards were arguing with Marcus and
Bentan. Josef snorted and walked over. Abbie just watched it with
horrified amusement.

"This man is under an order for lockup if he sets foot back in
Ravena. The order is on coded file. You understand why his name is
not on the order, but rather his number. The number will lead to another set of papers. I've had my office send them straight over to
lockup."

Marcus nodded. "Go on! You are under the direct orders of Roman Lyons. Josef Sheen has given you more information. Get to it
or you'll join him in lockup."

The guards took an uncooperative Bentan from the building.
She refused to look away, even as he threatened her.

Josef knew her well enough not to make a fuss and Marcus, thank
the gods, took that cue. "Ms. Haws, there's a conveyance outside
waiting for you and Mr. Sheen. It will take you wherever you need to
go. Mr. Lyons expresses his upset that such a person be allowed in
this 'Verse and wants to assure you it will be taken care of."

She swallowed hard, past the fear. "Thank you, Marcus."

Josef took her arm, under the guise that he needed it, and they
left the building.

Chapter 23

*A*bbie's hands shook on and off for the rest of the day, but she had work to do, and she'd be damned if she'd let scum like Bentan and Saul Kerrigan get in her way. Josef, in his own gruff way, stuck around on the pretense of wanting to talk with her about the licensing issue. And then he watched her in a hearing, saying he was still responsible for her, or his reputation was, and, by gods, he wanted to keep an eye on her and be sure she wasn't embarrassing him.

In the end, she'd forgotten about that horrible moment when she'd turned and seen Bentan, because Josef scared her staff so severely she thought Tasha would cry.

Assuring him she knew how to do her job and that she was fine, Abbie ushered Josef back out to the conveyance waiting to take him home.

She just had to get through the rest of her appointments, only two more, and then go home. Home to a hot bath, a drink or three and what she hoped would be a dreamless night.

Until she saw the man from the vid service walking toward her, smiling. She'd totally forgotten about that.

She smoothed down the front of her clothing, patted over her hair and waved at him as she made her way over.

"Roman! Turn on your screen," Marcus called through the open door.

He cursed as he turned it on to see Abbie, looking so very small and fragile but not betraying the horror she'd experienced that very day.

"Yes, I made my presentation today to the AC," she was saying to the interviewer.

The interviewer stood very close to her, annoying Roman to the end of his patience. The man smiled at her like a smitten young boy. Bah.

"How do you feel it went?"

"I'm pleased I was listened to. That's the first big step. Many of the Houses were particularly open to what I had to say. Asking follow-up questions and the like. I do believe many Families want what's best for the unranked in all the 'Verses."

"Many? So some don't?" The interviewer thought he was sly, not realizing Abbie had led him there in the first place.

"Oh, now, I didn't say that. I am sure there are many perspectives on the issue. I hope to tell you more after their next session. Chairman Deimos Lyons informed me they'd take the MRD's proposal up before their next official meeting."

The interviewer tried to get her to condemn someone and Roman kept expecting her to bring up Kerrigan, but she didn't. Hells, Roman wanted to scream it from the front steps. But she didn't and he realized he underestimated her and her commitment to the overall goal.

"She looks pale. You're going to her, aren't you?" Marcus came in, bringing a pot of tea.

"I'm in meetings until very late. Her comm has been off, so I left a message." He hoped she didn't blame him somehow for the debacle.

In an interesting turn, two of the members who'd been wavering on whether to support Abbie's proposal had gone to her side after Saul made such an ass of himself.

Deimos had been beside himself. Roman hadn't shared the details of what Bentan had done to Abbie, not overly specifically so, but he'd told his son the man had assaulted Abbie when she was young. That had been enough. The relationship between his boys and their maternal grandfather had always been weak, but Roman feared this stunt of Saul's would be the end.

And then the comms began, one after the other, as reps from the AC went back to their offices and the story began to unfold. On top of that, there'd been an actual skirmish between Federation and Imperialist troops on the Edge. It had been dealt with quickly, thank the gods, but now Roman had to deal with Wilhelm Ellis, the leader of the Federation military corps.

Roman wanted to go to Abbie, wanted to hold her and chase her fears away, but he had to be Roman, face of House Lyons, and that took precedent. He hated it, but that was reality. He knew Abbie not only understood but would expect him to do his duty. That only made him feel worse.

"Marcus," he said on his way out to a meeting, "could you—"

"I'm heading over there with Nyna once I leave. She's apparently still at her office. Daniel is going over there to pick her up and walk her home."

"Good." Daniel Haws was a dangerous man, more dangerous than his family knew, but Roman would leave it up to Daniel to share—or not share—with his family that he'd never left the corps at all. He'd protect Abbie with his life and that's what counted just then. "Will you give her this?" He handed Marcus an envelope.

"Of course. She'll understand why you can't come yourself."

Roman sighed. "I know. And I expect there'll be more attention on her, and me as it happens, for the next however long as this plays out, so keeping things very quiet would be the best thing." But he wanted to be there for her and the inability to do so chafed at him more than it ever had before.

"All the hells are breaking loose, Roman," Wilhelm Ellis, Comandante of the Federation military corps said without preamble as Roman entered the office.

"What the fuck now?" Roman fell into a chair and waved away a girl with a tray. He didn't need pastries, he needed answers.

"People are agitated, Roman. The 'Verses on the frontier and edge are most vocal, but we knew that would happen, especially after the connections Nondal had to this whole nightmare with Perry Walker. Now that the trials have started, it'll only get worse I expect. The Imperialists aren't stupid. They've been poking at it, making it worse when they could. Any sign of weakness is just blood in the air for them. They're vicious, and just because they got caught doesn't mean they've stopped trying to take our 'Verses portal by portal."

Roman sighed. "What's this about the fighting?"

"Small skirmish. Border issue. Shots were fired but in the air. Things are tense but peaceful. For now. The unranked are unhappy. This group that's been agitating lately, the"—he consulted his notes—"Movement for Representative Democracy? They could be a catalyst. I see they spoke before the AC today and Kerrigan brought his reprobate, rapist nephew in. To shake the Haws woman, no doubt."

Roman had long ago ceased to ask how Wilhelm knew the things he did. He simply knew things, understanding them in sometimes terrifyingly stark ways. It was why he was Roman's right hand. He rarely found it necessary to rein Wilhelm in, which, for someone with as much power as the Comandante had, was refreshing.

"Didn't seem to now, did it? Saw her on the vids. Looked a bit shaken but didn't give Saul a breath of attention. That must burn that bastard's ass." Wilhelm chuckled.

"I trust you'll take care of the Bentan problem."

Wilhelm Ellis's eyes lit a moment and then he nodded. "I don't like men who hurt women. And I don't like it when those Ranked muddy the names of the rest of us. I don't like being lumped in with people like Saul Kerrigan. It makes me terse."

"Indeed."

"I like her. Ms. Haws. She's got spark as well as one good-looking pair."

Roman narrowed his eyes and Wilhelm laughed again.

"She does, however, live in a building that's pretty exposed. Gets good light, I expect. But her windows, bedroom and kitchen area are very visible. If someone was looking, they might see something they weren't supposed to."

Roman scrubbed his hands over his face.

"I'm not going to see anything, of course. I personally think rules about intermarriage with unranked are outdated, and I'm glad I'm just associated and a third son. But there are people who might use such information to harm you and yours."

"Point taken. All right, do what needs to be done on the Edge. I want to know what's going on with the opposition Families, especially Solaris. I'm meeting with Walker and Pela after I leave here." He stood and Wilhelm did as well, dwarfing Roman with his nearly seven-foot frame.

"I've got your back. And you'll like Brandt's wife. She's one of my people, too. Smart, deadly. I'd wager Ms. Haws would like Sera a lot, speaking of Ranked men breaking rules and marrying the unranked."

Head hurting, Roman headed to the Council offices to meet with Ash Walker, who'd been sent by his father, Angelo.

Damn it all, if Wilhelm knew, it wouldn't be unbelievable if others would soon enough. His need to be with Abbie was relentless; it clawed at his gut. Just knowing she was upset and scared made him want to run straight to her. Just days ago he'd woken up, her body against his, sleep-soft and warm. He'd slid into her and she'd opened to him. It was simple and beautiful and he loved her. There was no way he could stay away from her just yet. He'd have to be extra careful, wear the disguise, but he wasn't giving Abbie up. Not yet.

Abbie grabbed her bag and when she turned back to leave, Daniel stood there, concern on his face.

He hugged her tight, kissing her cheek. "I heard. Damn it, I heard. I'm sorry."

"Not right now. I can't." If she spoke of it again, she'd fall apart. While she was at work she did not fall apart. She'd save it for her private moments.

He said nothing else as he took her bag and put an arm around her shoulders.

They walked, bundled against the cold, back to her place where she found Nyna and Marcus waiting for her. Nyna's arms were full and she knew her sister had brought enough food to feed a legion but it was her way of fixing hurts. And Abbie had some hurts that needed fixing.

She understood why Roman wasn't there. She'd checked her comm and saw his messages. His concern and anger on her behalf touched her. But she wished he was with her nonetheless.

"Hey there, you two. Don't you have, like, snuggling and stuff to do?" She accepted a kiss from Nyna and then from Marcus as she let them all in.

Marcus handed her an envelope and she recognized the tilt of the handwriting. *Roman.*

"He really can't be here right now. He wants to be. But you can't imagine the pressure he's under just now," Marcus said softly to her.

She took the note and tried not to cry. All she wanted to do was curl up and go to sleep, but instead she had to entertain what turned out to be a flat full of people as Georges showed up shortly after they arrived.

"I'm going to change my clothes, I'll be right back," Abbie called as she headed into her bedroom and closed the door, shutting everything out.

Quickly, she took a pill and hoped her hands would stop shaking.

She wanted to scream out her frustration. How dare Saul Kerrigan show up and infect her with fear again? Why wasn't she strong enough to simply not be affected by it?

She hated her weakness. Her need of Roman and his arms around her. Of course she would have to be in love with the most inappropriate and unattainable male in the entire Known Universes!

Gods, she was actually wallowing.

She sighed as she tossed herself on the bed and tore open the envelope. Roman's scent, masculine, sexy, forbidden, filled the room and she closed her eyes to savor it for a moment.

It was a simple note. Tender. He wanted to be there but couldn't. The 'Verse needed him but it was important for her to understand her safety was paramount and not to worry. He would protect her.

It wasn't as good as it would have been to bury her face in his neck, to have had his arms around her. But it was good. He cared. She was important to him and that was enough. It was all she could have just then, anyway.

"Abbie?" Daniel tapped on her door.

She wiped her face, tucked the note under her pillow and got off the bed. When she opened the door, no one but Daniel would have known she was upset.

"Come on out here and let us make it better. Mai is here, too."

Her mother looked around Daniel's body and like a child, Abbie sought her arms and let go. She and her mother sank to the floor, her mother rocking her, murmuring softly as she smoothed a hand over her hair.

Soon enough Daniel had her from the other side with Georges and Nyna following suit. She cried until there was nothing left but the occasional muscle spasm, and Daniel hauled her up, led her to the couch and sat her down. Her mother tucked a blanket around her and then sat beside her.

"Now, you feel better?" her mother asked softly.

"Sort of. I want him dead. And then I feel guilty because I wished another person dead. And then I feel guilty because I really don't feel guilty at all."

Nyna tsked and pushed a glass of something warm and alcoholic into her hand. "Take it. I know you took a pill. This will help you sleep through. Without the dreams."

"Is there anything private in this family?" Abbie sipped the mulled wine and let it warm her. She put her head on her mother's shoulder. "By the way, welcome to the family, Marcus. I'm sorry if you thought we were normal. Nyna will make you fat, I'll weep on you and Daniel will frown you to death."

Marcus looked stunned for a moment and then laughed. He took one of Abbie's hands and kissed it. "I like your family just fine. Jaron is at home of course but he sends his love. He's very angry on your behalf."

"So the news is everywhere then?"

Her answer came with a pounding on her door and Logan came in, rage on his face when Daniel opened up.

"Abbie, I heard." He sank to his knees in front of her and she touched his face.

"I'm all right now. My family wouldn't let it be otherwise." She smirked and Logan squeezed her knee.

"I spoke with Josef. He and I went by lockup but Bentan isn't there. There is simply no record of him at all. So we thought those bastard Kerrigans had done something yet again but Saul came in, crazy mad, yelling and accusing." Logan shrugged.

Daniel looked to Marcus, Abbie saw it, that gleam of approval in her brother's eyes once Marcus gave a slight nod. Well, now. Roman Lyons had stepped in at some point and made good on his promise to keep her safe.

"Maybe he fell into the space between portals and he'll wash up as 'Verse junk somewhere," Nyna said, but Abbie doubted anyone would ever see Bentan again in any form, and she didn't feel sorry for that at all.

She finally chased everyone out a few hours later when she was very drunk between her pill and the mulled wine. Her mother had been very stoic about her father's absence and Abbie had pretended she hadn't noticed just how much time he'd been spending with Robin lately. It was a game she tired of and she wondered why her mother took it. The countless affairs seemed to Abbie to be a bill she wouldn't want to pay. Her mother had a solid business, her health was in good shape finally, and she'd aged well. Abbie loved her father, faults and all, but her mother was far better off without him. But she wasn't privy to everything between them, maybe there was more than she knew beneath the surface. She could only hope.

Roman had used the disguise Daniel had provided for him and sneaking down back alleys and around corners, he'd finally arrived at her door. It was very late and he should have felt bad for disturbing her, but he couldn't.

He needed her.

He'd met with Ash Walker, whose mistress had informed Roman it was time to let the unranked have a voice and to stop playing games. Walker had thrown his support behind Roman against the opposition that'd begun cropping up. Brandt Pela had said the same on behalf of his family. It was still problematic because both House Walker and House Pela had suffered a huge setback with the charges of treason and collusion against their Family members.

Still, votes were votes, and House Walker had the most right after House Lyons, and Pela was very powerful as well. If Roman could line up several more Houses, he'd be in good shape.

Marcus had commed him and informed him about Abbie's breakdown at home. It'd taken every ounce of his will not to miss his next two meetings and go to her.

But he was House Lyons, he couldn't simply walk away when he was needed and he knew Abbie understood that. Still, he didn't want her to have to understand, he wanted to be there to put his arms around her.

So when he finished his last meeting, long after the second moon set, he headed out to see her. Even if only for a few moments. It was selfish, he knew it. She was probably sleeping.

He stood there, wrestling with himself, and finally tapped quietly. And then again when she didn't answer. She slept lightly; he knew this now that he'd had that luxury of sleeping with her. She should have heard the tap, especially the second one.

Was she all right? Had she sought comfort from her family and spent the night there? Or with Logan, the ex?

He pulled out the key she'd given him and let himself in. He stood in the dark until his eyes adjusted. Her shades had been drawn so that was something he didn't need to do.

"Abbie?" he called out as he headed toward her bedroom. Her scent hung in the air—sweet, long nights.

No answer.

He walked into her bedroom and she was there in her bed, alone. Breathing deeply, so deeply she snuffled a little bit on each exhale.

He grinned. She snored. Divesting himself of his clothes, he slid into bed next to her, not liking how cold she was.

She snuffled again and turned to him, nuzzling a very cold nose into the hollow of his throat. She hummed low and her eyelashes tickled as her eyes opened.

"You're here. I thought it was a dream. But I'm not supposed to dream so I knew it must have been true. And it was, so I'm not sad."

He pulled back enough to see her face and kiss her. Her voice was slurred. "Hello, gorgeous. I was worried so I let myself in. Are you all right?"

"Took a pill. Had wine and then forgot about the first pill until I took the second. I'm fine, just very groggy. Gods, you're warm. And why do you always smell so good? I love the way you smell. I like when I wake up and you're in my bed. I wish that happened all the time."

Despite his amusement at her state of inebriation, he was concerned for her as well. Two pills? And wine?

"What pills do you mean? Abbie, are you supposed to take two pills?"

"The pills to keep the dreams away."

He rolled her onto her back, trailing his fingers down the front of her heavy nightshirt. "The dreams?"

"The dreams of the bad time. I don't have them very often. But sometimes they come. Today." Her hand found its way to his cock and gave him a pump and then another.

"Gorgeous, wait. I didn't come here for that. I just wanted to hold you. And I woke you because I was worried when you didn't hear me at the door."

Her hand fell away and her sweet, talented mouth opened on that little snuffling sound. She'd fallen back into sleep. He pondered waking her again, worried about how much medication she may have in her system but she'd said it was fine when she'd first awakened. Right?

Snorting at how fucking cute she'd been, he snuggled back down into her bed, pulling the blankets up and tucking them both in. And made a mental note to deal with getting her into a building right on a vent, damn it.

Chapter 24

*A*bbie woke up with one spectacular headache. She slept hard when she took the pills. Full consciousness came very slowly, and as it did, so did the realization she wasn't alone in bed.

Her eyes snapped open to find Roman looking down at her, concern and amusement on his features. "Good morning."

She mumbled at him and made her way into her bathroom, closing the door. Gods! He looked like a damned entertainment model and she looked— A quick glance in the mirror had her groaning. Certainly *not* like an entertainment model.

She turned on the water and, shivering, shucked her clothes and got in. If she was going to deal with a beautiful, sexy man in her bed, she'd do it looking human.

She heard the tap at the door and the breeze as he opened it and came in. "Oh, good idea." He grinned at her.

And within moments he'd crowded in to join her.

What? Was she going to complain? Was she stupid? As it happened, her headache had lessened, she was clean, warm, and in very close proximity to a naked man. No complaints there.

"Good morning. Are you supposed to be here?" She kissed his chest, licking over one of his nipples.

"You seemed pretty pleased to see at least part of me when I came over last night."

"I did?" She felt herself blush even in the heat of the water.

He laughed. "I was worried. I knocked and you didn't come so I let myself in. I hope you're not upset. And when I got in bed with you, you were a bit, um—" He struggled with a smile and she rolled her eyes and got out, drying off quickly.

"So we fucked and I don't even remember it? Well that's not very fair." Gods, she must have really been out of it to not remember that.

He followed just moments later, getting out and drying off. "Abbie, I'd never fuck you in that state. You grabbed my cock, said how good I smelled and fell back to sleep."

She laughed. "Oops. Sorry. It's the medication. I usually only take one but I took a pill and then had wine and took another before I remembered I'd taken one earlier. They put me into a very deep sleep. I haven't had to take two in a very long time."

He pulled her close, kissing the top of her head. "Damn it, Abbie, I'm so sorry about yesterday. I'm sorry you have to take pills to drown out dreams of something so horrible. And I'm sorry I couldn't come straight to you. I tried to stay away, to let you sleep, but I found myself on my way here and I couldn't stop my steps. I had to hold you, to know you were okay."

Gods, why did he have to be so good? Why did he have to go and be tender and caring?

"Thank you. My family came by. Nyna with loads of food. Marcus to keep her company and gaze upon her adoringly every few moments." Abbie smiled.

Roman picked up a brush from her counter and began to work it through her hair. With a happy sigh, she stood and let him minister to her.

"Daniel frowned a lot. Georges told jokes and my mother patted my back. They made me drink mulled wine and no one would leave until I got into bed. That feels wonderful, by the way."

"Good. After yesterday you deserve to feel wonderful."

"*Pfft.* By the way, were you back behind a curtain or something? Watching me all unobserved like?"

He snorted. "You've outed me. Marcus and I were up in the viewing gallery. I wanted to see how you did. Abbie, you did a marvelous job. I'm very impressed. You made some very fine points. And even after Saul came in with that piece of garbage, you held it together so well."

She waved it away. His praise meant more than he'd ever understand. "Thank you. We'll see what happens by the next meeting. The first trial starting in the treason cases is going to make all sides tense."

She walked from the bathroom and he trailed behind. "There's an extra robe there. You can wear it for now. I'm going to put some kava on. I need the energy."

"Don't open the window shades!" he called out.

"Why?" Alarm raced through her.

"Let's just say I got a friendly tip that your windows, when opened, showed everything going on in here."

"Ew! Are you kidding me? People are spying on me? You have that kind of spying?"

He put his hands up. "No," he assured her hastily. "One of my people knows, but he was warning me to protect me."

She relaxed a bit as she began to heat the water and measure out the kava. "Well I suppose you should be extra careful coming here." She bit her lip. "Or maybe, maybe it's time to not do this anymore. I can't imagine how awful it would be if you were found out and it harmed you. I'd never forgive myself. I don't want to be the cause of any harm to you, Roman. I love you."

In two steps he had his arms around her. "I love you, too. Gods, Abbie. So much I can't . . . I can't let you go. Not yet. I can't."

She let her anxiety go for the moment and slid her palms up his back. He was warm and solid and real. Not a memory, not a nightmare. He'd come for her when it risked so much.

Effortlessly, he picked her up and placed her on the counter before stepping between her widened thighs. One arm banded her waist, pulling her close, while his mouth sought hers, delivering the sweetness of his kiss.

His hands wove through her hair, yanking so her head went back and her neck arched, offered for his lips. She groaned and he echoed it. He shoved the top of her robe apart and down, exposing her body but also binding her arms back as he feasted on her nipples.

"So sweet. How can I let you go?" he said against her skin.

She wanted to clutch him, to bring him close and never let go.

The kettle whistled and he let her go long enough to turn it off. She hopped down and poured the water though the press. But just moments later he picked her up, tossed her over his shoulder and stalked to her bedroom.

She landed on her bed with a laugh and he was on her again.

Their robes fell away and she hissed as his warm, naked skin slid along hers. Gods, he felt good. She dug her nails into his back, urged him closer as she wrapped her legs around him.

He groaned, licking and biting her nipples. Good heavens above and below, he felt good. He licked and bit a path down her belly and right straight to her pussy. He ate her like she was the first thing he'd tasted after a fast. Like he couldn't get enough. He stabbed his tongue up and into her gate repeatedly and then dragged the flat of his tongue over her clit, pressing down until she whimpered.

But before he made her come, he got to his knees, his cock in his fist. He moved to fuck her but she held a hand out to stay him.

"Wait. I want to see how you hold yourself. Make yourself come, Roman. Show me what you like."

"Mmmm. Good idea. Then I can come on these." He reached out and pinched a nipple.

He moved up her body, straddling her so she got a very good view and his balls rested against her belly, hot and heavy.

His gaze locked with hers, he began to pump his fist up and down around his cock. Slowly at first.

The eye seeped and Abbie was unable to resist reaching out and sliding her fingertip through it and licking the salty taste. His mouth opened as he gasped air.

"Gods, you're going to kill me."

"Come on my tits first," she said, her voice low, threaded with suggestion.

Satisfaction roared through her at the way his pupils swallowed the iris of his eyes for a moment.

She broke their eye contact to watch how he handled his cock. Sure, even a bit rough. He pumped all the way down to the root, hard enough to sound the slap of his hand against his belly.

Up and off and back again. The way he handled his cock en-tranced her. It was beautiful to watch him in such an unguarded way. She dug her fingers into the blankets beneath her to keep from reaching out.

The head of his cock gleamed with pre-come, his chest began to heave with his breath, and all she wanted was to taste him.

"I love it when you look at my cock and lick your lips like you're hungry for it."

She looked up at him. "I am hungry for it."

He muttered a curse and laughed. "No one like you. Never will be."

"Come on me," she urged.

"Oh, I will, gorgeous. Don't worry about that. I've wanted to paint those breasts with my come since about ten minutes after I met you."

His movements got jerkier, less fluid. She knew he was close and she watched his cock hungrily until he groaned low and long, and warm, silky seed landed on her breasts and belly.

Each electric touch of his come sent her closer to her own cli-max. Never had anyone done this to her, with her. He'd marked her in a sense and she felt *possessed* right down to her toes.

He backed down her body with a satisfied exhale, but before he could bring the edge of a robe to clean her up, she slid her fingers through it. He froze in place as she looked up at him with a smile.

Roman had never actually done such a thing before, and gods it was hot. The memory of his come jetting over those pretty pink nipples would be burned into his memory forever.

He'd been ridiculously sated until she'd reached up and slid her fingers through his seed, dragging them over her nipples, glistening with him.

Her eyes on him, she took that gleaming wetness and slid it down her belly. He moved to the foot of her bed and she'd spread her thighs open wide, exposing the swollen, wet folds of her cunt to his greedy eyes. Yes, he'd been eating that right before he came. He licked his lips, ready to head back to it. Until she took fingers wet with his come and used it to lube herself over her clit.

Words flitted away from him as he took her in. His proud, sexy Abbie. A woman totally in charge and unashamed of her sexuality. With him she was free, and it made him feel like shouting it from the top of her building.

Instead he watched as she played with one nipple with the slippery fingers of her left hand while she circled her clit with the fingers of her right.

She lay before him, a feast of sexy woman, playing with her pussy and nipples, wet with him. Her eyes never left him as she did it.

He couldn't decide where to look so he just made the circuit back and forth between her fingers—gods, she fucked into her gate with them and they came out even wetter. He scented her cunt, rich, sexy, heady. Her movements sounded slick between them in the air as she held him transfixed.

He said nothing, not wanting to break the spell.

She was a cipher. A siren. A magical witch who held him in her thrall and he went willingly. Offered himself to her to be bound.

Her clit, slippery and swollen, played peekaboo around her fingers as she sped her movements.

He watched, rapt. He knew it wouldn't be long and it wasn't. Shortly after she sucked in air and her pretty nipples darkened. Two of her fingers stabbed into her gate while she thumbed over her clit hard and fast.

With a gasp she arched, her hips churning, riding her fingers until she sighed long and slow, and leaned back, looking boneless against her bed.

He laid back down, covering them both with the blanket as the scent of sex and kava painted the air. A perfect combination for a perfect moment.

Delivering a kiss to her nose, he used his robe and cleaned her breasts up. She turned to him, wrapping her arms around him and burying her nose in his neck as she wriggled to get close.

"I love you," she whispered.

"I love you," he replied. Because nothing in the 'Verse had ever been truer.

Chapter 25

A bbie sat in the courtroom, trying not to think of the morning before. Roman had loved her. Not just sexually but emotionally. He'd come to her, risking himself in the process and had touched her. No one other than her family had ever done that before.

But she felt him slipping away. Knew it had to happen even if neither one of them wanted to face it. The ache of it, the impending sense of desolation, hung over her. Her mood wasn't helped by the fact that she'd become the topic of discussion all over the capital. Her business was now a curiosity. That wasn't her plan, and damn it all, it really made her cranky.

And her father had been sniffing around, acting agitated, and she feared what would happen at the next MRD meeting the following evening.

Abbie went through the motions, making her arguments, questioning the witnesses, totally relieved when they were done for the day. Until she saw Logan outside the doors, his arms crossed.

"Why hello, Ms. Haws. Remember me? Let's walk, shall we?" He linked arms with her and walked out the front doors. The air was cold, her nose would be running in just a little while if they didn't go back inside.

"Logan, I left you a message."

"I've come by your office several times and commed you. What? Suddenly I'm not even your friend anymore?"

They stopped and he turned to her, hurt in his eyes. She touched his face.

"Of course you're my friend. The day it happened I worked until very late and then Daniel ambushed me, took me home to a flat filled with my family. You were there. Yesterday I just tried to keep my head down. It's not like I was avoiding you. But I am sorry if you felt ignored or if I made you feel unimportant to me. You should know by now that's not the truth."

He hugged her and kissed her forehead. "I'm sorry. I've just been worried about you. All this gossip and the way you looked that day, you sounded awful and you looked pale and I wasn't there. Are you mad because I wasn't there when it happened?"

"Don't be silly. Truly, I'm all right now. Well . . ." She tugged him to get him moving again. "I'm not thrilled with all the gossip, but that's to be expected. Luckily I'm so busy with work and the treason trials have started and are on the vids all day so I'm being pushed from the consciousness."

"I've heard rumors," he said, his voice very low. "You and Lyons."

"Where did you hear this?"

"Lockup. The guard over there, the one at the door. He mentioned it to me. Sneered at me even."

How the fuck would that piece of garbage know? He had connections to Kerrigan, she knew that. He was related to one of the boys who'd attacked her.

Abbie hoped like hell she sounded nonchalant, because she felt anything but. Once people found out, *if* they found out, it would be the end. And it would hurt Roman. "What kind of rumors?"

"Don't. Abbie, I know you. I may have been too stupid to know what I had, but I know you. I saw how you looked at him. But—are you going to throw away everything you believe in to be a woman on the side? You deserve more."

"Of course I do. Now I have to meet with a client, so I have to run. Thank you, truly, for being concerned about me. But I'm all right." Maybe if she said it often enough it would be true.

"Just . . . just be careful. And remember I love you and I'm here if you need me." He squeezed her hand and let her go.

Straight into a vid crew waiting in the lobby.

"Ms. Haws! Do you have any comment on the statement recently released by House Kerrigan?" the reporter asked.

She steeled herself, standing tall. "I have no idea what you're talking about, but I'm on my way to meet a client."

"Saul Kerrigan has made an accusation that you're attempting to use your relationship with House Lyons, an *inappropriate* relationship with Roman Lyons specifically, to manipulate the system and force through your proposal for a takeover by unranked representatives."

She blinked several times. "My. There are so many things wrong with what you just said I don't know where to begin. Let me be very clear. Anyone in the AC who heard my proposal on the part of the

Movement for Representative Democracy can tell you that we are asking for an advisory council to the Governance Council. We want a seat there. We are not proposing to abolish Family Rule. Only to enhance it with representation by *all* her people. Now, I have a job to get back to. You all have a nice evening." Abbie sailed past them and onto a lift, knowing security would stop them from going to her floor.

Once inside and with the doors closed, she slumped in the corner, her heart beating so rapidly she felt a little faint.

And she felt no better when she got to her office and saw Alexander Lyons sitting in her chair.

She exhaled sharply. "This day keeps getting worse. I have a client meeting just now, Mr. Lyons. I don't have time to be accused of whoring myself out for democracy or whatever else Saul Kerrigan has been telling you. I'm really quite at the end of my rope with all of this so please *do* excuse me."

"I can see why he enjoys you so." Alexander stood in one smooth movement. "We do seem to clash every time we meet. Why is that?"

"May I be frank?"

One corner of his mouth rose a tiny bit. "Please, yes, let's."

"Because you're an uptight, entitled asshole who thinks the 'Verse owes him something because he was lucky enough to be born to a Lyons instead of a Haws. It offends me. Your ferocious sense of entitlement. As if hard work and ambition are somehow beneath you while this endless plotting to bring down someone you don't even know is not. I find it repugnant." *Did she actually say that out loud?*

One of his eyebrows rose very high and then he laughed. Great gales of laughter. "Oh my, Ms. Haws, I do like you. Honestly, I do.

Roman is such an unlucky fool to not be able to have you. Because, if I may also be frank, you are everything a man like him needs. Alas, I get the feeling you would not be so inclined to join me after your brief involvement with my brother ends. Which, I suppose, is what makes you so appealing."

She put her face in her hands. "What are you doing here and what are you talking about?"

"I like that you're not giving my brother up. You know, despite our differences, I care about him very much. He's a good man. Deimos tells me you're the real thing, as he puts it. I hope so, because, Ms. Haws, dark days are upon us. I came to warn you. I've stepped away from the move to have your license revoked. Dem has told me many things. I've recently begun to realize I may not have always been correct in my political stands." He shrugged. "Watch yourself." He touched her arm as he moved past. "Please."

*R*oman sat in yet another meeting, his skin crawling with his need to get out and see Abbie.

But it wasn't going to happen any time soon because the treason trials were starting and he had to be the face of the Council several times a day, every day. And he had to meet with people and reassure them. His entire life had suddenly become all about trying to calm people down.

And it didn't help that the Imperialists had been pushing at him, had been encroaching in Edge 'Verses. Breaking treaty rules to goad him into making a rash decision.

But he wasn't a rash man. Except for Abbie. Wasn't he allowed to have one small thing? One beautiful thing that made his life all right?

He realized someone had been addressing him and he sighed inwardly as he struggled to concentrate.

Thankfully, the meeting finally ended and he shuffled from the conference room, took the stack of papers Marcus handed him and kept moving to his next meeting. A meal with the Five. The Five were the five highest-ranking Families, and together they dominated the Council and governance in general.

Because the treason trial of Perry Walker had begun just days before, all five Ranking members or first or second sons were in the capital to watch the proceedings.

Marcus had arranged a dinner at Roman's home, so he hurried into his conveyance. At the door he turned to his assistant.

"Marcus, go home. Jaron's trial begins this week and you need to be there for him. You've been working nonstop lately. Get some rest. Mercy will have everything handled at my home."

Marcus looked relieved. "Thank you, Roman. Comm me if you need anything."

Abbie knocked on Marcus's door, not surprised when he opened it to find Nyna there as well. Since they'd had a meal at her café, her sister and Marcus had been nearly inseparable.

"Abbie, what an unexpected pleasure. Please come in." Marcus kissed her cheek and took her coat as she stepped inside.

"I . . . I didn't know what to do so I thought you might know."

Concern marred his handsome features and Nyna came over. "Abbie? Is everything all right?"

"Rumors. Oh gods, there are rumors about me and Roman. Alexander came to see me in my office. He warned me. And Logan heard, too. From Haerv at lockup. I think House Kerrigan knows. I don't know. I'm—" She tossed her hands up and began to pace before Marcus shushed her and gave her a hug.

"Abbie, it's not the end of the 'Verse if you're found out. Tell me exactly what was said. Maybe it's just jealous people seeing you get access. You know how Saul is. He's a low human being. He'd naturally assume things."

"A vid crew was in the lobby of my building asking me to comment on the statement from House Kerrigan that I'd used my improper relationship with Roman to get things! I avoided that part and addressed the rest. Logan said Haerv sneered about my involvement with Roman and then Alexander was in my office. Sitting at my desk! You have to warn Roman."

"He's at a dinner with the Five tonight, Abbie. The trial has stirred up all sorts of stuff. I'll speak with him tomorrow when he comes in to the office. He has early meetings, so I can catch him quickly. It sounds like someone somewhere knows about you two."

She sighed heavily. "I need to go home. I just wanted to get word to Roman, to warn him. I'd hate for him to get surprised by this."

"Are you going to be all right?" Nyna asked.

"I'm losing him. It has to end now before he's exposed and it can be used against him. I can't be that to him." It would break her heart to know she caused him hurt.

Marcus took her shoulders. "Abbie, you stop it right now. He knew what he could be in for when he started with you. And I've never seen him throw away the rules for anyone or anything before. You mean something to him. The time you two have had, he's been lighter, happier than I've ever seen him. That's not hurt. I just wish—"

"Don't we all?" She shrugged back into her coat. "I've got to go. I've got work to do. Just tell him. Please."

Nyna kissed her cheek and hugged her, as did Jaron and Marcus, and she was off again, alone.

Chapter 26

The high ceilings of the grand adjudicant's courtroom soared overhead as Roman sat in the audience. Perry Walker's testimony would be heard that day, and he needed to be there to put a Family face on the proceedings.

Ash Walker sat on his right along with his father Angelo. As the second most powerful family, the Walkers had suffered a huge backlash when it came to light that three of their members had been part of the treasonous conspiracy with the Imperialists that had led to the deaths of hundreds of Federation citizens.

Their position was precarious, and House Holmes sat on Roman's left in solidarity. They all needed to stand strong and united in the face of this mess. To be sure those guilty were punished and to keep the Federation 'Verses moving forward instead of mired in personality issues and power squabbling.

House Pela sat behind them, along with House Khym. The Five stood united against the threat posed by upstart Families like Licht and Gayle, who currently agitated to try and shake up the Five and have a less powerful Family put into the Five.

The last thing the Federation 'Verses needed was *more* instability. The Council should all be standing together but instead, Roman had to deal with a constant barrage of petty infighting.

Roman had come straight from home to the courtroom. He needed to get in touch with Marcus at the next break. Marcus had left him several comms but Roman had been so busy he hadn't been able to contact him yet.

When the break finally came, he went outside to use one of the nearby Family offices to contact Marcus but he saw Abbie walking out from another hallway. The light glinted off her hair, so black it was nearly blue. Her forehead was furrowed, and as he neared her, he saw the dark circles beneath her eyes.

"Ms. Haws. How are you today?" he called out.

She stopped and smiled when she saw who it was. "Mr. Lyons, I trust you're well?"

"I'm attending the trial." He didn't need to specify, even to Abbie, who had her own stack of trials.

"Oh. I meant to try and stop in but I had a meeting. The MRD." She licked her lips and his cock hardened. "Did you speak to Marcus? Things are complicated. I need to talk to you."

She sighed heavily and he moved closer, lowering his voice, "Things are very bad just now, Abbie. Ever since the plot with the Imperialists has been exposed, our relations with them have deteriorated. 'Verse-wide relations have suffered as well. The Families are fighting amongst themselves. I'm walking a fine line and I'm afraid if I make a mistake I'll plunge millions upon millions into war." He needed her to understand just what he was up against. The stakes were very high, and with the pressure on House Walker, he feared, truly feared, what the outcome of agitation from the unranked would be.

"Are you asking me to wait?" Abbie had eaten him up with her gaze as he'd approached. He was so beautiful, powerful and sexy. She clutched her bag. The truth was, of course, she wanted representative democracy. But not at any price.

He looked at her, his gaze sharp at first and then softening. "Where did you come from? You're like a miracle to me and I can't have you. There are times when I'm in my bed, alone, when I'd trade it all just to walk at your side."

She blinked back sudden and unexpected tears. Not here, not right now.

Suddenly Saul Kerrigan approached with Parvi Licht. A vid crew hovered just beyond, and Abbie wanted to throw up right then. It was coming and she couldn't stop it.

"Roman Lyons! Do you have any comment on the allegations of your romantic liaison with Abigail Haws?" the vid crew seemed to all ask at once.

Abbie blinked, trying to control her emotions. Selfishly all she could think of was how she'd never hold him again.

"My personal relationships are no one's business." Roman stood taller.

"They are when you're rutting with a woman who seeks to tear apart the very foundations of our rule! You're thinking with your cock and not your head. Isn't it enough that one of our most highly ranked Families has betrayed us? Must you compound that by your relationship with this woman? How can we trust you when you say her proposal is sound?" Saul accused.

Abbie said nothing. What could she say? This was Roman's situation, his problem to deal with.

"I'm not going to discuss my private life. Not with you, Saul, and not with a vid crew. I'm happy to discuss matters of 'Verse rule. I'm happy to discuss the future and our plans to deal with the devastating blow those in House Walker have dealt us all and also how Angelo Walker plans to move forward. But my leadership has been solid and trustworthy since I took the helm of House Lyons, and I will not have my integrity challenged this way. Lastly, Ms. Haws gives her life and her time to doing the business of justice here in Ravena. Saul, it's clear you have a personal issue that stems from your highly inappropriate harassment of an elderly woman formerly in your employ, whom Ms. Haws defended successfully. That woman raised my wife—your daughter, Lindy. That you have no honor and loyalty says far more about your accusations than it does about me. Now, good day. I have work to do."

He shook Abbie's hand, urged her to go down the hall to escape the vid crews and then headed off in another direction.

Abbie only barely stopped herself from running. Instead, she kept her back straight and headed around the side of the building and across the walk to her office.

From there, she told Tasha to cancel her appointments and hold her calls, that she was sick and leaving for the day.

Roman's hands shook as he closed the door and headed in to comm Marcus.

Marcus's face showed up and it was clear the vid feed had been live. "I'd been planning to speak with you about some rumors floating around. I see I was too late."

Roman nodded. "I need to get back to the trial. Please talk to the boys for me. They'll need to hear it from one of us if possible. I'm going straight home when this is over, but I suspect I'll need to deal with my father before the day is through."

Marcus hesitated. He wanted to say more but it wasn't possible, so he sighed heavily and signed off.

Ash stopped him before they were seated. "Roman, I saw what happened just now. I'd like to speak with you later. In private, if I may."

"Of course. I'll be at home this evening."

He heard nothing. Only saw lips moving as he sat there thinking about Abbie. About how he'd had to let her go just then when all he'd wanted to do was protect her.

And she'd slipped through his fingers like smoke. One moment he'd had her, the next it was impossible to keep her.

Chapter 27

Abbie trudged to her door after having wandered the capital for most of the day. Night had long since fallen, and the cold had fully come to settle into the bones of the city.

She'd avoided her family. Her father had commed her several times and she knew that would be a big bucket of shit to deal with, but she didn't want to just then. Her mother would be concerned, as would her siblings. Logan had commed but Abbie hadn't looked at any of the messages, just knew they were there. She should have felt comforted by them.

But she felt nothing. Just a desolate emptiness inside she knew would only worsen as her days passed. Would she even be able to say her last good-bye to Roman, or was it over totally? Would those horrifying moments in the hallway be their last? She'd never run her fingers down his spine as they were ready to tip into sleep. He'd never kiss her awake again.

Once inside, she didn't bother to turn the lights on as she headed into the bedroom and through to the bath on autopilot. Now that she'd entered her place, the reality of the cold and how chilled she truly was had become apparent. Her teeth chattered as she started her shower.

She stepped in, feeling as if her life had moved into slow motion, and she watched herself from another place, until the water hit and she gasped in a breath, allowing herself to feel it all.

She didn't hear the tap at her door as she sank to her knees, weeping as the water swallowed the sound of her grief.

Roman avoided vid crews, official requests for statement and comments about Abbie, and was grateful for the security detail who surrounded him as he rushed from the building into the waiting conveyance.

Home was a riot of noise and people. A crowd with cameras had gathered outside the gates, but fortunately the guards kept them all back.

Deimos and Corrin waited for him in the entry.

"Oh Dai, are you all right? How is Ms. Haws?" Deimos asked as he hugged his father.

"No, I'm not all right, and I don't know how Abbie is. I was in that blasted trial all day, listening to Perry Walker try and explain away his treason as if it were of no consequence at all that nearly four hundred citizens were murdered by this complicity. I wanted to shoot him in the head."

"Right after grandfather Kerrigan, I expect," Corrin said. "He's commed here several times today. Not happy with the house arrest you've placed him under."

"My people are working to find a way to hold him there for as long as I can. He can molder and die in that manse, for all I care. Boys, he devastated Abbie today and for no other reason than because she defended your mother's old governess. I can't abide that. And he's caused a great deal of upheaval at a time when I have more than enough to try to manage with these trials."

"Come on through. Mercy made a meal and Ash Walker is here, waiting in the family room with Brandt Pela," Corrin said.

Roman heaved a sigh, straightened his clothing and headed into the family room to greet his guests.

Ash stood when he entered, as did Brandt. Roman waved them to sit. "Please, here I'm just Roman, all right?"

He sat and Mercy materialized, left food and drinks, disappearing again just as quickly.

"Roman, do you love this Haws woman?" Ash asked.

Roman scrubbed his face with his palms. "I really am not up to this right now. Yes, I had a relationship with her. She's a good woman. But I don't want to discuss it or make excuses for it."

"Some time ago, more than ten standard years now, I loved a woman. An unranked woman. I'm a second son so, like you, I wasn't able to marry where I liked. I had to marry politically and the woman I loved left rather than become my mistress. Do you remember this?" Ash asked.

"I do. Gods, of course. Sera, Brandt's wife and your mistress now, right? You three are in a permanent triad, yes? I met her the other day. She's lovely and now I understand why you're here." He sighed. "Yes. I love Abigail Haws but like you ten years ago, I can't marry where I like, especially not now, with all this chaos brewing. And like Sera, there is simply no way Abbie would be my declared mistress, even if I wanted that, which I don't. All I can do at this point is break things off and move on."

"Roman, you've given House Lyons two sons. You don't have to do anything right now. You can have a lover who is unranked and perhaps in a year or two, you can revisit the issue. Things will smooth out after the trials and the unranked realize we will give them justice," Brandt said.

"I can't do that to her. She's active in the MRD, this movement to create an advisory council for unranked to be adjunct to the Council here in Ravena. She's a barrister. She will be open to enough scrutiny as it is. What can I offer her? A life where she can never be part of official events? She can't visit here as my lover. I shouldn't have ever started with her but I couldn't resist."

"Roman, listen to me when I tell you, letting go of someone you love will kill something inside you both." Ash spoke from the heart, and Roman heard the pain of the memory in his voice.

"Excuse me, Mr. Lyons, but your father is here and demanding you see him immediately." Mercy looked unimpressed by Roman's father's bluster but he also knew he couldn't avoid this confrontation forever.

"I'm sorry, I'm sure you realize why I need to deal with this." Roman stood, Ash and Brandt doing so as well, each shaking his hand.

"Comm me if we can help in any way." Ash waved, sadness on his face, as they left.

His father's step-click gait sounded as he used his walking stick and before long, Noah Lyons entered the room and heaved himself into a chair, glowering in Roman's direction as he did.

"What the blasted seven hells are you playing at, Roman? Saul Kerrigan is an oozing boil of a man, but you've given him a weapon to use against House Lyons and I don't like it. Do you have no sense of just how precarious things are right now? You couldn't just fuck a

Ranked woman? I've seen her, this Haws woman, on the screen. All day today, as a matter of fact. No doubt to her appeal. She's smart, too. Tough. I had my people check her out, I know what Bentan Kerrigan did to her but now so does half the 'Verse. Can't be easy for a woman to have to relive such a horrible event."

Roman heaved a breath. Noah might be insufferable on many issues but he was right. Abbie would suffer all because Roman couldn't resist her.

"I know you, Roman. You're not a womanizer like your brother. If you had something with this woman, she must be peerless. I'm not hurling stones at her character or even her background. But facts are facts, and she is not Ranked. You are not only Ranked but you are House Lyons. You cannot have her. You must give her up tonight and not look back. Do not act with shame; it would only hurt her and make you look like a cad in the offing. We've got enough Family looking bad right now. So deal with it. Make your good-byes but keep to them."

Roman nodded. "You're right."

"Of course I'm right. And we've begun discussions with House Holmes and House Khym for a suitable wife match for you. You can meet her. I know you'd want to court her and like her and all the things men of my generation couldn't have cared less about. But you've been single long enough, and an alliance with another strong House would be beneficial, especially right now." Noah pushed himself to stand and Roman followed his father to the front door.

"Resolve, Roman. You've always had it. Don't lose it now."

Resolve. Wonderful. That's what it was to break the woman he loved? Resolve?

Since he was now going to break off things with Abbie, Roman didn't bother hiding as he entered her building. It was very late so it was fairly deserted, but he wouldn't have been surprised if someone had been hiding behind a bin ready to film him.

The lobby was quiet, so he only had his thoughts to keep him company as he took the lift up to her door.

He tapped, and then again to no avail. Worried about her sleeping too deep again, and perhaps a bit that she was avoiding him, he let himself inside. The place was dark but he heard the water running and headed toward her bathroom.

That was when he heard the sobbing and it nearly drove him to his knees. He pushed the door open to find her on the floor of her shower in a ball, her hair covering her body like a dark, wet cloak. But the sound of her grief caught at him, driving home just exactly what his future held. And it didn't hold her, the thing he wanted so very much.

"Abbie, honey, please, let me help you out," he said softly.

She looked up, her eyes red and swollen. "Why are you here?"

He turned off the water and wrapped her in towels, trying not to look at her body, the body he loved so much. Briskly, he rubbed up and down her arms and then over her hair.

Her hands shot out from beneath the towels as she huffed indignantly. "I can dry myself. Are you all right?"

"Me? To answer your first question, I'm here because I had to see you, to—"

"Say good-bye," she said simply.

Roman heaved a breath and followed her into her bedroom, which still smelled of the two of them.

"I don't want to. You must know that." He was desperate for her to understand.

She turned, letting the towel fall away. He was unsure if the trembling was from the cold or nerves. "I understand. I know. We both knew it had to end. I'm just sorry it hurt you in the process." Moonlight shrouded her skin as she bent to grab a sleep shirt but he reached to her. Something bound within him unfurled when she moved quickly to slide into his arms.

"I don't want you to have to understand. I don't want this. I want to be with you and I want this thing between us and I hate the way things are."

"Stop moaning about what you cannot change. Stop it and stop wasting time. You're here and you won't be again so make it last. Burn yourself into my being because that's all I'll have of you after you walk out the door." Her hands slid beneath the hem of his shirt, against his bare back, her nails digging in to pull him closer.

He closed his eyes and fell into her. For the last time. His mouth hovered, just above the skin where neck met shoulder and he breathed, tasting her, smelling her, taking her essence inside him.

He groaned as he licked her skin, salty-sweet, and she arched. Desperation beat at him but he tamped it down, wanting to savor every last breath he had with her.

"I'm naked but you're not. I don't like that state of affairs."

"Mmm. But I like you naked very much." He took her breasts in his hands and then rolled and pulled the nipples until her pretty lips parted and she took quick, gasping breaths.

His mouth replaced his fingers, his tongue drawing under and around the nipple, first one and then the other. Her fingers dug through his hair, holding him to her as he took his fill of her skin, of the soft, needy sounds she made.

He lapped at her, loving the way her nipples hardened, elongated at his attentions. The air in the room had warmed with the air from her bathroom and her scent hung heavy—the scent of her flowery shampoo and of the heady honey between her legs. Her trembling from the chill had transformed to trembling in her knees and thighs. The good kind of trembling.

Once he'd gotten his fill he dropped to his knees and inhaled, pressing his face into that downy triangle at the vee of her thighs. She took a step back but he banded her thighs with an arm, holding her in place.

She was all he saw, all he smelled and breathed, and when he slid his tongue in between her labia, all he tasted. All her balance rested on him and he allowed her to rock back, landing on the bed, legs akimbo and nicely spread.

"I'm going to eat that sweet cunt." He was on her barely moments after he'd said it, licking from her pretty asshole to her clit. He would drown in her, revel in every delicious drop of her body as he ate.

She writhed beneath him, her hands grabbing at the blankets, and when he pulled his face away she cried out, her body arching up toward him.

"Hold yourself open, hold your legs open for me."

She obeyed quickly, her fingers digging into her calves as she held her legs up and spread for him.

Roman loved how she tasted, how the soft, swollen furls of her cunt felt against his lips and tongue. She let go and gave him every last bit of herself. Even then, as things were ending, she held nothing back, taking her pleasure in return.

His thumb slid back and forth against the pucker of her rear passage. She was so wet, the way was eased by her lube. He pressed just slightly inside as he pressed his tongue into her gate and she groaned, low and feral.

If they had more time he could have breached her there. But there wasn't enough time. He closed his eyes against the wash of pain at the realization that tomorrow wouldn't hold Abbie, waiting for him to take her, to make love to her, to fuck her and ravish her and give her his all.

Abbie knew there'd be bruises where her fingers dug into her legs to hold her body open for him. Knew it because she poured her emotions into that grasp. It was that or cry again and she couldn't. Didn't want to mar their last moments with tears and regrets.

He felt so good, so right there as he delivered the devastating pleasure only he could, touched her the way no one else ever had. Surely, boldly, and with total love and adoration. His mouth on her was worship and she'd never felt so beautiful as she did that moment.

Her orgasm built slow, despite the urgency within her. Every moment was just so, nothing too much, nothing too little. He filled her slowly from toes to the top of her head and when she ran over, when orgasm grabbed her, it was right. She knew it was there, knew it would happen even as tears pricked her eyelashes and she ruthlessly shoved them away.

She let it run its course, let it fill her and then drain away until she opened her eyes to see his face just above hers, eyes alight with love and sadness just before he kissed her.

Her taste simmered on his lips like soft words and they slid back into her system, changed by having been on him, in him. Like she had.

One-handed, she shoved his sweater off, pausing in the kiss only long enough to yank it over his head. She shoved him onto his back and scrambled atop him to kiss his neck. To sip from him just beneath his ear and to feel him buck as she knew he would. Knew he liked it, knew no one else would affect him the way she did.

She sucked the fleshy lobe of his ear into her mouth, nibbled a bit before moving to kiss along his jaw, pausing at his chin to nip it and head to his lips again. Abbie lost herself in those lips for long minutes until his hands cupped her ass and she remembered she had other things to kiss as well.

She found the warm, spicy hollow of his throat, the angle of his collarbone and the flat, solid muscle of his chest on her way to his nipple. She swirled her tongue around it before sliding her teeth against it.

He squeezed her ass cheeks in time and she knew he wanted more. So she gave it to him, kissing down his belly, down that sweet, beguiling trail of pale hair that led to the waist of his pants, quickly opened, allowing her to shove his pants off his legs, ridding him of his shoes and socks first.

When she got back on the bed she looked him up and down, so princely there. She closed her eyes for a time, just committing him to memory.

"Abbie, don't. Just . . . just love me right now." His voice was strained, nearly cracking at one point, and she shook her head, dragging the back of her hand across her eyes to rid herself of the tears.

She bent over him again, this time after she'd retrieved some lube from her bedside drawer. He sent her a curious look but she shrugged and placed it within reach just before she grabbed his cock and slid her mouth down, taking him in as far as she could. Once, twice and three times.

She let his taste make a home within her as she built him up, slowly and surely. Abbie dribbled the lube down his balls, sliding her fingers through it, massaging his sac until he gusted a deep, aroused growl.

And then she slid a questing finger down, past his perineum and over his ass. He tensed at first, until she slid her finger back and forth, the lube heating, adding sensation as she fired up those nerves she knew had never been fired before.

He relaxed, widening his legs as she probed a bit more, sucking him, keeping him aroused while she slowly pressed her finger into his ass. She kept it slow, slow enough to let him adjust and to keep him trusting she'd be gentle.

The lube slicked the way and his cock hardened impossibly more with each inexorable bit she moved within him. Until she brushed against that hard, smooth bundle she'd told him about and he made a sound, involuntary, deeply turned on. His cock throbbed against her tongue, hard, so very hard. His breath came out in short puffs.

"Gods, that's—" He swallowed hard. She stroked it softly while she continued to suck his cock until he groaned and muttered, nearly savagely. "Fuck, I'm coming. It's too good."

He flooded her with his taste and she took it all, not wanting to let go of any part of him.

She kissed his belly once he'd sort of calmed, excusing herself to clean up and try to get herself back under control.

When she returned, he'd closed the window coverings and turned the lamp on. A yellow glow cast his body into muscular hills and valleys. Roman Lyons was ridiculously beautiful.

"That was unexpectedly incredible." He grinned at her, holding the blankets back for her to climb in next to him. "I want the lights on for the next part. Once I recover, I want to fuck you and watch every part."

She buried her face in his neck and he stroked a hand up and down her back. They said nothing for the longest time. There was nothing else to say. It wasn't that she didn't know he loved her. It wasn't that he didn't know she loved him. But they both knew what would happen and that it was unavoidable, and so they enjoyed the moments they had left.

Finally, the fingers on her spine slid toward the side of her breasts and down to the nipples. She turned to face him completely, to offer him everything he wanted to touch and his eyes lit with pleasure.

"Will you ride me? Fuck yourself onto my cock so I can watch you? I want that memory of your hair sliding forward, of the sight of my cock disappearing into you, wet and dark from wanting you so much."

She nodded, kissing his breastbone as she climbed above him. He was ready to go and she angled him enough to slide back, taking him into her cunt. She shuddered at the ripples of pleasure echoing through her as he filled her up.

At first she didn't sit and ride as much as she rested her upper body against his and slid back on him, grinding her clit against the stalk of his cock.

It allowed her to kiss him all she liked, to feel the beat of his heart against her, to revel in the crinkle of his chest hair against her nipples.

After a time she sat straight up and swiveled in circles, his cock deep inside. He looked up into her face and she smiled.

"I love you. If you take nothing else away from this, know that you are my heart. Nothing and no one will ever fill the spot you'll leave empty," Roman said quietly.

"I love you, too. So much, I don't honestly know how I'm going to make it through tomorrow."

She laughed, only slightly bitterly, and smoothed the lines of concern from his forehead.

"I'll survive. That's who I am and I knew, we knew." She paused as he brushed against her sweet spot with the head of his cock. "I'd rather have had you for this short time than never at all."

"Gods, look at me. Look at me, Abbie, so I can see how beautiful you are. I have all I want and still I want more. But what I want most, I can't have. I've never had that feeling before. I can't say that I like it."

He reached up to cup her neck, her eyes locked with his, and she tried not to cry. Tears wouldn't make a bit of difference.

When she came it was with deep, rolling muscle contractions that made her limbs warm and heavy. His lips opened and he exhaled softly as she felt his cock jerk inside her.

Roman kissed the top of her head as she rolled from atop him and to the side. All he ever wanted was right there in his arms.

"You're going to need to keep an eye on Saul. I've got people on him now to try and protect you but I can't stop all of it. I can't stop the gossip and I can't stop the speculation. I wish I could."

She sniffed her tears away though her eyes shone with them and he wanted to howl his misery.

"I know. I'll talk to Daniel tomorrow. Today I guess. My father . . . I'm afraid he's going to try to use this. I'll do what I can to rein him in. I'll have Tasha keep all communication between her and Marcus or Deimos's assistant. I know we can't associate."

She sat up and he looked at her, beautiful and tousled from sex. He swallowed hard. "Abbie, my Family is talking marriage negotiations. Things are so bad in inter-Family relations, infighting, lesser Families fighting to try and shove Walker and Pela out of the way to take over. A marriage would stabilize things a bit. I—I'm sorry and

I want you to know I wish to gods it wasn't happening but it will be. I love you. I want you and if the 'Verse were different—"

A tear slid down her cheek, her bottom lip trembled and the cold, sweet splash of the tear fell on his belly. "But they aren't. I knew you'd marry again. I'm not ready for it. I'm not ready to see you love anyone else. But I know it will happen."

"Abbie." He sat up and took her chin in his grasp. "I will never love anyone else. You mean everything to me. And if it was just me, I would walk away from it all. But it's not. It's my children and the entire Federated 'Verses in such an unstable time. I've made mistakes and we're already on the verge of war. There will never be anyone else in my heart. You own it. Always."

She licked her lips, the tears flowing now. "Go. It's very late. I know you have to go and people will be watching you. I love you. Just know that, all right? Do what you have to."

He got up and pulled his clothes back on. "Stay here. I don't . . . I can't take it if you walk me to the door."

His last look at the woman he loved, the way he'd loved her most, was at that last moment before he turned and left the room. Her soft sobbing echoed in his ears all the way home.

Chapter 28

Oh gods, if one more person stuck their head into her office with that look on their face, the one that dripped with pity and yet, their eyes lit with curiosity, she was going to hurt someone.

Logan pranced in, boldly yanked her from her chair, laid a kiss hard on her mouth and then plopped down across from her, a smirk on his face.

She laughed. It had been the first time she hadn't felt like crying since that moment in the hallway the day before.

"Hello, Logan. And how are you today?"

He shrugged. "Better now. Thanks for the kiss. I feel all manly now. I'd ask how you were doing, but I know you and I like my balls unkicked. So how about you and I have dinner? We can go to Nyna's. I'm afraid with your new level of celebrity we'd be bothered anywhere else. Or I can make you a meal at my place. It's up to you

where, but not if. We are going to have dinner because I like to look
at you. Even if you look like seven types of hell."

She sighed. "All right then. Nyna's it is. Your flat, I'm sorry to
say this, always reeks of female. Usually pussy. And you're a horrible
cook."

One of his eyebrows rose. "I do like this general turn in your
language. And I'll pick you up here." He looked at his watch. "You
have another three hours and then you are done for the day."

He sniffed and swept from her office, leaving her shaking her
head with a smile.

She still had that smile when she heard someone enter sometime
later. And promptly lost it. Her father stood there, hair wild, eyes
wilder. Gods, he was *on a mission*. She'd known it would come to
this, so she steeled herself emotionally.

"Close the door and sit down." She wished she'd taken a blocker
for the headache she was sure she'd have by the end of the conversation.

"I can't believe you didn't tell me!"

"Tell you what?" She knew him well enough to know to keep her
voice calm and even. To give in and let him infect her with whatever
mood he was in would only make him worse.

"And you haven't returned my comms! You had the perfect in
and you wasted it. Well," he leaned back and crossed his arms, "now
you have another kind of leverage. If Lyons wants you to stay quiet,
he'll give us our way and right quick."

She held her pen very tight and looked straight into those wild
eyes. "I didn't comm you back because I knew you'd be on about
this. Not that you'd care that I just lost someone I loved very much.
Not that you'd care that my business has become the topic of con-

versation all over the capital. But that you'd want to use that for
your own gain. A fine example of your parenting."

A shadow of guilt slid into his gaze and she was momentarily
chastened. Just momentarily.

"Now, I'm telling you this in private to save us both the embar-
rassment. The MRD is my organization. I run it. I started it and I'm
the one who made the inroads with Georges's help. Not because I
slept with anyone, but because I've kept my eyes on the goal."

"The goal, Abigail? Having sex with a wholly unsuitable man
and letting him use you?"

He was so ugly sometimes. And a hypocrite.

"No, that would be you. Did you think we would never notice all
your special *protégés*? All the women like Robin who came into our
home and made our mother cry softly at nights because the places
you saw fit to house us in had thin enough walls we could hear her
misery? I'm not married. Roman isn't married. As far as I can tell,
that puts me miles ahead of you."

Rage. Rage at the way he'd ignored them for his mistresses and
his causes, his kids in the schools who worshiped the ideal instead of
who he really was, swept through her. It'd taken a lot of years for it
to bubble up. Abbie had wanted him to do right but he never would,
and suddenly that thin love he'd doled out when it was convenient
for him simply wasn't enough. It would never be enough. He wanted
her to be as soulless as he was, and she simply snapped.

"You will keep your mouth shut and you will follow along with
my plans for the MRD." She put her hand up to silence him, coupled with a severe glare. "And you will not challenge me, go around
me or make trouble for me. Or Roman. You will, for once in your
life, be a father to me and do as I ask. As I need you to. I've never

asked you for anything. Not ever. Not even when I was in the hospital and you didn't come see me once because you were off on a trip with yet another one of your protégés. I'm asking you now. But if filial duty won't move you, you should know I've had more than enough from you and the rest of the world today and I will *make* you behave if you won't do so because I ask. We both know I have enough to discredit you. I'd rather not hurt you. Despite your horrible parenting, I do love you and I certainly love my mother, whom you do not deserve. Now, get the hells out of my office before I say anything else I'll regret."

He opened his mouth but no sound came out. Shame-faced, he got up and left without another word.

An hour later Logan came in and she said nothing, did nothing but place her arm in the coat he held out.

They walked, the cold air peeling away the layers of apathy she'd shrouded herself in all day.

"I saw your father come in earlier. Are you all right?" Logan put his arm around her shoulders.

"I said some pretty harsh things to him, Logan. But I've thought about it a lot since it happened and they needed to be said. I hope he listens to me and backs off. If he doesn't, I'll have to go through with what I told him I'd do."

He took a deep breath and exhaled, a shroud of fog around his face a moment as they got near the door to Nyna's café.

He stopped, turning to face her. "I've known you a long time. I've loved you almost as long. You are many things but rash isn't one of them. I know that if you said what you said to your father, it needed to be done. And I know you must love Roman Lyons very much to have risked what you did." He kissed her forehead as tears returned.

She wiped them away with the back of her hand, her glove sucking up the wetness. "You're making me cry. Just when I was pretty sure I had no moisture left in my body to cry with. Thank you. I love you, too."

Nyna came bustling over, kissing Logan's cheeks and then hugging Abbie tight, murmuring into her hair. "I'm glad you're here. Come on into the back. I've got a huge feast going. Daniel and Georges are here with Mai. Marcus and Jaron, too, is that all right with you?"

"Why wouldn't it be? Marcus and Jaron are my friends. I can't avoid all mention and association with him, you know. He's the leader of everything. Now come on. I need food and I need a drink."

Nyna squeezed her again and led the way into the back room. Several people sent her glances, most of them friendly. This was her base, her place, and these were her people. That was enough for the time being.

Marcus saw her, his face a crystal clear indication that he knew the extent of her situation. "Is it all right that we're here?" he asked as she sat down.

Abbie grabbed his hand. "Of course. Marcus, you're my friend. You're my sister's man. Of course you belong here."

He smiled and kissed her cheek. "Thank you. I'm . . . I'm damned sorry, that's what I am."

Her mother simply caressed her hair and kissed her cheek. "Honey, would you like to come home for a while? Stay with us? Or would you like me to come stay with you? I can take care of you for a few days. I ache for you. You're such a good girl. Roman Lyons is a fool to not see that."

Abbie smiled. "He's not a fool, Mai. He knows. But the 'Verse is what the 'Verse is. I can't have him. He can only have me as a mistress.

As it happens, I'm worth more and he has to seek a political marriage. It was a dead end, but I don't regret a moment of it." She shrugged. "I love him. I was loved. What more is there, really?"

Her mother nodded. "Yes, I agree. It's only that I love you so much. I want you to get everything you desire."

Abbie smiled. "Aww, Mai, if only, huh? If only."

Chapter 29

*B*learily, Abbie watched the vid screen in her living room two weeks later.

"Abbie, turn it off," Nyna warned.

"I can't! Nyna, at least I can look at him."

"Not like this. Come on. Why don't I just poke you in the eye? We can just go straight to the horrible pain part and skip watching this."

Unable to help herself, Abbie laughed at her sister. "Shut up. I'm trying to hear them fawn over Roman."

She turned back to catch a tall, genetically perfect woman deliver a sugary, peppy, fannish bit about Roman:

> *House Lyons' handsome leader, Roman Lyons, has never com-*
> *mented one way or another about his involvement with barrister Abi-*
> *gail Haws, but it's clear he's moved on.*

> *Lyons patriarch Noah Lyons has entered into negotiations with*
> *House Khym and House Holmes to broker a marriage. Will the golden*
> *Lyons choose the tall, lithe bloodlines of Holmes or the more politically*
> *powerful Khym, with some of the most beautiful and sought-after*
> *daughters in the Known Universes?*
>
> *Roman Lyons is being closemouthed about it except for one brief*
> *statement acknowledging that he is indeed looking for a wife. It'll be*
> *nice to grow old with a woman to take care of him after all these years*
> *of raising his sons alone.*

Perfect Polly there smiled dazzlingly into the screen and Abbie
curled her lip as she shut the feed down.

"I've never seen a woman I wanted to shove into the meat grinder
more," Nyna said. "Well, until we see the hag Roman will marry.
We will tear her to bits, of course."

Abbie sighed and went to sit back next to her sister.

"I feel sorry for her. Whoever she is. Can you imagine just being
traded off like that? Like you're a sack of grain or a pretty bauble?"

"That's well and good, Abbie, but she's getting in your way. Roman loves you. Marcus says he's miserable and is terribly grouchy
all day long."

"Even worse, then. Being married to a man who loves another
woman! And good. He should be miserable. I'm miserable. I'm miserable because he made me love him and there he is all pretty and
cultured, and even if he doesn't love this woman, he will make her
feel cherished and she'll be the one next to him at night where I
should be. And I can't, all because my father wasn't Ranked."

She stood up and began to pace.

"I ask you, Nyna, how fucking fair is that? I've been good. I've
helped people. I'm working to make the 'Verse a better place. I

never railed against my fate after the attack. I *deserve* this man! And she's going to have him. Why?"

"Finally. Gods, I've been wondering when you'd get mad. Watching you mope around for the last nearly two weeks has been ridiculous. Get mad. It is stupid. It's fucked up."

"And then, the AC was supposed to meet to tell me what was going on with our proposal, but that got delayed because of the trials and this damnable mess. You'd think fucking me was as bad as a mass execution. I am a good person! I don't need to have people shoving cameras in my face asking me how good Roman was in bed."

"You did show remarkable restraint by not shoving that camera up his ass." Nyna put her feet up on the low table in front of the couch.

"It's not fair!" Abbie pounded her fists against her thighs. "I've never felt this way about anyone and it has to be the one man I can't have? Why? What did I do? His precious Familial system! It's hateful and backward and I hate it! I hate it. I hate his duty. I hate his honor. His resolve to do the *right thing*. Well, I'm the right thing. He says he loves me. I *believe* he loves me. But he walked away. Am I not allowed to have this one thing? Is he not allowed? Is that what this is about? He's had everything with sparkles on top his whole life so now when there's something he really wants he's being punished somehow?"

She bent, resting on her haunches and screamed, low and guttural. And collapsed on the floor.

"I hate this time in my life."

"You deserve to. Abbie, you're such a good person. If anyone in this 'Verse deserves happiness, it's you."

Abbie heaved a breath and sat up. "I'm over it now. Not really; I'm lying. But I don't want to talk about it anymore."

Nyna snorted. "Fine. Why don't you tell me what you said to

Dai to make him keep his mouth shut. I know you had words. It got around."

"It doesn't signify. It needed saying. It's over. So far he's keeping out of my way so hopefully he'll continue with that. Anyway, why are you here? The arguments in Jaron's trial start tomorrow. Doesn't Marcus need the company?"

"The mother is here. She came to visit, got some official leave from her priests. Can you believe in all this time since the arrest she hasn't even been here? You couldn't keep me away from my child like that. But why should she bother now, she tossed him away when he was a baby." Nyna shrugged.

"I like you with Marcus. I can't imagine why he would care that you were there. He doesn't love Jaron's mother. Hells, he barely knows her."

"He wanted me there. I guess I felt weird."

Abbie rolled her eyes and pulled her sister from the couch. "Get the fuck outta here. Go to him. Be with him. I saw him earlier, he's a mess." She shoved Nyna's coat on, slapping the hat on.

Nyna hugged her. "You're the best. My best friend. You do deserve to have Roman. I wish I could make you happy."

Abbie shrugged. "That's life. Now go." She shoved her sister from the doorway and watched her rush to the lift, anxious to be with her man.

She heaved a sigh and shut the door behind her.

Abbie took a bracing breath and headed toward the courtroom door. It was day one of the murder trial for Jaron. Tensions were high all over the capital.

Vid crews blocked the way, and internally, she clicked off her emotions and readied herself.

She only said, "I cannot comment on an ongoing case. As you all well know." Satisfaction slid through her when a particularly burly security guard made way for her to get to the door by shoving people back. She hoped it hurt.

Once inside, the scene was only barely calmer. The room was packed, given not only the nature of the crime but also the connections Jaron had to House Lyons and of course, oh so luckily for Abbie, her own.

Oh seventh hell! What was Roman doing here? She clenched her jaw and sailed past, pretending not to see him and not making eye contact. The last thing she needed was to have him on her mind even more. Gah! Could she smell him? She should hit him on the head with her case, that's what she should do. Teach him to be so attractive.

He was messing with her ritual. *Okay, okay, focus, Abbie.* She found her way to the lead table and sat, taking deep breaths. She pushed out the chaos and the noise and she opened herself up to quiet, calm and focus.

She opened her eyes soon after and found that inner place of calm before turning to pull her file from her case.

Marcus leaned in and kissed her cheek. "How are you?"

She smiled, letting him see the bloodlust in her features. "We're going to do this, Marcus. We're going to clear your boy." She shouldn't have made promises like that. She never did. One had no idea what would happen in a trial. But for some reason—mainly due to the huge amount of evidence—Abbie just *knew* they'd walk out of there having cleared Jaron's name.

* * *

*R*oman watched her walk past without even looking his way. His gut twisted as he caught her scent. He'd wanted to reach out and touch her, to grab her and take her out of the room and away, far away where there was no House Lyons and no Ranked marital rules.

But where was that? He'd asked himself that question repeatedly since walking out her door two weeks prior. Earth? Now a wreck barely able to support her less than a million inhabitants. The Edge? No matter what, he could not escape the facts. She was unranked, he was Ranked. He couldn't very well make an argument that the Haws line was old enough and well-connected enough to make it an Associate House like he'd done with Kerrigan.

Abbie was beautiful, masterful, as she stood and addressed the adjudicator. Her back was relaxed. *Damn she is small.* Still, her presence was large as she made her opening case.

The inquisitor made her opening argument. Roman wanted to laugh when he noted it was her archenemy, the fiancé-fucker, as Abbie had referred to her. Abbie seemed to take an effortless glee at winding the other barrister up and getting her upset.

Roman had done this long enough to remain impassive on the outside while he laughed on the inside. Abbie amused him greatly that first morning as she laid her case out. He had every hope she'd prevail. It was her nature, he realized, to do so.

The light from the high casement windows gleamed off her dark hair, off her luminous skin, and he cursed his situation for the millionth time. He wanted her. Not some mindless, helpless twit from Holmes or Khym. He'd met three potential wives already and each one of them made him feel a thousand years old and his balls had crawled up into his body.

Nothing. Not just sexual unattraction but revulsion. They were all very young, and each a pale, pale substitute for the woman who paced slowly, sensuously, before them all as she outlined her case.

He hated to imagine her watching it on the vids. Hated that he hurt her. When he caught the vid shows and saw how she'd been hounded because of their relationship, he'd wanted to rush to her. But he couldn't. It had to be a clean break or it would only hurt everyone involved.

So he'd taken care of two things he needed to do for her and had tried to stay away. But he had to come today. Had to be in the room for Marcus and Jaron and, yes, Abbie, too, because he believed in her skill and Jaron's innocence and he wanted them all to know it.

He felt less warm-hearted toward Logan, the ex-fiancé, when he came in and sat near the defense table. He felt downright homicidal when he noted how the man touched Abbie's neck and leaned in close to speak to her during a brief break.

Realistically, Roman knew she'd move on, too. Hells, he was brokering a marriage! But he didn't have to be fair when he was raging in his head, he didn't have to be logical and he didn't want her loving anyone, didn't want anyone taking his place in her bed and in her life. He knew it was selfish but he felt it anyway.

At the end of the day, Abbie wrote a note and gave it to Marcus. "Please give this to Roman. I'm going to need him to testify on Jaron's character. Deimos, too, if possible. I don't know what to expect. Right now things are looking good. The inquisitor hasn't done much I'm worried over. But surprises crop up all the time. I want to hit hard with our case, use every single weapon we have, and they don't come much bigger than Roman and his son."

Marcus smiled at her. "Okay. You want to ask him yourself?"

She laughed, rueful. "No. I can't be seen speaking to him. It's not a good thing. And right now, I want this to be all about Jaron. I don't want any nonsense from the vids to cloud the case."

Marcus kissed her cheek. "Done. I'll see you tomorrow."

Jaron followed with a hug. "You're doing a great job, Abbie. Really."

"This will all be over soon, Jaron. I'll see you and your dad tomorrow."

They left and she gave them time to speak to Roman on the way out as she gathered her things. If she so much as looked at Roman she'd fall apart. So she just kept her focus on her things, on the papers in her hands and putting the correct folders into her case. Over and over.

Logan stood at her elbow. He'd been such a good friend to her in the weeks since she and Roman had split. Abbie wasn't sure she'd have been as together as she was if it hadn't been for him.

In a way, she wished she could love him again as more than a dear friend. Even the way she might have before Roman. She couldn't contemplate loving anyone else right then, much less investing in the emotional energy it would take to trust Logan after all he'd done. Friendship, yes. She trusted her heart to him that way, and that was enough. More than enough; it saved her just then.

"You did a great job today, Abbie. Come on then, let me do the male thing and lug your case. Then you and I have a date with the cinema."

"I really should work." She looked up at him and snorted. Not very likely.

"I know you. You've already planned out every single possibility and have created three alternative ways to deal with it. So come on.

A film, some down time. I'll have you back to your flat in plenty of time to get a good night's sleep."

"Treats on you? I know you just got a rise in credits."

He laughed and for one small moment, she connected to that love she had for him long ago. So lost in so many ways, was Logan. "You drive a hard bargain. Especially since I know you won't let me sleep with you when I bring you home." He gave a put-upon sigh. "But all right. Treats on me."

"Then you have a date." She took the hand he held out—the other was filled with her case—and let him lead her from the room. She didn't even mention that his little friend the fiancé-fucker was still glaring at them both from her table. See, she had self-control. Really.

Chapter 30

"This is ridiculous. House Kerrigan steps too close to outright treason for my tastes. House Khym moves to have House Kerrigan's Associate status revoked." Leong Khym, leader of House Khym, glared at Saul from the screen he appeared on.

Saul had simply given Roman all the ammunition he needed by breaking his house arrest to come and agitate there at the Council meeting, so Roman was content to let the man continue to dig himself deeper.

"I'm saying nothing many Houses aren't thinking." Saul sat, smug.

"Kerrigan is not a House. Kerrigan is an Associate House at the sufferance of House Lyons. Your status is up to me. I gave you Associate status due to the length of time Kerrigans had been here, and their overall relation to House Lyons. But I have had it with you, Saul." Roman was quite close to losing his composure.

"I am saying House Lyons's recent indiscretions with an un-ranked woman have put us in further chaos. I am saying we cannot trust the perception of Roman Lyons when it comes to this Movement for Representative Democracy or anything else. He is not thinking about what is best for the Federation but rather thinking with his cock."

"I have had enough!" Roman stood and the room silenced immediately. He rarely lost his temper, usually being the most calm person in the Council, but he had had it with Saul's behavior. "I suggest House Kerrigan produce evidence of malfeasance or neglect on my part or cease this line of inquiry immediately. I, that is to say, House Lyons has lost all patience with this temper tantrum. I will tell you, Saul, your behavior is destructive and not conducive at all to unity in this time of setbacks with the Imperialists. With the trials happening, your timing with these attacks on me is destructive, and I have to wonder just what exactly you think you'll gain. You'd risk making us all less safe for what?"

"You put me on house arrest for attending a meeting. That is not rational. I am saying what I think is best. You need to step aside. We can't rely on your leadership."

"House Kerrigan, as an Associate House, has no standing to make such a motion in this body." Angelo Walker spoke from his screen. "House Walker is not impressed with this behavior."

"Coming from a House being tried for treason, I'm not sure that's so very moving." Monitan Licht spoke from his screen.

"What was that? I'm afraid it's difficult to hear what's being said so far down the table," Proctor Feist said.

The Houses and their representatives all began to argue until Roman rapped his gavel and muted the screens. "That is enough! I will not have this insanity. The Imperialists encroach on our territory every day and we play these games with each other. I am sickened. Saul, I will meet with you later today about your issues if you do not have proof of my supposed illegal deeds now." He turned to Saul who put his hands across his chest like a sullen child. "Get out."

He made eye contact with Angelo Walker, then Gabriel Holmes, Vicktor Pela and lastly Leong Khym. He knew the Five were united on this issue and that's what mattered. Roman also knew the other high-ranking Houses were on his side. Time to squash this stupid infighting. The Imperialists had exploited their weaknesses long enough.

"Now that that is taken care of, let's address the real issue here. There will be no movement of House status. Period. I am well aware there is a move by lower-ranked Houses to try and use this time of strife for personal gain and I will not have it. Do you all understand me? House Lyons is a peaceful House; we have led with a gentle hand. But I will smack any House who continues with this destructive behavior. We cannot be scattered right now. Our enemy sees our petty fighting, sees these trials, and they want to use it against us. Will you let them because you are so mad with lust for position you simply turn a blind eye?"

Roman stood and began to move, slowly, surely, making eye contact with each House leader. "Will we turn on each other right now when we need to stand together? I want to make a few things clear to you, so let me be very honest. The Five are totally united on this. None of the other houses can make a move without at least two of the Five on their side. Moreover, I am aware that the majority of the other ten houses are also opposed to this silly behavior. You have no chance of succeeding with this. If you continue, House Licht, House Stander, and House Gayle, I will strip you of your status and award it elsewhere. Do not underestimate me simply because I have been merciful up until now."

He pivoted and looked at them again. "Yes, I know who you are. I am not stupid. Now get the hells out of my sight before I send in my troops to take your Houses now."

Roman stalked from the room, furious, and headed back to his office where Saul Kerrigan had better be waiting.

$\mathscr{W}$hich, of course, he wasn't. *Fool.*

"I want Federal troops at Saul Kerrigan's door right now. I want him brought into custody and I want papers drawn up stripping House Kerrigan of Associate status and I want it all done immediately," Roman told Marcus before he stormed into his office and slammed the door.

Not even ten minutes later, Saul Kerrigan was shoved through his door, red-faced and indignant.

Roman looked up after he'd finished the paragraph he'd been reading and addressed the soldiers. "Thank you. Please keep watch outside the door. If this man leaves without my permission, I want you to shoot him." The soldiers nodded once and stepped out. Roman couldn't help but feel a savage satisfaction at the pale look of Saul Kerrigan.

"Do not," Roman said as Saul began to speak. "I'm speaking now, and in case you've forgotten, I am House Lyons. You have been a disease in my 'Verse. I've given you multiple chances and you've ignored them in lieu of making trouble. I warned you when I put you on house arrest. I've been kinder than I should have been out of respect for who you are to my wife and children. But no longer. I have evidence you've been working to destabilize the Council in a power grab. Accordingly, I've issued a declaration revoking Associate status for House Kerrigan. You are now unranked. I will let you keep your secondary residence but staff paid for by House Lyons are being transferred to my residence and offices as we sit here." Roman paused to let that settle in. Saul began to speak but a widening of Roman's eyes stopped the other man before he said anything.

"Your other grandchildren will be allowed to finish their Family-funded education. However, your Family-provided employment has been terminated. I told you it was unwise to rankle me. I told you it was stupid to attack me and attempt to cause division in such times. And I told you not to harass Abigail Haws. You have violated all of these mandates, and for that you will pay. Now get out. If you do not comply, you will be thrown in lockup. Do not bother to try to raise voices against me, Saul. I have control of the Council. I have the power. I have the credits and I AM HOUSE LYONS!" Roman reined his temper back. "Get out now. You are a fool, and if I get any wind of you attempting to harm Abigail, or anyone else for that matter, you will *never* see sunlight again. If you don't believe me, ask Bentan. If you can find him." He went to the door and opened it. "Get this filth away from me."

Saul, spine bent, totally silent, was removed from the room. Roman knew he'd try something, so he'd put people on watch, and the moment Saul stepped out of line, he'd be in lockup.

Marcus came in a bit later bearing cookies and kava. "If I were female, I'd be offering to bear your children just now. Have a cookie, you deserve it."

"I wanted to shoot him in the head."

Marcus patted his shoulder. "I know, Roman, I know. We all do.

But he's gone for now. Not forgotten, though. You know he won't quit."

"I imagine he'll attempt to go to my boys. That's why I've summoned them here. Speaking of boys, how's yours?" He sipped his kava, feeling very satisfied.

"Today is a break in the trial. Jaron's home, trying to pretend he's not nervous. Abbie stopped by earlier to talk with him, reassure him and run through what it would be like when he addressed the adjudicator. She's been so good. Reassuring. She's very thin these days though. I could see her shoulder blades sticking out earlier. Nyna is worried. Abbie isn't sleeping, I'm told." He paused and shook his head. "I'm sorry, Roman. I just . . . Let me change the subject."

Pain and helpless rage, his constant companions of late, rose within him. "No. Marcus, I want to know about her. I want to know she's all right although it sounds as if she's not. Gods know I'm not. But I'd hoped she was faring better. I saw her with that Logan fellow."

Marcus snorted. "He's a friend, Roman. Nothing more. He takes her to the cinema, to dinner. Keeps her focused on other things. She doesn't look at him like she looked at you. But eventually, you know it will happen. She'll move on. It's not fair of you to think she won't."

"I know she will. Part of me wants her to, just so she's not suffering and alone. A small part, I admit. Listen, I have something for her. Take the rest of the day off. I want you to have this delivered. Not from you. But from a courier." Roman handed a thick envelope to Marcus who took it without question.

"All right. Why don't you come by tonight? It's just me and Jaron. Nyna has to work."

"Why don't you two come to our house? I'll have Mercy do up something special. The vid crews can't get into the compound."

"Good idea. All right, we'll see you later today then."

The news of House Kerrigan being stripped of its Associate House status was all over the capital and Abbie had to hide her elation. Saul Kerrigan was trash and it was about time he got his.

Still, she wished she could have spoken with Roman about it. Abbie knew he would be hard when he had to, but it couldn't have been easy for him, making such a decision. House Kerrigan wasn't huge, but there were several dozen people who would feel the choice. At the same time, a House is only as strong as the person leading it. It was up to the members of that Family to be sure they were being represented fairly and appropriately.

It also didn't help her sympathy when a vid crew had burst into the hearing she'd been in and shouted the news, asking for her reaction to it.

What it meant was that she would not be asking Roman to testify at Jaron's trial. It would just add a level of sensationalism that wouldn't be fair to Jaron or anyone else. It would also open Roman up to questions about his relationship with Abbie, because his truthfulness would be in question. And whether he'd lie to protect a lover would be reason enough to ask him about their affair.

So for the first time in her career, she'd let her personal life affect her professional life, and the guilt of it nearly eradicated her pain at not being with Roman.

"What the hells is wrong with you, Abbie?" Daniel walked into her house like he lived there.

"Why, hello, Daniel. I must have missed your knock."

"I didn't knock. I'm hungry. Got any food?"

She sighed and made him a sandwich. "Why are you here harassing me instead of finding a woman? Then you can harass her." She put the plate down and he inhaled the food in minutes.

"Good gods, Daniel! You know I'd like to remind you your mother and sister run a café. You can get food with them if you feel unable to procure or make your own."

He wiped his mouth on the back of his hand and she grimaced, handing him a kitchen towel.

"I know. I was just there a while ago. You were the topic. Everyone is worried, so I was enlisted to come and figure out what your problem is."

"Lovely. Look, I broke up with someone I love and he's planning to marry someone else. It's not a puzzle."

"Abbie, you're too thin. You look less than healthy and I know you, it's more than the Roman thing. You can't feel bad that House Kerrigan lost association. If you do, I will hurt you."

She sighed and told him about the whole testimony thing.

"Oh, so you're taking on the weight of this because you were in love with someone, did a favor for him and his friend by taking on this case. And because he is all-powerful and can't be seen to touch unranked flesh, it's your fault. I see. Makes total sense. Because this should be the fault of the unranked, too. Saul Kerrigan using his rapist relative to try and shake you. The tantrum he threw in public. The way he's been planning with Licht to try and shove Walker and Pela from the Five. This is all your fault."

"Daniel, how do you know about that stuff with Licht?"

"I just do. I'm telling you this because I want you to understand a few things. This shit is not your fault. It is Roman's fault. He never should have touched you, but he did, and of course it got found out.

How he thought people didn't watch his every move, I don't know. In any case, you have not endangered Jaron by this. Deimos knows him better anyway, you said. And you have many character witnesses. The friend of Jaron's father isn't as powerful a witness as the also powerful Ranked friend of Jaron who's known him since they were tots. So stop taking the 'Verse on your damned shoulders. You aren't that important, honey. I love you more than anyone else in the Known Universes, you know that. But you can't make yourself responsible for everything because you actually allowed yourself to have a life."

"What are you talking about? What's that about Roman being watched? And—" Daniel put two fingers over her lips to silence her.

"Stop interrupting me. House Kerrigan are traitors. Period. Roman did the right thing, and while part of it was about you, it was the right decision. You need to eat more and sleep more and stop eating guilt like sweets. You are not responsible for everything in the world."

She crossed her arms. "I do no such thing. I don't take on everything that way."

"You've been Dai's chief apologist for many years. It took you this long to finally tell him to shut up and back off. No, I don't know what you said but I'm glad you did. He needed to hear it. And for what it's worth, I'm on him, watching him to be sure he keeps shut. Just, you know, live your life. Not with Logan. He's a nice guy, but no matter what he's doing now, he'll cheat again if you take him back. But you're a beautiful, intelligent woman, and you are old enough to be looking for a man who'll love you forever. Who you can build a future with."

Abbie sighed. "You know, I'm not an idiot. I know you're doing more than consulting with that security firm. Also, does Roman know people are watching him?"

"If you know what I am, stop talking about it. And I imagine Roman does now, yes. Now, you and I are going to eat a meal and then you are going to sleep. You have a big day tomorrow with the trial, and of course, in the wake of all of the Kerrigan stuff, the vid crews will hound you more. I've assigned someone to you; a bodyguard, if you like. He will be with you from the moment you leave here in the morning until you return. I've also got people outside."

She stood up. "Oh, no, you did not! Daniel, this is silly. I'm fine. I know how to walk past a vid crew."

He stood and took her upper arms. His features were taut and a part deep inside her felt fear. This was Daniel, her rock. When he was worried, things had to be bad.

"This is inevitable. So accept it. There's a lot of stuff going on right now, Abbie. Dangerous stuff. You're a target for those who are upset their way of life is being challenged. You're a rabble-rouser, a small woman with a big mouth, and you're trying to tear down their unquestioned rule. Worse? It looks like you may succeed and their precious House Lyons is protecting you. This puts you in danger more than you know, and I'm going to protect you. More than just me; this is from above me as well. I'm telling you because you deserve to know. Whether you like it or not, I don't care."

"Why, Daniel? This is ridiculous. I've been rabble-rousing for years. It's my daily bread. All this is because I fucked Roman?"

He kissed her forehead. "Gods, you're naïve. You know things are bad. You've seen the vids, you've read the 'Verse-wide feeds. House Lyons just disassociated a House. Things are dangerously unstable.

And you, Abigail Haws, are a fucking one-woman conduit. For the unranked who are sick of waiting, for the Ranked who are scared of finally accepting that after millennia they have to share power and things will change. Hells, even for the Ranked who want the change. I've been out and among people. You haven't seen it because you're on the defensive over this affair stuff. Abbie, you're a symbol. A folk hero, they used to call it."

"Great, I'm a symbol." She threw her hands up. "I can't be a symbol. I'm too busy."

He laughed and let her go. "Honey, better you than someone like Dai, right? Anyway, it's you because you're busy. You're decent and honorable and you've spent your life helping people." He tossed her coat at her. "Come on, Nyna is waiting."

"You just ate!"

"That was a snack."

A knock sounded on the door just as she was opening it. A courier stood there and another man loomed at the end of the hall near the lift. He nodded to Daniel, who'd shoved himself into the doorway. Daniel tipped his chin and then stood back. This would get old very fast.

"Are you Abigail Haws?"

"Who's asking?" Daniel asked gruffly.

The courier produced identification, which Daniel didn't even bother to let her see before handing it back to him.

"He's legitimate."

"Yes, I'm Abigail Haws."

He handed her a thick envelope. "From the Ministry of Housing."

She took the envelope and signed for it. The nervous courier quickly left and she stepped back into the flat, closing the door and locking it again.

"Why don't I open that?"

She pulled the envelope out of his reach. "I have some suggestions about things you can do, if you like. At least I know it's not a criminal complaint or a summons. Housing doesn't send those," she mumbled, slitting the envelope open and pulling the contents free.

After a quick view, she had to sit.

"What? What is it?" Daniel practically danced around trying to see the papers she'd clutched to her chest.

"I've been on a wait list to get a flat nearer to a vent for three years. I apparently finally reached the top."

"Why do you look so upset? This place is cold, you complain about it all the time. A building nearer to a vent means it'll be warmer and you'll have a better energy feed too."

"It's not just near a vent, it's *on* a vent." The thought of it, of the glorious heat in the cold season and the cool from the fans in the hot season, made her slightly giddy. But. "But, Daniel, the wait list for a flat on a vent is much longer than three years. And there's more. I've received a higher water allowance."

She wanted to cry at the kindness of the gesture. Not baubles, not dresses—heat and water.

"Why do you look like you're going to cry? Gods, Abbie, just explain yourself, because I have no idea why you'd be upset about this. Who cares if you got bumped a bit? Come on! Do you have to be totally good every minute of your existence? Sometimes it's okay to let yourself enjoy something, a bit of luck, if you will. Because we both know Roman did this. And so the fuck what? He loves you and he wanted to make sure you were warm. That's what a man does. He takes care of the people he loves. Let him do this."

Warmth replaced her sadness. He'd done this for her. A simple thing, and he'd done it because he loved her.

"I will." She stood. "And you're going to help me move next month."

Chapter 31

Abbie saw Deimos in the antechamber of the courtroom. "Hello, Mr. Lyons. Thank you so much for coming down here to-day. I know you're very busy."

He stood when she spoke and bowed over her hand. "Of course. Jaron is a friend and he needs me. And you asked. All you have to do is ask, and if I can help, I will. By the way, I thought I'd tell you in person that the AC has decided to recommend your proposal up to the Governance Council at their main meeting in a week."

She smiled at him, at that very good omen. "Thank you for telling me that. I'm thrilled that I'll be able to take this news back to my organization."

"An official notice has been sent to your office containing all the details. You'll need to address the Council and be prepared for a question-and-answer period as well. It may be—rough from certain quarters. But I will be in attendance along with the other four main

Houses the AC represents. We supported you, that is, those five
Houses, unanimously."

She nodded. He'd just let her know it wasn't totally unanimous
but the most powerful seats in the AC supported her. Okay then,
she could work with that.

"Thank you for your help in this. There's one person who needs
to finish testimony once the break ends and then you'll be up. You
should be aware that my relationship with your father may come up.
Just be honest and don't let the inquisitor goad you. She's that type,
but you're a Lyons."

He smiled and she saw his father in that unguarded moment.
Abbie fought touching him; she'd grown fond of Deimos, not just in
her limited dealings with him but through his father.

"Someone will come to retrieve you. You can stay in the room
after you've finished, if you'd like."

Roman watched Abbie question her witnesses. Watched each one
of them paint a picture of the same boy he knew so well. At first he'd
been hurt when Marcus had relayed that she didn't want him to
testify after all. But then after Marcus had begrudgingly explained
why and then told him how badly Abbie felt, how she'd felt personally responsible for hurting the case, his hurt had turned into anger. Silly woman had no idea how much she did for people.

Deimos came into the room and Roman liked the ease with which
his son inhabited his own skin. Deimos wouldn't be a good leader
some day—he was a good leader now. He'd step into his father's
shoes with confidence.

The questioning went well until the inquisiton had its turn to
address Deimos.

"How do you feel about Ms. Haws?"

Abbie simply sighed and stood. "Mister Adjudicator, the defense objects. Mr. Lyons's feelings on me are not relevant."

"But they are. It goes to the witness's motivation in testifying here today," the inquisitor said.

"Ms. Proctor, I will give you *very limited* leeway here. I don't like where this is going, so you'd better be sure it stays on track. Or you'll spend the night in lockup." The administrator looked to Deimos. "Answer the question."

"Objection, Mister Adjudicator," Abbie interjected calmly. "The question is very broad."

"Indeed. Rephrase the question, Ms. Proctor."

Abbie sat and Roman saw a slight upturn to the corners of her mouth.

"Mr. Lyons, would you say you were friendly with Ms. Haws?"

"I'm friendly with many people." Deimos cocked his head as if he didn't understand, but Roman knew he did.

"Be that as it may, it's a yes or no question."

"Yes, I would say I was friendly with Ms. Haws on the few occasions I've dealt with her."

"Would you do things to make her happy?"

"Things?"

"Would you alter your testimony for the sake of her friendship?" Marcala Proctor finally asked.

One of Roman's brows rose at the woman insinuating his son would lie or that Abbie would seek to have him do so.

"I am a man of honor, Ms. Proctor. As it happens I'm fortunate to have known Jaron Mach over the course of pretty much my entire life. It is nothing but my honor to stand up here and tell the adjudicator what a good and kind person he is."

"Yes or no, Mr. Lyons. Would you lie to protect your father's mistress?"

Abbie stood and objected. It was only Marcus's hand on his leg, pushing hard, that kept Roman from standing as well.

The courtroom filled with outraged whispers and derisive tones until the adjudicator banged his gavel and spoke loudly. "Order! There will be order or I will empty this room right this instant."

Abbie walked around the table. "Mister Adjudicator, I object to the words used in the question. Furthermore, I'd ask that the inquisitor be advised to be a professional or face sanctions."

The adjudicator looked at Ms. Proctor, who suddenly seemed to realize she'd gone too far. There was no peer panel in this trial; the adjudicator would decide. A man who'd spent most of his adult life as not just a barrister but as an adjudicator.

"Yes. Except Ms. Proctor has had"—he looked down and shuffled through some papers—"four such warnings for her unprofessional conduct. Therefore I will fine her one thousand credits and find her in contempt. I'm also placing a notice of this in her file and recommending to her superiors that she enroll in a professional responsibility course. Now, the next step is five thousand credits and three nights in lockup. Let's consider this closed. You asked if he'd lie, he said no. If you can prove your assertion, if you have one, through accepted avenues, please do so. Until then, this line of questioning is closed."

The rest went more smoothly. She had nothing really, and after she tried her little stunt about Abbie, all Deimos did was look even more earnest and paint Jaron to be more like a good, gentle boy.

"Thank you, Mr. Lyons. You're dismissed."

Deimos came to sit next to his father and Abbie caught Roman's gaze for one very long moment.

relentless   289

*A*bbie simply accepted that she'd always love him, and why not look? He was just right there, after all. So close that in two steps she'd be able to touch him. Stupid Marcala. The woman had been thrashed by Abbie in three of the four times they came up against each other, and she still didn't know Abbie at all. All that little stunt did was make Abbie angry. And when she got angry, she only wanted to win more.

She brought the two boys she and Roman had interviewed that day—it'd been so carefree then—to the stand and made no attempt to hide their histories, giving them no reason to lie and also giving Marcala nothing to try to prove.

When they'd ended for the day, all that was left were closing statements to the adjudicator. She'd already prepared her final brief. The case was ridiculously circumstantial and Abbie couldn't see, other than a rush to take someone into custody that first night, why they'd gone forward. It was a very weak case. It wasn't often as a barrister representing the accused that she got a case like this. Most of the time it looked pretty bad for her clients. Perhaps it was the gods making up for taking Roman from her.

*R*oman paced in his bedroom. Seeing her that day had stirred him up immeasurably. Seeing the love in her eyes as she'd finally looked at him, really looked at him, had shaken him, shaken his resolve to break off contact.

He sat back at his desk and looked out over the gardens in the grounds around the house.

He picked his pen up again and began to write.

Abbie,

When I saw you today, saw you in the courtroom so strong and self-assured, all I wanted to do was stride up that aisle, grab you and take you far away.

I wanted to rip the clothes from your body to expose your bare skin to my mouth, my hands. I wanted to touch you the way only I know how to touch you until you began to make those needy sounds that make my cock so hard.

You'd look up at me, eyes wide and seeing right to my very soul, and you'd give yourself to me. You'd hold your thighs open while I ate your cunt, making you come on my lips over and over again.

And then when you thought you had nothing left, I'd take you from behind. Lay you flat on your belly and slide your leg up high just how you like so much. I'd give you my weight to let you know it was real, to let you know I was your man there to fuck you for as long as I wanted.

Your cunt would welcome me, slick from orgasm, hungry for my cock and I'd thrust, fast and then slow. That wet sound of fucking would wrap around us as I entered you over and over.

I'd do this to you for days. Just gorging myself on you, letting you sleep here and there and taking you again once your eyes opened.

He stopped, his breath coming faster and his cock aching as he imagined her face, her scent, the sticky-sweet feel of her cunt, her thighs, the way she tasted. He fell into such a desolate spot when he knew it would be unfair to send the letter, just as unfair as the fact he'd never do those things with her again.

* * *

"*R*oman, you need to choose. Three women, all lovely, all amenable to marriage. Just blasted choose." His father glared at him from the head of the table. The letter still lived in Roman's head, and he'd far rather be with Abbie right then than discussing marriage with his father.

"Grandfather, he's a little busy right now. Let up," Corrin interjected smoothly.

"Bah. Busy. I heard you were in a courtroom with that woman today. You promised to stay away from her."

"Marcus's son is on trial for his life. Of course I went. Deimos was there, too. Anyway, I haven't said a word to her since we spoke last. Three weeks and I've done your bidding. I've escorted women out to the theater, let you negotiate to procure one for my wife even. Stop complaining."

"You're mouthy."

Roman looked at his father and then to his sister, who hid a smile behind her napkin. "I am. I'm told I come by it honestly."

"What are you going to do when she addresses the Council next week?" Alexander asked.

"Listen to her proposal. Given the current climate, I will most likely not speak until everyone else has."

Deimos looked at him and put his glass down. "You'd not support her? Her proposal is sound, you know that. If you supported her right off, she'd have an easier time of it."

"Or it could harm her because everyone would think he supported her because she had sex with him," Alexander said with a shrug. "I think you should simply not go that day. I'll take your place, or have Deimos do it."

"Why let her speak at all?" his father asked.

"Because she makes sense. Because right now I have had to order federal troops out into the streets of several cities across the 'Verses to keep the unranked calm after yesterday's testimony at Perry Walker's trial for treason. We can't ignore the unrest."

"Last time I checked, we were in charge. Why let them lead us around like pets?" His father sent an arched brow right back at him.

"I know you're being deliberately provocative but I'm too tired to play with you tonight. I had to endure a terse and tedious comm with Supreme Leader Fardelle. The man is oily. He denied, of course, that he had anything to do with the recent problems on the Edge. Said the skirmishes in the border 'Verses were provocations on our part. He demanded to negotiate on the so-called shared governance of three border 'Verses."

"I hope you told him to shove his proposals up his arse!" Deimos laughed.

"In more diplomatic terms, yes, but I did tell him we weren't negotiating to hand over any of our 'Verses and to back off the edge. Ellis got involved then. The man is frightening when he gets very gruff. He stared Fardelle into a stammering mess." Roman had been very proud of his comandante at that moment.

"I hear tell the unranked in some of the 'Verses have been hanging banners with Abbie Haws's likeness on them. She's becoming a symbol, Roman." Alexander paused and took a drink. "Be sure she's not martyred."

Roman nearly choked.

"What? Do you think I'd endorse assassinating our lovely Ms. Haws? Do you think so little of me?" Alexander's question sounded genuine.

"I don't know what to think of you. But I don't think little of you. I just think little of some of your opinions and how you go about your romantic entanglements. I think you're a good man to my children, to your sister, to your parents and, yes, to me. But I'm wary of this seeming change of heart on your part. What makes you suddenly so concerned about Abbie?"

"Your Ms. Haws cares more about Ravena than just about anyone I've ever met. I had her investigated, of course, when Saul first came to me. I learned much about her. And then every time I had any interaction with her, she simply proved to be an astonishing person. Bold. Pushy. Mouthy even. I can see why you want her. Even as I can see why you'll never have her. In any case, I'm not in favor of tearing down our entire system of governance. But that's not what she's asking. She's brave, your Abigail. I like that. I'd seduce her as quick as a blink if I could, you should know that. I'd love to possess a woman like her. But Deimos and Corrin would be angry with me and she'd expect me to marry her or some such nonsense." Alexander waved it away, attempting to fall back to shallow, and Roman realized, although not for the first time, how complex his brother was and what a shame it had been for their father to have been so focused on the first son and none of the rest.

Thank the gods he'd made every effort to include Corrin and let him know his worth. The boys didn't seem to have the same sort of rivalry and resentment Alexander and Roman had. Corrin preferred to create art and travel, which was a relief to Roman. He didn't want to have to choose between his boys that way.

"Thank you for your honesty, Alexander. It occurs to me that I have many meetings and only so much time. If I could impress on you to perhaps represent the Family at them more often, that would help me greatly."

Sophia smiled at him and then at Alexander, and Roman branded himself a fool for taking forty years to reach this point. But as the whole damned Federation seemed to be teetering on insanity just then, it was time to make steps, new steps, toward a better sort of unity and understanding.

Chapter 32

A bbie had been up since long before the sun, as she always was on a summation day of trial. She went out for an early morning walk in the cold. Snow fell but melted before it hit the ground. The cold narrowed her focus, kept her sharp as she ran her summation through her head. The bodyguard she wasn't supposed to notice hung back, and a new one kept ahead of her. She supposed it was the lovely death threat delivered to her building's doorstep the day before.

Daniel had gone off the deep end, insisting she either let him stay there or she stay with him at his flat. His cold, very small flat, reeking of single male. She'd tossed blankets and a pillow at him and made up her couch for him.

On her way back she stopped at Nyna's and got some kava while her mother chatted to her and made her breakfast. Daniel sauntered in and sat next to her. Her mother simply kissed his cheek and put two plates out. She must have known Daniel would show up.

"Mai, can you make up some kava and rolls with some meat and cheese? The guys watching me are probably cold and hungry."

"Abbie, they're working, not on a holiday." Daniel groaned but he took the hot kava and breakfast rolls out to them himself.

"Your brother is a good boy. Thank the gods none of my children got their character from their father."

Abbie never knew what to say to things like that. So she took her mother's hand and kissed it. "You're the best, Mai. I couldn't have asked for a better mother."

"I would have done so many things differently."

"And none of us would be who we are. I think we're all pretty good people. But if you wanted to make some changes in your life, I know we'd all support that and help you however we could."

"I'm too old for that. I have the bakery. If my intuition is right, I'll be planning a wedding soon for Nyna and Marcus. All you kids are my life. Now eat. It's summation day."

Daniel came back and the two ate quickly and companionably before heading back to Abbie's flat.

"I checked your new building out. It's very nice. Warm. Your flat is on a lower floor, so you should get hot water quicker and heat quicker, too. It's on a corner, so you have a lot of natural light and you're closer to work. Get that look off your face, Abbie. You're moving. It's a safer, more secure building. It even has a doorman and lift keycard access."

She tucked the last bit of her hair back and slipped into her shoes. "I feel guilty, Daniel. Other people have waited longer for that flat! Why should I jump to the front of the line because my ex has power?"

"Abigail Haws, everything in Ravena is about power. Stop pretending it isn't. How many times have you traded yours for someone else with less? I've seen you do it over and over. You are entitled to a little bit of selfishness. You've been on that list for three years. Take it, Abbie. Let him do this for you, if for no other reason."

"You're giving me that face." She let him help her into her coat.

"It always works on you. Just give in now and save us both the wasted time of a charade that you won't."

"*Hmpf.*"

She didn't really think about anything until she'd finished her summation. She walked into a crowded courtroom. The vid crews had shouted rude questions at her about the death threat and about her opinion on which bride Roman should choose.

Marcala began her summation, which was stilted and awkward. More so than usual because they didn't have a case. And because Marcala was a thousand credits poorer and most likely had spent most of the day before after they adjourned being yelled at by her bosses for acting like an idiot and making the adjudicator censure her.

She had not proved her case. In Ravena, the charging party held the burden to prove guilt, and they hadn't. Abbie didn't bother to take notes. Nothing Marcala said was worth rebutting anyway.

A nod to Marcala, a polite good morning to the adjudicator, a hand squeeze to Jaron, and Abbie stood and began to speak. It all spilled out, the evidence and the lack thereof. She believed Jaron was innocent. She believed the inquisitor was wrong and she let her emotion, her belief guide her argument.

And then she sat down and sound rushed back to her. Her heart began to slow, returning to a normal rhythm as the adjudicator told them he needed time to decide and would call them back when he had.

Marcala rushed out without looking at Abbie.

She turned to Jaron and Marcus. "I don't think it's going to be long but you never know. Keep your personal comm with you and I'll contact you. Go and get something to eat, all right?"

Jaron hugged her, surprising her. "Thank you, Ms. Haws. That speech you gave, well, it meant a lot to me to hear just how passionate you are about my defense."

"You're innocent, Jaron."

Marcus hugged her and took his son out.

She didn't go back to her office but stopped in at several places she needed to, filing some papers here and there, visiting a few clients, speaking with opposing barristers in a few cases. Just work to keep her brain busy. She didn't want to leave the building because she just had the feeling it would be today that they heard.

And as it happened, it was. Not even two hours later, the comm came. She notified Jaron and headed back. That's when she was waylaid by a vid crew.

"Will you be at the wedding then, Ms. Haws?"

She sighed and tried to move through. Her bodyguard made a hole and she headed through it. But just as she got to the doors she caught sight of a monitor to the right, and on it, Roman stood with his father and a tall blonde woman. The caption read: *Agreement nearly reached in the marital negotiations between House Lyons and House Holmes.*

"Go on. You can't undo it. Don't let it mess with your head," the bodyguard whispered in her ear and pushed her through the doors and into the safety of the room.

Of course it would happen. She knew it would. Roman had told her it would and the negotiations were on the screen every minute of the day. But once the papers were signed it would only be a matter of weeks until the nuptials. There was a cooling-off period where either party could back out until the nuptials and so, over time, nuptials had gone very quickly after the deal was made to keep anxious parties from backing out.

She reached deep to find some calm, but that spot was very low on positive emotions. Abbie sat in a daze as Marcus and Jaron came in, as the room filled again and order was called.

When the adjudicator found Jaron innocent and freed him, she still felt nothing. She hugged father and son and accepted their thanks. The noise and chaos of the crowd moved around her as she headed to the doors.

Roman stood off to the side and when she made eye contact the tears came and she rushed out, her head down, her bodyguard rushing with her, holding an arm around her to keep people back.

"She knows," Deimos said to his father.

"I know." Inside he was devastated. His emotions had been tumultuous and then had flattened into nothingness, an empty, cold place until he'd seen her face and known the pain on it.

"She got a death threat last night," Marcus whispered into Roman's ear as they hugged.

He froze. Fear for her sped his heart. And then anger that he hadn't been informed cooled his blood. "I'll contact Ellis right away."

"Are you coming to the celebration tonight? It's at Nyna's. I'm going to ask her to marry me. I wanted this to be over with first, but now that it is, I want to move forward with my life."

"Congratulations, Marcus." Roman smiled, meaning it. "Nyna is an amazing woman. You two are good for each other." He paused. "But I can't. Holmes is upset about the rumors concerning me and Abbie. I need to stay away from any contact with her. I can't risk it and it won't help anyway."

Marcus sighed. "You don't have to do this, Roman. You're House Lyons. You make the damned rules."

He shook his head. "Go on. I'll talk to you in a few days."

He didn't speak to anyone on his way to Ellis's office. Frustration that he hadn't been told mixed with pain at having hurt the woman he loved so very much. He'd hoped absence from her would lessen his feelings, but in truth, he'd only come to appreciate her more. He watched her from afar, having known her intimately. He got to know her in a public sense. He saw how she handled the vid crews who shoved themselves into her life at every turn.

What woman could compare? The tall and pale, beautiful Hannah Holmes was cultured and soft. She was raised to occupy a certain space and she'd make a fine political match. But not a partner. Abbie would take up his life, fill it with laughter and passion, something he'd felt. And now the absence of it chafed. Left him unsatisfied in a way he'd never experienced before.

He entered Ellis's office without knocking. His military comandante merely looked up from his vid conference and then back.

"I'll get back to you. Be sure to keep an eye on her at all times. Comm with Daniel on it a few times daily."

Wilhelm Ellis looked back to Roman. "I hear congratulations are in order."

"Knock it off. Why wasn't I notified of the threat against Abbie?"

"Believe it or not, Roman, I don't conference you about everything that comes across my desk. Imagine how time-consuming it would be for us both if I bothered you with every little thing."

"I'm not amused, Wilhelm."

He laughed and sobered quickly when Roman didn't join in. "Her brother is in charge of the guard team on her. He's staying in her flat. She has two guards on her every minute of the day now. There are no surveillance cameras in her building, so we don't have any real leads on who left the threat. It's in a busy area, lots of foot traffic all day and night. I didn't tell you because I knew Marcus would and because I wanted some deniability that you were using my office for personal favors for your ex-lovers."

"I want to know everything, Wilhelm. I may not be able to be with her, but I love her and I want her safe. If that takes a team of ten people on her, make it so. I'll pay for it myself. Send the bill to my home, not the office. This is not a joke. It's her involvement with me that's made her a target. I can't let that stand."

"Roman, it's a combination of things. I hate to poke a hole in your ego and all, but she's an icon right now. Over the last months her popularity as a symbol of increased freedom and visibility of a more empowered unranked class has grown exponentially. In the fourth ring there are banners with her likeness hanging from the public buildings. In the third and moving into the second ring there are fliers on the post boards with her face, quoting her words. Without you, she'd still be a target."

He sighed. It wasn't like he could prevent her from being Abbie, even if he wanted to. "I don't want her to end up a martyr, Wilhelm. She's addressing the Council in just a few days. Has the security been adjusted as necessary?"

Wilhelm smirked. "Believe it or not, I've been doing this for a little while. Yes, it's been adjusted. I'll send a report to your home comm with all the details. She'll be all right, it's my job to keep her that way. Now get out of my office, I have work to do and so do you."

"Gods, one of these days I might get a staff who shows some deference," Roman groused as he stood to leave.

"I respect you, that's better."

Roman snorted and left. It *was* better.

"*B*y the gods, Abbie, you're taking years off my life." Daniel paced behind her as she packed.

"This isn't about you, Daniel. I have to get out of here. I can't see this vid coverage. I can't. It *destroys* me every time I see it. There's nothing left inside me but pain, and I cannot live this way. I'm sick of being strong. I'm sick of pretending I'm not broken inside. I am broken. My heart is broken. So I'm taking a few days. I have the time built up at work, that's for sure. And Marcus was kind enough to offer his flat in the foothills. No vid screens. Just time alone. I can read and go on hikes and try to steel myself for this presentation I need to make."

He hugged her from behind. "All right. You're right, you deserve the time. But you can't be alone. The second threat note sent to your office is more than enough reason for you to let me and an-other guard come. I'm sending someone ahead to make sure the flat is secure and safe. Don't argue; it will make no difference."

"If two other people are there, I'm not alone. It defeats the whole, *I need to be alone* purpose." She put her hands on her hips but recog-nized the look in his eyes. He was implacable and she knew it.

As if things weren't already crappy, when she opened the door to leave, her father was raising his hand to knock.

"Come in." She stepped back, dropped her bag and shut the door behind him.

"What are you going to say to the Council? You haven't informed us of what you'll be saying."

She sighed. It was too much to have expected him to really change, she supposed.

"In fact, I have. I gave Georges a copy of my presentation and he posted it at the offices. I know he did because when I was there yesterday I saw it."

"We don't like that you've made yourself into a symbol. You're not the only member of the MRD." He glared at her.

"What are you talking about? Your complaint was that I hadn't informed you of what I'd be speaking about. Which I had. Now it's what? That I was asked to speak and not you? Is that the problem?"

"Of course that's the problem. He can't stand it that you're in the spotlight but you don't really want it. He can't bear to imagine you getting attention he craves. Isn't that right, Dai?" Daniel sauntered into the room and their father jerked to attention.

"You don't know a thing about it. I'm not the only one upset. This is an organization and she's the one putting her face all over the place. This isn't the Abbie Show. What about the rest of us?"

"I've been having the worst time of my life excluding the months I spent rehabbing from my assault. My personal life has been splashed all over the vids. I've been getting death threats and I have kept doing my job and the work of the MRD. I didn't design those posters. I didn't seek out that attention or notoriety. But, to be blunt, I'm the better face for it than you. I'm the one speaking to them and I'm not interested in making a personal platform for myself for my ego like you or Robin would be. Now, if you'll excuse me, I'm on my way out."

"Do you think I'm so uncaring? Really?"

"I think I just told you I received death threats and you didn't bother to follow up. I think I just had to watch the person I love on the vid screens next to a woman he'll be marrying soon. I think I've had enough and you don't care. Not really. It's not that you're evil. I don't think that. But I know you've been trying to agitate the staff against me and I have to ask myself, what kind of father does that? I don't even have any tears left for you. But I'm done making apologies for you. I'm done being the one child in the family who says, *'Oh, he doesn't really mean it that way'* because," she shrugged, "you don't care. Do not mess with this presentation I'm doing next week. This is our chance. At long last our chance. And if you mess it up because you're upset you won't get yourself a few groupies to fuck on the side while you've got a wife at home who cries herself to sleep, I will bring you down. I can and I will. Because I do care. This is our time. This is the time the unranked will finally get a voice in their own future. If you destroy it, I'll turn them all against you. You don't know how I wish I didn't have to make that threat. I really wish I didn't. But I know you. I can see the greed in your eyes at the attention you wish was yours. This isn't about you. It's not about me. It's about representative democracy, and I will not let you destroy all we've worked for. Now get out of my house and remember what I said. You might be entertaining an idea that I won't go through with my threats. Get that thought out of your head right now. I can and I will."

"Abbie, you've gotten hard. You're losing sight of the goal."

"The goal isn't making you into a viddie celebrity. I think that, of the two of us, I'm the one who knows the goal, the real goal. But you're right about one thing. I have gotten hard. I need to be, apparently."

He shook his head and left without saying anything else.

"I'm having him watched. Just so you know. Georges is also keeping an eye out. We can't risk him going solo on this issue. You're doing a great job, Abbie. You are. And you're precisely the person to do it. Don't let him shake your belief in that." Daniel hugged her to his side. "Now come on. We've got some traveling to do."

"First we stop by the celebration at Nyna's and then we'll be off."

Chapter 33

A sign hung on the front door of Nyna's café telling patrons there was a private party in progress and welcoming them back the following day.

Daniel and Abbie went inside and Abbie grinned at the sight. So many people had gathered, all of them smiling and laughing. Jaron sat at a table, looking like the boy she'd suspected lived within the scared shell of a boy she'd known since the arrest.

Marcus saw her and waved, with Nyna ensconced in his lap. Her mother bustled over and looked down at the bag in her hand with a scowl.

"What is that?"

"I'm going away for a few days. Marcus has graciously allowed me to use his flat. I'll be back the day before I address the Council. Don't fret, Mai. Daniel is coming along."

"Of course I fret. Did your father go to see you? He was in a right mood earlier today. I told him to stop acting like a spoiled child. I doubt he did."

"He did and don't worry about it. Now, I'm starving. You two have any food around here for a hungry barrister?"

Her mother looked as if she wanted to argue but let it go.

"Abbie! Come and join us." Marcus clapped his hands and stood up.

Abbie sat and her mother shoved a mountainous plate of food before her.

"We owe this evening to Abbie. Abbie, who muscled her way into lockup and got Jaron taken care of. Abbie, who argued until we got him out of lockup and allowed to be at home. Abbie, who investigated and hunted and found the people she needed to prove Jaron's innocence. And Abbie, who nearly reduced that room to tears. So here's to Abigail Haws. Thank you for living up to your promises." Marcus raised his glass and many others did with a cheer as well.

"Thank you. Now sit down! It's my job. And of course Jaron is free; he's innocent. Now let's eat." Abbie blushed.

"One more thing I want to thank Abbie for—she brought me here and introduced me to Nyna. My love and my heart. And, I hope, my wife."

Nyna's eyes widened and she leapt into Marcus's arms with a happy yelp. More cheers and toasts. A pledge ring was produced and slid onto Nyna's finger.

Things were good. Not perfect, but good.

After the excitement of the engagement had calmed a bit, Marcus approached. "Abbie, I wanted to introduce you to Thaniel. He's my cousin and he's just arrived from Borran." Marcus indicated a

very handsome man to his left. As ploys went, it wasn't exceptionally sneaky, but how hard would it be to sit and chat with a pretty
male over some food?

Thaniel was quite charming and clearly interested. They chatted for some time. He told her about his business. He conducted
charter flights for tourists and visiting dignitaries back home but
was looking to expand to Ravena. He was unmarried but wanted to
marry and start a family at some point.

When she readied to leave to catch her train out of the capital,
he stopped her. "I understand you're still probably healing from
your recent break with Roman Lyons. But I'll be back here when
the thaw comes. May I contact you then? Perhaps we can go to the
cinema or have a meal."

She swallowed hard. The thaw was four months away. What
harm would it be to have him call her then?

"All right. I'd like that. It was nice to meet you."

He didn't press. Didn't try to kiss or hug her. She liked that he
respected her space and the time she needed to heal.

"Enjoy the flat. It's fully stocked. Roman sent someone out to do
it." Marcus snorted. "He wants to help. So do I. We're going to be
related soon, so let me help."

Abbie smiled. "Thank you, Marcus. Congratulations. I like you
and Nyna together. You'll make a good team."

Abbie held the envelope, annoyed that Daniel had waited until
they got to Marcus's hillside flat before giving it to her.

"What if it's bad? You'd have traveled upset the whole time. This
whole area to that stand of trees and the stream is safe. I'll leave you
alone to read it." Daniel kissed her cheek and left her sitting on a

carved wooden bench. She pulled her cap down and snuggled into the warmth of her coat and opened the envelope.

His scent reached her nose and damnable tears pricked her lashes once again. She hated that she cried so much of late.

> *Dearest Abbie,*
>
> *By now you've seen the news of the nuptial agreement. I could tell by your face that you had. I only have yet more apologies for you. I wish things were different.*
>
> *I wanted to congratulate you on your success with Jaron's trial. Your skills as a barrister are masterful and I remain in awe of you on so many levels.*
>
> *No matter what, remember this—you own my heart.*
>
> *R*

Great, for all the damn good it did her to own it. It wasn't like it made a difference. He'd marry someone else and have babies with her. The children she would have given him will bounce on Hannah Holmes's knee. Or, more likely, Mercy's knee, and Roman's. Hannah Holmes had that look about her, the kind of woman who was raised to be sold away for power and position. She'd breed because that was part of her agreement, but she didn't seem maternal. And it absolutely wasn't fair of Abbie to judge her, but life wasn't fair.

Well, she had to deal with it. It'd been several weeks and nothing was going to change, so wallowing would not do anything positive. She had to learn to live with part of her broken. There was nothing else to be done but move forward.

How she'd deal with it, she wasn't sure. But she had a job, friends, family who loved and needed her. Many people survived each day on far less than that.

So she spent the next days hiking and playing cards with Daniel and Andrei, her bodyguard. She worked so hard that she had nothing more to do at the end of each day than to simply close her eyes and fall into a dreamless sleep.

Abbie had no idea what the vids were saying, but she convinced herself she didn't care. And when she got off the tram and walked back to her building, she turned to Daniel.

"I'm not moving."

He cursed and then sighed. "I knew it."

"How can I? Come on, Daniel. It isn't fair and it would be exactly what they're saying about me. That I used my sexual relationship to get special treatment from Roman. I can't. I don't want people to think that of me."

"Fine. Fine. I know there's no arguing with you. I had a feeling you'd be this way."

"But I will take the water allowance," she said as they got off the lift and headed to her door. "There's no waiting list for that, so I'm not taking it from anyone."

When they went inside she went to unpack and tossed her dirty clothes, along with everyone else's, into the laundry while Daniel and Andrei spoke in hushed voices in the other room.

"So tell me," she said when she was ready to deal with it.

"There was another threat. This time it was an envelope with toxic fumes inside. When Tasha opened it, she passed out."

"Oh my gods. Is she all right? Is everyone all right?" Abbie moved toward the door but Andrei stood in front of it and Daniel actually growled at her.

"You will not take your tiny little fragile self out of this place until I say so. Yes, Tasha is all right. She spent the night in the hospital; they flushed her system, transfused her. She's home now. Two other people needed to be hospitalized, some kid from the mail room and the assistant who sits next to Tasha. Everyone else is fine."

"Why did they not comm you at the flat?" A sinking feeling hit her then. "They did! You've known all this time and you were arguing with Andrei on how to tell me. Don't even try to lie to me, Daniel."

"Yes, I knew. But you needed the time and there's nothing you could have done. I kept in contact. You know if Tasha had really been bad off I'd have not only told you but arranged to bring you back here immediately."

She threw up her hands. "I have had it with people deciding what's in my best interests."

"Tough. Don't give me that look, Abbie. I'd do it again. You have color in your face for the first time in ages. You laughed, you played cards, and I saw more in your eyes than ghosts. I'll be fuckall if you think I'd infect your time to heal with something you couldn't have changed. Tasha knew you were away, and what's more, she instructed her doctors, your boss and then me not to tell you until you returned. So there. She's fine and at home and you beating yourself up over this isn't going to make her better."

"I'm going over there."

"Fine. But you're going to have a full security detail. This is serious business. People aren't just threatening you, they're trying to make good on it. You're to be guarded at all times."

"Says who?"

"You're acting like a brat."

"Because I asked who has made this choice?"

"Comandante Wilhelm Ellis of the Federation Military Corps. And through him, Roman Lyons, Leader of House Lyons. Ellis is very concerned for your safety. There will be heightened security tomorrow for the address to the Council as well."

She snorted. "Fine. But you know, in the future, when someone tries to kill members of my staff, I want to know."

She grabbed her coat and the three of them headed out.

Chapter 34

$\mathcal{A}$bbie took a deep breath and nodded to Andrei and her new bodyguard, Cynthia, to open the doors. Other security guards had been alerted and were waiting to escort them down the hall. According to Daniel, Saul Kerrigan couldn't make a move without everything he did being recorded and watched so she felt safe on that front at least.

Today she would make history. She, Abigail Haws, an unranked barrister who grew up with nothing, and yet would be one of only a handful of unranked to ever address the Council and the first to ever be granted an audience to officially petition for expanded governance for the unranked.

With her were her mother and father, her sister and brothers. Her father had delivered a slightly tearful speech to her under her mother's watchful eye. Abbie believed most of it and had asked him to come along. Marcus would already be inside to attend to Roman, but it would be good to have another friend in the room.

She wore her best suit, one purchased specially for this event. Her hair was up in a tight but complicated knot her mother had composed at the nape of her neck. She wore a pin on her lapel, a pin that had belonged to her grandmother and her mother before that.

The significance of the moment was framed most excellently by the physical space itself.

The building the Governance Council was housed in sat in the exact center of the capital. The spires rose high into the clouds. Paintings and photographs, statues and certificates lined the walls of the wide, spectacular Hall of Heroes.

Abbie had never been inside the building before and the effect was not lost on her. Generations of history surrounded her, reminded her that despite having a monopoly on power, the Families had done a good job on many things.

Doctors who'd pioneered the first vaccines for diseases that used to kill millions of citizens. Engineers who harnessed the vents to create heat and power to run all of Ravena. Military leaders like those who fought at Varhana, the battles that pushed the Imperialists and their slave traders back past the edge and underlined the Federation values they all held. Freedom from slavery, education for all, life and liberty. It hadn't been perfect, but it was theirs and she was proud of it.

A crowd had already assembled, and the closer she got to the Grand Council Chambers at the end of the hall, the more people had lined the walls.

Shit, that's what those banners look like? She noted the huge banners people held with Abbie's face and the MRD motto—*A voice for the voiceless. Hear us now*—emblazoned upon it.

"You're making history, Abbie. I'm so proud of you," Daniel murmured as he leaned close. "This is a momentous occasion. We are getting drunk when you're done here."

She laughed. "You are so right about that." Hells, she'd have pounded back a few that morning if she hadn't already been on the verge of throwing up from sheer nervousness.

Sunlight, filtered through the tall glass lining the upper part of the hall, marked squares of progress to the doors at the end. Abbie counted them in her head, seeking the calm in the rhythmic activity.

The noise from the crowds faded, even as she registered a less-than-friendly tone in some quarters. Not all would be for her plan. Not even all the unranked. Change was scary; she understood that better than most.

The crowd pushed in and she was jostled a bit, but her guards held them back and the security guards pushed to keep the way cleared.

The doors opened, revealing the burnished wood and gleaming surfaces of the Grand Chamber within.

"Ms. Haws, if you'll follow me? I'll lead you to the upper chamber. You'll remain seated there until it's time for you to speak."

Abbie looked up and up some more until her neck hurt.

The giant of a man nodded at Daniel and Charlie. "I've got it from here."

Abbie was surprised to see her brother nod and take a step back.

"Excuse my manners, my mother would whack my hand for that." He bowed. "I'm Wilhelm Ellis. I'll be your bodyguard here within the Grand Chambers. Everyone out there"—he lifted his chin, indicating the hallway outside—"has been run through weapons scanners just as you were."

She placed her hand on his forearm and left her group, following him up a staircase to a promenade of sorts, facing a tiered seating area. Audience chambers sat to either side of the tiered seating.

"So, um, are you saying you're expecting someone to try and kill me or something?"

"Ms. Haws, someone did try to kill you but got your assistant instead. I'm not letting you get harmed. Not on my watch. No way. It offends me."

She couldn't help but snort a laugh, making him smile.

"You'll address the Council from here." He indicated a podium. "A speech broadcaster is built in right here. Just use your normal voice. If you want to move a bit, it has a good range. You're going to be great. I've read your proposal and I think you make sense. Just speak from your heart and be aware that not all of them will want to hear it."

"Thank you. I do appreciate that."

He inclined his head and took a seat next to her.

That morning, Roman had awakened with a sense of calm. He wouldn't send Alexander in his stead. What would that say to Abbie? No, he would be there and watch her, send her some sort of moral support as she made a very difficult proposal.

He would see her, eat her up with his gaze. His beautiful, intelligent Abbie.

He arrived at the Council building to see a crush had already developed. He worried for Abbie, worried for her safety. He'd nearly had a heart attack when he'd been given the news about the poison delivered to her office. Thank the gods she'd been out of town and surrounded by guards.

His own guards materialized and led him into a side entrance. The noise from the Hall of Heroes was nearly deafening. Roman wondered how this day would end. Nothing of this sort had ever happened, and he had to lead it, lead through it and guide a solution. He hoped he made the right choice.

When the time came, all fifteen Family leaders filed out onto their seats. This was a special meeting of the Council, and each leader was there in person rather than by vid conference. They'd all attend the final day of Perry Walker's trial the following day. The ritual was in high form. Each man wore his Council robes, all lined with their House color.

Row by row, bottom to top. He sat in the middle on the very top tier and saw her right away. Wilhelm was with her and Roman relaxed a bit. If anyone could protect her in a crisis, Ellis could.

He used the amplifier on his seat as he stood. "Order in the chamber. I would like to admonish the crowd to hold down the noise. Any party making an outburst will be escorted from the chamber immediately. We rarely have such large gatherings here, so please be patient as we work through the process. We've dealt with routine business issues in a special private session and now will move on to our guest, Abigail Haws, of the Movement for Representative Democracy, as she makes her proposal to this body."

He turned from the crowd to face Abbie. She sat, looking perfectly calm, but he knew her, knew she had to be nervous because this meant so much to her. But for both their sakes, he had to remain as neutral as possible.

"Ms. Haws, please take the podium. Your time will be displayed on the clock to your left. At the conclusion of your remarks, there will be a question-and-answer session with the assembled Council."

Roman sat and Abbie stood and walked slowly to the podium. She had no notes. No paper. Just herself. And that's all she needed because her speech was written into her very bones.

She waited a moment and then thanked Roman and the assembled Council. And then she thanked the crowd.

"I was born here in Ravena. In the outback. My father was a teacher. My mother took in mending and also cooked and baked for other families for extra money."

Abbie fell into the story, *her* story, the story of the unranked, and didn't bother to look at the clock. She knew just how long it would take.

She spun through her life briefly before launching into her proposal.

"We do not want to steal your power. We want to share it. We are all citizens of the Federation. We all work hard and build lives here. We raise families and watch the fireworks on Varhana Day. We do not dispute the fact that the Families only wish the best for all their citizens, nor do we dispute that for the most part, especially here in Ravena, we lead good lives. But we have no say in the direction our governance goes in. We do not vote; we are not asked. We simply let governance happen to us. And it has created a sickness that resulted in the worst sort of betrayal."

Gasps sounded but Abbie did not flinch from the truth. The Families had brought this crisis on themselves and now they had to face it.

"We have been voiceless for generation after generation. And yet we have done service in the military corps, we have built 'Verse after 'Verse from the sewers to the portals. We seek an advisory committee with an unranked, *elected* member from each 'Verse, to serve as an adjunct to this body."

Abbie went through the details of how that would happen and ended with, "The time for a greater democracy, the time to give voice to the voiceless, is now. Thank you."

Thundering applause sounded from the chamber below, drowning out the boos of some of the assembled people. She caught sight of her mother's face, the pride there, and then her father's and it touched her to see his smile, his approval.

Roman let it go on for several moments and then admonished them to be silent, which, thankfully, they did.

"I'll take questions from this body," Roman said.

Deimos, sitting with the rest of the AC to the right of the Council, stood and raised a hand, Roman recognized him.

"The Auxiliary Council, by majority vote, endorses the plan as proposed by the speaker."

Abbie watched the Council and knew her little bask in adoration was coming to an end.

"House Licht has the floor," Roman said.

"My family has led for millennia. I was trained to do this. What makes this woman think she's capable of such a thing as leadership? I do not dispute the beauty of our sewers and portals, but one can hardly compare such things to running a government."

It went on and on that way with Licht, Stander, and Gayle lobbing hostile questions at her.

Roman watched as she handled each one with such unflappable calm he wanted to laugh out loud even as he wanted to smack those who questioned her ability.

Still, his ire was raised at how little respect his fellows paid her. It was fairly clear to him they indeed believed the unranked were incapable of intelligent leadership.

His mind began to spin.

Vicktor Pela stood. "House Pela stands in support of the proposal."

"Your daughter-in-law is unranked, of course you would!" Monitan Licht shot back.

"But she *is* Ranked, Monitan. In fact, her Rank is higher than yours. She's also a capable and strong leader who saved all of us from the plot that killed so many of our citizens." Vicktor smirked and Roman liked the man even more.

House Walker stood next. "I was admittedly not in support of this plan until I listened to my son and then heard Ms. Haws speak. House Walker supports the proposal."

House Khym also stood in support but House Holmes wavered. Roman knew it was about Hannah and their apprehensions about Abbie.

Each House spoke and it appeared he would have to speak to provide the extra weight she'd need.

Someone in the gallery screamed out, "This whore should be banned from this body! She fucked her way here. She isn't worthy of this honor. Even Lyons thinks so. Who's he marrying?"

Abbie met his gaze and he saw her breath hitch but she stood tall. White noise sounded in his head and he realized what a fool he'd been all along. She struggled and he put her into a warm apartment. One she'd turned down because she didn't want to jump the line ahead of people who'd waited longer than she had. He'd not given her what she really needed, what he wanted to provide from the first, but had been so blinded by tradition he'd never imagined a different future for either one of them.

He'd hedged around the one thing he knew he could do to be with her. The marital rule existed for very good reasons, even if over time they'd become less and less relevant. Making a change, especially right then, with so much upheaval, seemed foolhardy. He did not want to destabilize things any further, and while it was often thought of as *fun* to have so much power, to hold that much power came with deep responsibility. Roman was in charge. That meant he had to do the right thing.

This woman stood before them making an intelligent and rational argument as to why she should have a voice in her own future, while they all decided on whether they should share as if they were more special by nature of birth.

Which they were, in a sense. But it was Abbie Haws who deserved leadership and a voice. More than anyone he'd ever met. And he'd given people the idea that she was a whore because he'd fucked her and discarded her, even though he loved her.

He was ten kinds of fool and totally unworthy, and he'd missed just exactly what the right thing would be all this time.

He stood. But he'd spend every moment of his life trying to make it up to her.

"House Lyons supports this proposal. The proposal passes by a majority."

Chaos reigned and he looked down toward where she stood. She wrestled with her emotions but kept it together like the professional she was.

"Order in this chamber or you shall all go to lockup, House members included!"

Stunned, the audience quieted.

"After today, Deimos Lyons will lead House Lyons."

Deimos looked up at him, surprised for a moment, but he hid it quickly.

"Because I will be marrying. Ah, I shouldn't make that assumption. She may not have me." He looked up at Abbie, who held her hand to her throat. "Abbie, I've been a fool. My last official act as leader of House Lyons will be to eradicate the marital rule. Will you take me back? Will you marry me? I have a feeling your life will be very busy after this; you might need a consultant. I know a bit about governance, so you'd be getting a good package deal. A man who loves you more than anything in the Known Universes and an expert consultant. What do you say? We can live in a house on the vent so you're never cold in the winter."

Abbie looked up at him, totally stunned but filled with the kind of joy she'd never imagined. She fought her tears. No way was she going to cry at the happiest time of her life.

She stepped to the amplifier. "House Lyons, speak you true?"

"As true as my love for you. Be my wife, Abbie. Make brothers and sisters for Deimos and Corrin. I hear you might have a connection for good cakes for the wedding."

She laughed and looked to her mother, whose shoulders shook with happy tears.

"Deimos Lyons, what say you?" She wanted to be sure his children were all right with this.

Deimos stood. "I say welcome to House Lyons and that I hope you can talk sense into my father and urge him not to step down."

Abbie smiled. She might be principled and she might have turned down that apartment, but no way would she walk away from this man who held her heart in his hands. "Yes, Roman."

All seven hells broke loose as Roman strode from the tiers and into the crowd. Guards shoved people back as the assembled Council alternately clapped and frowned.

Within moments Roman was at her side, pulling her to him and the noise died away. It was just the two of them.

"I'm sorry. I've been a coward. I love you."

"I love you, too."

His lips met hers and a sense of homecoming stole through her. Her mouth opened on a sigh and his tongue slid in. She met it with her own as she held on to him tight, not wanting to let him go ever again.

His hands unerringly went to her hair and she wanted to laugh out loud when it began to fall from the knot.

His taste found its way home again within her and the pain of his absence began to lessen just a bit. He was hers and that would not change.

She sucked his tongue slightly and he arched a bit, letting her feel just what that had done to him. Abbie wanted to climb up his body and fuck herself onto him right then and there. She probably would have, had Ellis not cleared his throat loudly, reminding them he was there.

Chuckling, Roman pulled back from the kiss, licking his lips and still gazing at her. "Sorry, got a little carried away."

"I'm amazed, Roman, that it took you so damned long to come to your senses," Ellis commented. "But if I may interject, you should get back to work. It's sort of chaotic down there."

Abbie looked down and nodded. "Go and calm them down. I'll be here. And Roman? Listen to Deimos. Don't step aside."

"Protect her with your life, Ellis," Roman said before kissing her hard and fast.

"Do I tell you how to do your job? Maybe I should. I would have told you to eradicate that stupid marital rule long ago." Ellis glowered quite well, and Roman squeezed her hand before dashing away.

"Is he going to be all right?" Abbie turned to Ellis as she asked.

"It'll be rough but he has support, enough to survive. He is House Lyons, after all. And he just did something none of them have ever had the courage to do. Some will admire that. Roman is tough. He was born tough. None of them can stand against him for long."

She smiled at him. "I find myself quite happy you seem to admire him so."

Ellis laughed. "He's an admirable man who has been instrumental in making me what I am today. There are many highly placed people who can say the same. None would want him to step aside. Deimos can do the job and do it well, but it's Roman's place. I hope he sees that."

Abbie agreed.

"Comandante Ellis, Mr. Lyons requests you move Ms. Haws to the rear antechamber until he's finished with their private session. Ms. Haws, he requests that you wait for him if possible." Marcus grinned at her from the top of the steps.

"All right. Will you inform my family, please? I don't want them worrying about where I am."

"Of course. I've had some food and drinks put in for you to snack on. Private sessions like this one can take a while. And congratulations. I'm, well, I'm thrilled for you and Roman." Marcus winked and disappeared down the steps again.

"I don't want to try and get you through that gallery below. Come through the side with me."

He pressed a panel to his left and a pocket door popped open.

"Nifty."

"It does come in handy to know the back way sometimes."

She followed him through the door and down a hallway. Exterior light came through the top of the passage and she realized they were on a modified sort of catwalk over the chamber below. Now she'd have to get back in the gallery to see how noticeable it was.

He punched a code into the wall panel and it took a retinal scan and the door slid open to a set of stairs that they took downward and into the antechamber. True to Marcus's word, food and drink was laid out on a sideboard and a comm station had been unlocked for her to work on.

She sat and it all hit her so hard she had to put her head down on the table. Everything was right there. Everything she'd ever wanted and by the gods she wasn't going to let anyone take it from her.

Chapter 35

"You're out of your mind. That's all there is to it, Roman. You cannot mean to do this." Gabriel Holmes had barely waited for the door to close before he spoke.

"This is the sanest thing I've done in my entire life. I've been in love with Abigail since about five minutes after we first met. I'm too old to throw love away like a fool."

"You cannot mean to step aside."

"You're talking about me naming a successor?" Roman was confused.

"Roman, I would have welcomed a marriage between our Families and I ask you to remember you have two unmarried sons and an unmarried brother, but I can't stand in the way of your love for this woman. She's clearly intelligent and well-spoken. I do not agree that any of us should be in each others' pockets on this sort of personal issue," Gabriel said.

Well, that was unexpected. "Oh. How say the rest of the Five?"

"House Walker supports you continuing in place, although we will not be revoking the marital rule ourselves." Angelo Walker spoke.

The others stood behind Roman. He hadn't felt bad about naming a successor. He'd trade this job for Abbie in a heartbeat. But Deimos had urged him not to and now that he'd had time to think on it, if he didn't have to step aside, why should he?

If a majority of them, a healthy majority of the Families felt he should stay, he would.

"We should take this up tomorrow. House Licht needs time to formulate a response." Monitan Licht's lips were pursed.

"A quick show of votes before we adjourn, then," Vicktor Pela said. "House Pela supports Roman Lyons continuing as leader of House Lyons. Not that this is any of our business. This is up to House Lyons."

"This affects us all! He shoves through this Advisory Council and *then* he asks the woman to marry him and repudiates millennia of Family tradition," Monitan Licht said angrily.

Roman sighed.

"The vote for the Advisory Council was eight to six with House Lyons making the ninth vote. That's not *shoving* anything through. That's a solid majority and it's no longer up for discussion."

Roman loved when Angelo Walker got snotty.

"Just take a damned vote as to where everyone stands on Roman holding his position as leader of House Lyons and then we can all go. If it's an overwhelming show either way, we can go from there," Leong Khym said.

A quick show of hands had nine in favor and four against, the four Roman had figured would vote that way anyway.

"I don't see why we need until tomorrow then." Vicktor Pela stood up. "I'll see you all at next week's meeting. Congratulations, Roman. I hope to meet this Abbie in person very soon. I imagine after all this time apart you're rather anxious to get to her." He smiled and Roman stood, too. Hells yes, he was anxious.

"Council is adjourned until next week's meeting. Thank you, gentlemen. I'll be off now."

Roman nearly ran from the room into the antechamber where she sat, laughing with Wilhelm. By the gods, she'd charmed his usually dour comandante. He grinned at her, leaning to hear what she said.

"My goodness, I can't leave you alone for a moment or you're making more men fall in love with you."

She looked up, her smile widening when she saw him. "Are you all right?"

"Come on, Abbie. We're going to my house where it's warm and we can be alone. Yes, I'll live to lead House Lyons another day," he added quickly when she started to ask him again.

"I'll escort you out to the conveyance." Ellis got up and spoke into his comm before opening the door and leading them out.

Abbie knew she had to contact her family, but all she could think of was Roman. Of taking joy in touching him openly for the first time since she'd met him. At the conveyance, he helped her inside and slid in next to her.

Finally it was silent as the door closed and they pulled away from the front of the building.

"You did such an amazing job today. I was so proud of you. You did it, Abbie. You reached your goal through hard work and persistence."

His words meant so much to her.

"Thank you. Thank you for supporting it. House Lyons supporting the proposal makes a huge difference. Despite what some will say."

"Fuck them. You made this happen. You did. Not what we have together, but your work. And soon you'll be House Lyons, too. Gods." He hugged her to him and she buried her nose in his neck, loving that she still fit there just perfectly. "I've missed you so much."

"I've been broken without you. And then people wanted to hurt me and I wanted to run to you but I couldn't."

His arms tightened around her and they pulled to a stop. "Come on, let's go in. I want you here from now on. It's safer than your flat and it's at my side. Will you do that for me?"

She nodded, not able to express just how happy she was.

He helped her out and she followed, still amazed at the size and scope of the outside of the manse.

Dazed, she nodded until the door was flung open and the house manager—Mercy, Abbie thought her name was—rushed out and hugged Roman and then Abbie.

"Welcome, welcome! Oh it's going to be wonderful to have a lady of the house again. And such a pretty one. Come inside! I've warned the boys they can only visit with you for a short time and then you two will need to be alone. Oh, I've been waiting for you to come to your senses, Roman."

Abbie hid a smile at how the woman led them into the house, more like a mother than an employee. She liked that Roman's staff seemed to like him as well as respect him.

But right then, she wanted to rub all over him. It'd been four weeks since she'd touched him. Four weeks with a broken heart, feeling alone and scared, like she'd never be happy again.

And there he was, his arm around her shoulders, openly loving her. It was nearly too much. She wasn't sure what to think or do, part of her wanted to curl up and take a nap just to hide for a bit.

"Dai! Congratulations!" Corrin came in with Deimos and they both hugged their father and then looked to her.

"Abbie, it's such an honor to welcome you into our family. You make our father whole. I can't wait to get to know you better." Corrin looked sort of tentative, and she supposed he had reason to be. He didn't even have that small bit of exposure to her that Deimos had had.

"I look forward to that, too. Your father talks so much about you, boasts about your musical and artistic talent. I'm quite looking forward to seeing your paintings and drawings. I know neither of you know me that well, so it's got to be a bit uncomfortable for you. Rumors will be flying around. I'm sure they are already. Will you promise to talk to me if you have questions or concerns?"

Corrin and Deimos nodded. The stiffness in Corrin's spine had eased, which made Abbie feel better.

"Boys, Abbie and I have been apart for four weeks. We've got some stuff to talk about." Roman glanced at the chrono on the wall just opposite. "Let's meet back here for dinner in two hours, all right? And Mercy, will you arrange to get Marcus, Jaron, my parents, and Abbie's family here, too? Make it a big party?"

Mercy smiled. "It's already in the works. You two go on. I put some things in your room and I hope you don't mind, Abbie, but I spoke with your brother Daniel and he's going to be bringing some of your things over tonight."

"No, I don't mind. Thank you."

Abbie let Roman tug her arm as they walked up a staircase as grand as the one in the Grand Council Chamber.

"Are you warm enough?" he murmured as she gawked at the majesty of the upper hall on the way to his room.

"Right down to my toes. I can see marrying you is going to be worth it."

He laughed. "I have all the hot water you can use, too. But I think I might have some other uses you may be interested in." He shoved open tall double doors and she wanted to gasp and only barely succeeded in holding it back.

"You sleep in here? My entire flat could fit in here." The room was massive and sumptuous. The kind of place you could go at the end of the day and the world would fall away. Thick, lush fabrics covered the bed and a sunken seating area formed a half-circle before a large stone fireplace.

"Do you like it?"

"I'd like it more if you were naked. But this place is beautiful. I love it." She turned around to take him in. The gaze that had been happy and filled with love just downstairs had darkened. The love was still there; the happiness, too. But want burned through his eyes, most likely mirroring her own.

"The doors are closed, mine—rather, ours—is the only room on this floor on this side of the house. Make all the noise you want. I know I will." Abbie watched, fascinated, as he slid off his suit jacket and then unbuttoned his shirt. When he peeled it away, her heart thudded against the wall of her chest.

"So handsome," she said. "I've dreamed of your body since the day you walked out my door."

His hands paused on his belt as he toed off his shoes. Pain sparked through his gaze. "Never again, Abbie. I will stand with you until I cease to draw breath. Can you forgive me? For not being there when you needed me? For hurting you?"

She shucked her jacket and rid herself of her shirt, tossing it to the side as she moved to him. "It's over. We're here together right now, and that's what counts. You were hurt, too, I know that. And I know you sent Ellis, and through him, my brother, to watch me. We'll talk about that later."

She shoved her skirt off and smiled when he caught sight of the bows holding up the stockings at the garters.

He fell to his knees before her, pressing his face to her belly and then against the front of her panties. The heat of his breath echoed off her skin, even through the material.

A tide of desire, of raw-edged need, rolled through her and she buckled. He caught her, lowering her to the rug that was soft and thick.

She watched, intoxicated with him as he stripped the last of his clothes and turned back to her, gloriously naked. "Hold on." He got up and she angled her head to watch him move to the fireplace, and in moments he'd turned on a switch and flames merrily danced, casting a lovely glow about the room along with heat enough to make her languid like a feline.

"You spoil me," she said, arching into him as he came back to her.

"I plan to for the rest of our lives." He made fast work of her bra and panties but refastened the stockings. "These, my darling, are absurdly sexy. Who on earth were you wearing them for?" One gold eyebrow rose as he leaned in to kiss, ever so lightly, the distended tip of her nipple.

"You. In my head, of course. I had no idea you'd be—oh, that's so lovely—willing to toss aside your job, *your life*, for me so you'd see them."

He nibbled on her, nipping the soft skin on the underside of her
breast, up and around, carefully avoiding her nipple.

"You *are* my life. Gods, the scent of your pussy is making me
crazy."

She laughed, widening her thighs and wrapping them about his
waist. "I'm so wet I'd be embarrassed if I didn't need you so much
right now. The moment you looked down at me earlier, it shot straight
to my cunt. You have magical powers over me, I think."

"If I do, I'd use them to keep you naked, here in our room.
Maybe not totally naked. You can keep the stockings. And I can
come in to fuck you any time I like. I'm not the kind of man who
will lose interest in you sexually after we marry. You should know I
plan to fuck you every way, in every place I can think of, every time
we get the chance."

He teased along her gate with the head of his cock, just barely
dipping inside and pulling away.

"Good to know. I'm not the kind of wife who plans to be ignored. So put your cock in me right now."

He kissed her. Softly at first, but once she opened to him, he
groaned into her mouth and the need licked them like flame. His
tongue slid along hers, teasing, seducing. All the while he'd busily
pulled the pins from her hair, running his fingers through it as he
continued to kiss her.

Gods, he was on fire for her! The slide of her soft, bare skin
against his own sent little flickers of electricity through him. His
woman beneath him. *His.* The freedom to love her, to have her, to
share his life with her, made him giddy. All he'd ever wanted resided
within the walls of his home. His children, healthy, successful and
happy, and now a woman he could give himself to, trust to take care

with his heart, with his family. Abbie was all of that and more. He looked forward to learning more about her each day.

He was so hard, each throb of his pulse bordered on pain, but it had been entirely too long since he'd had her like this and he planned to take full advantage. He kissed across her jawline, over to that spot just beneath her ear that made her make *that* sound.

Her hips jutted forward, taking the head of him into the heated, soft gate of her pussy.

He plunged into her fully and she gasped, arching to take him. She was tight, so snug around him he nearly lost his control, it felt so damned good. He pulled back and thrust again and once more before pulling back out and kissing her nipple. First one and then the other.

He pressed them together so that he could lick and bite them more easily. She whimpered and he blew across her sensitive skin.

"I love that sound," he said around her nipple. "Needy, achy. I know you want me to fuck you. And I will. But first I'm going to bury my face in your pussy, licking you the way you like. Then, when I've made you come, then I'll fuck you."

Like she would argue with that?

"If you think I'd stand in the way of that, you don't know much about me after all."

He kissed down her belly, his gaze locked with hers as she leaned up on her elbows to watch—take him in as those big, capable hands pushed her thighs wide. And then he broke his eyes from hers to look long and greedily at her pussy. Her breath caught at his perusal, at the way he made her feel—adored, beautiful, desired.

He didn't waste time with his usual long, slow tour of her body. Instead, he dove in with a ferocity that made her gasp at the intensity of it. He pressed his mouth into her, tongue swirled over and over from gate to clit, steady, rhythmic, until her thighs began to tremble against his palms.

She'd needed him for so long, had been alone for what felt like forever. Her body had been numb but his touch brought it roaring back to life. Orgasm came, an irrefutable onslaught of intense physical and emotional sensation bringing tears to her eyes and a muted cry to her lips.

Abbie reached down, fumbling to grab his cock, but he had better use for it, slicing into her body as she melted around him, sending so much pleasure into him his eyes rolled back into his head.

He stilled for moments until he grasped a tiny amount of control and began to move again. Roman braced his weight on his arms as he fucked into her body. His gaze roamed over her, taking in the seductive bounce of her breasts as he thrust, the wet gleam on her lips as she licked them, the puff of her breath as she was caught in the same web of sensation he was. Her eyes were wide but still blurred with her orgasm. Her pussy fluttered and clasped around him as he pushed in deep and then pulled out.

Her scent was deep within him, mixed with the beauty of her taste on his lips.

"You're written into my bones, Abbie."

She blinked, the blur disappearing until those clear, beautiful brown eyes locked onto his. "You do know how to make me weak in the knees, Roman. I love you and I'm not giving you back so the rest of the Known Universes just have to deal."

He could tell she tried to be flip, but the breathless quality to her voice told him she was as affected as he was, and that she was close to coming again.

"That smile makes me all tingly. It usually means you've got something enjoyable in store for me."

"Indeed."

Adjusting himself slightly, he moved down her body a bit, changing his angle so the line of his cock slid over her clit each time he pressed into her body. Right away her breathing changed, hitched. Her honey slid over his balls, hot and sticky.

"Mmm. Just like I like you, panting and ready to come. Give it to me, Abbie. Come all over my cock."

Her mouth opened as if her body's response had been a surprise, her back bowed and her nails dug into the flesh at his hips where her hands had been. She squeezed him with her thighs as her cunt grabbed him and he knew he was lost to the magic they made each time they touched.

Chapter 36

Seven Standard Months Later

"You know I'd keep you just for our bathroom, right?"

Wearing a smirk and little else, Roman looked down at her in their bathtub. "You're worth it. I must say my bathroom is much nicer to be in with a sexy, wet, naked woman in the bathtub."

"Well, I don't have as much time as I'd like to enjoy it."

"Abbie, darling, you'd be in here every moment of the day if you didn't have a full time job as a barrister and weren't the newly elected leader of the Unranked Advisory Council."

She frowned at him a moment. "I'm going to have to lower my caseload. I spoke with my boss about it, and he's making me a super-visor like he is. His second-in-command, he says." She then laughed and he loved her more for the fact that, regardless of the size of her house and that she didn't have to work at all if she didn't want to, she still found joy in a promotion.

"Are you all right with that?"

"Why are you getting dressed? I'm here, naked and ready to be tussled with, and you're putting pants on. This is not the direction things should be moving."

"We have a state dinner to be at. Remember?"

She sighed, pouting those lips he loved so much for just a moment. "Oh yeah, the Mrs. Lyons thing. That's another job." She stood with a fake, put-upon sigh and he handed her a towel even as he delighted in the way the water slid down her breasts and belly.

Another thing Roman enjoyed about his wife was the way she went from wet sylph to the wife of the leader of the Known Universes in just a few minutes. She was wonderfully independent and not fussy. Complicated, yes. Moody at times. Aggravating in her insistence that she keep her job as a barrister through the creation of the Advisory Council and then the election cycle. But through it all, she'd remained his most strident and solid supporter. Abbie understood policy with an eye he'd come to respect and appreciate. In truth, his wife was his chief advisor, and while there had been grumbling from several quarters, she'd comported herself with so much dignity and strength, she'd won over many of her original detractors.

She loved his sons and they her. She'd even managed to charm his father, who now chastised anyone who spoke ill of her. And she simply accepted it.

Abbie slid into a gown in a style she knew Roman favored. The deep, bloodred coloring accentuated her skin and hair. Twin golden lion heads fastened the slim braided straps at the very bottom curve of her back.

When she entered her dressing area just outside the bathroom, she wanted to laugh at the very idea of a dressing area, but she did love it. Loved the gleaming table where she frequently found new presents from Roman. Little bits of jewelry and things for her hair. Loved the space that was so feminine and luxurious.

"My, you do know what that dress does to me."

She smiled into the mirror at his reflection. "When you fucked me in the antechamber of the hall where we married, yes, I did get the idea you enjoyed seeing me in it."

"Only my bride would marry in such a gown. The talk of the vids for weeks afterward."

She laughed and made quick work of her hair, fastening it with pretty clips. "Well, that one was pale blue. This one is red but in the same design. How many women own such a thing?" She motioned at herself. "I love this dress so I wear it when I can. I can't very well argue cases in it."

"You won't hear me complaining that my wife is the sexiest woman in all the 'Verses."

He kissed her neck, his clever fingers pinching her nipples through the silky, cool material of the dress.

"Sera Pela isn't anything to sneeze at."

He shrugged. "She's lovely, yes. But she has two men already. Good thing I find you much more compelling."

She turned, tiptoeing up to kiss him quickly. "Good. That'll come in handy when I'm huge from the baby and all."

Wearing a smile, she left the room as he gaped at her.

Laughing, he followed after her and made them very, very late for their dinner.